## Praise for *Shroud of Ice*

"*Shroud of Ice* is a remarkable novel, one that lingers in a reader's memory long after the final page has been turned. Sharon Krasny crosses 5,000 years to create a drama with themes of dignity, loyalty, resilience, and community; extending the tale began with her first novel, *Iceman Awakens*, a memorable read in itself. Gaspare may have been shrouded in ice for centuries, but in these pages, he lives and breathes again, as emotionally complex as any modern character. Krasny's research is impeccable and her writing is tight, often lyrical, tense where it needs to be, and always elegant. *Shroud of Ice* stands as a significant work, one that honors any bookshelf upon which it might sit and any reader who might undertake its journey."

—Greg Fields, author of *The Bright Freight of Memory*
2025 American Writing Award for Literary Fiction
PEN/Faulkner Nominee

"A poetic, rich, imaginative journey, not just for Gaspare the Iceman but for the reader as well. Grim and compelling, it's about so much more than survival in an age of primitive conditions. This novel speaks to the deep motivations of each of us: the search for freedom, redemption, and true brotherhood. Haunting."

—Maryel Stone, author of *Child of the Scales*

"Sharon Krasny has done it again! Years after Gaspare was reduced to slavery in *Iceman Awakens*, she continues to flesh out the mysterious, frozen 5,300-year-old mummy of the Alps in such a way that I saw him as a living, breathing human being with hopes, dreams, and fears not so unlike ours today. I felt as if I were with Gaspare and Haliam every step of their journey toward freedom. Krasny's exquisite writing style, which ranges from lyrical descriptions to sharp, staccato, emotion-filled sentences, made me see what they saw, hear what they heard, and feel what they felt. Her intensive research and passion for her subject have created a book not only of the heart but of the mind as it brings to life the culture and people, both bad and good, of the Copper Age."

—S. A. Smith, author of *The Rain Gypsy*, *The Cemetery Tender*, and the upcoming *Sweetgrass in the Rain*

"*Shroud of Ice*, the speculative fiction story of Gaspare and his life in ancient times, will keep you as spellbound and delighted as it kept me. The themes of friendship, home, and family run deep.

"The difficulties of life in such a harsh environment will keep you turning pages as you move toward the inevitable conclusion. Death and danger are Gaspare's constant companions as he escapes his enslavement in the copper mines to return to his home and family.

"Gaspare is the name the author has given Ötzi, a man who died centuries ago and was found in what Ms. Krasny correctly calls a shroud of ice in the title of this book. Her first book, *Iceman Awakens Book I*, led to recognition of her talents as an author. Now, *Shroud of Ice* continues her journey as an author and seeker of knowledge about a man who could never have foreseen what he would contribute to our understanding of history.

"I highly recommend *Shroud of Ice*. It's a winner!"

—Charles Tabb, president of The Virginia Writers Club and author of *Floating Twigs*, a Kirkus Reviews recommended book

"*Shroud of Ice* is a riveting family saga of love, betrayal, and belonging. Deeply imagined and exquisitely written with a rich historical context, I took my time with this one, savoring every page."

—Julia Sullivan, award-winning author of *Bone Necklace*

"Krasny's research and command of language urge us to walk alongside Gaspare and listen deeply to what is said and not said. Through the lens of the ancients, we come face-to-face with our strengths and vulnerability as a species. His journey, real and imagined, is a compelling lesson in the complexity of our roots, our innate drive to survive, and our profound need for safety, community, and freedom. *Shroud of Ice* is not just history, plot, and character. It is epic poetry, extended metaphor, and a masterpiece of literary fiction for our age."

—Katherine Mercurio Gotthardt, award-winning poet and author of *The World Has Changed from When I Last Was Here*

"Historical fiction at its most visceral, Sharon Krasny's *Shroud of Ice* unflinchingly portrays a story of nature's hardships alongside human fragilities. Krasny's powerful storytelling rewarded me with an epic tale of betrayal and resilience that kept me up into the late hours…"

—Nic Winter, author of *A Season to Kill (Darcy Sinclair Novel)*

# SHROUD

## OF

# ICE

# SHROUD
## OF
# ICE

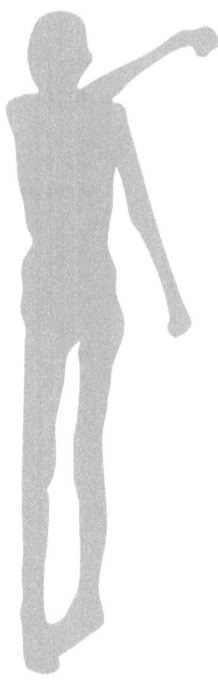

## SHARON KRASNY

Brandylane
Publishers, Inc.
*Publishing books since 1985*

ISBN (Paperback): 978-1-966369-21-9
ISBN (eBook): 978-1-966369-22-6
Library of Congress Control Number: 2025910828

Designed by Sami Langston
Project managed by Ashley Barnhill

Published by
Brandylane Publishers, Inc.
5 S. 1st Street
Richmond, Virginia 23219

Brandylane
Publishers, Inc.
*Publishing books since 1985*

brandylanepublishers.com

# DEDICATION

For Magdalena, Jakob, and Josefina—you three guide me to a better
sense of home.
Lots of love,
Mom

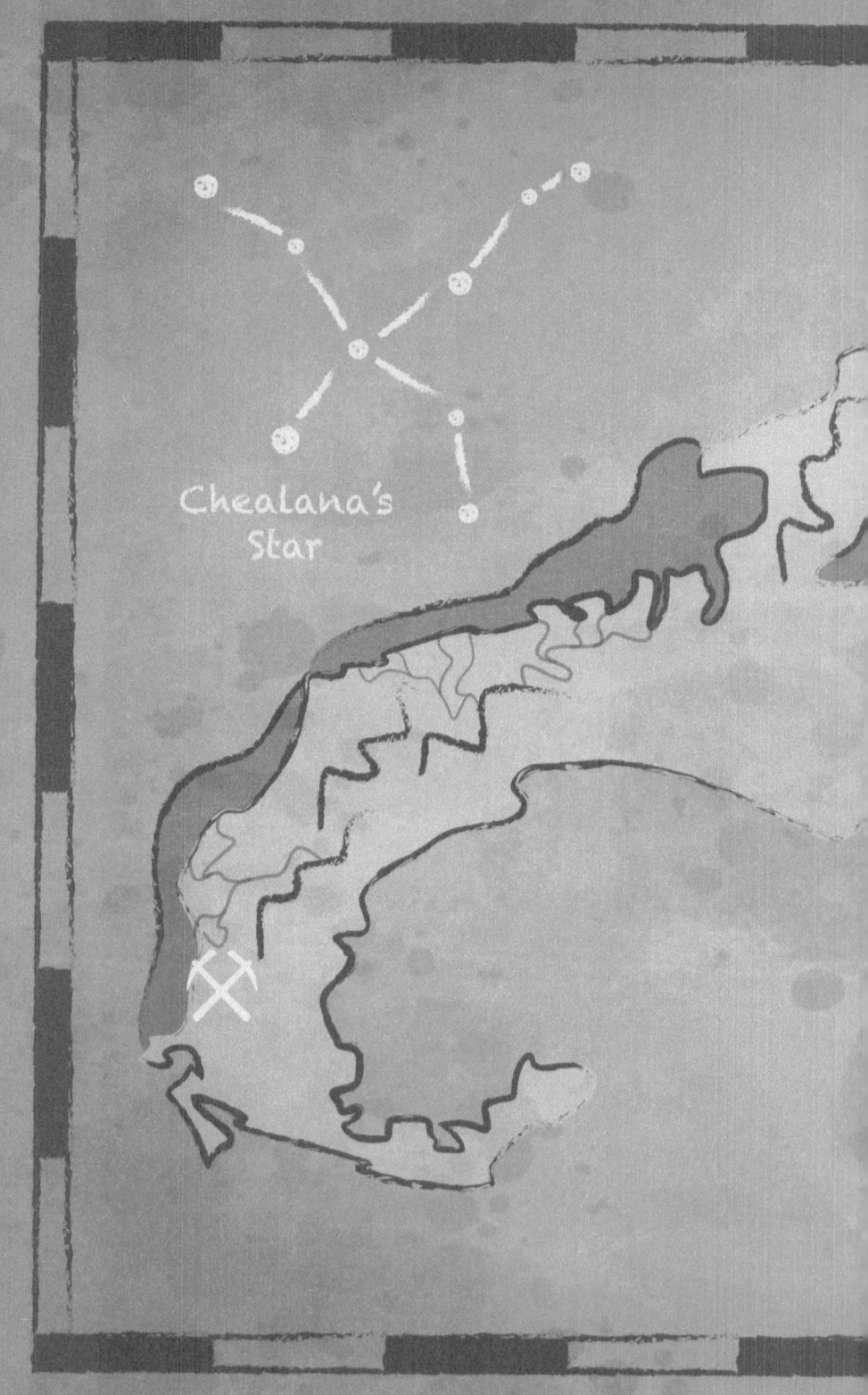

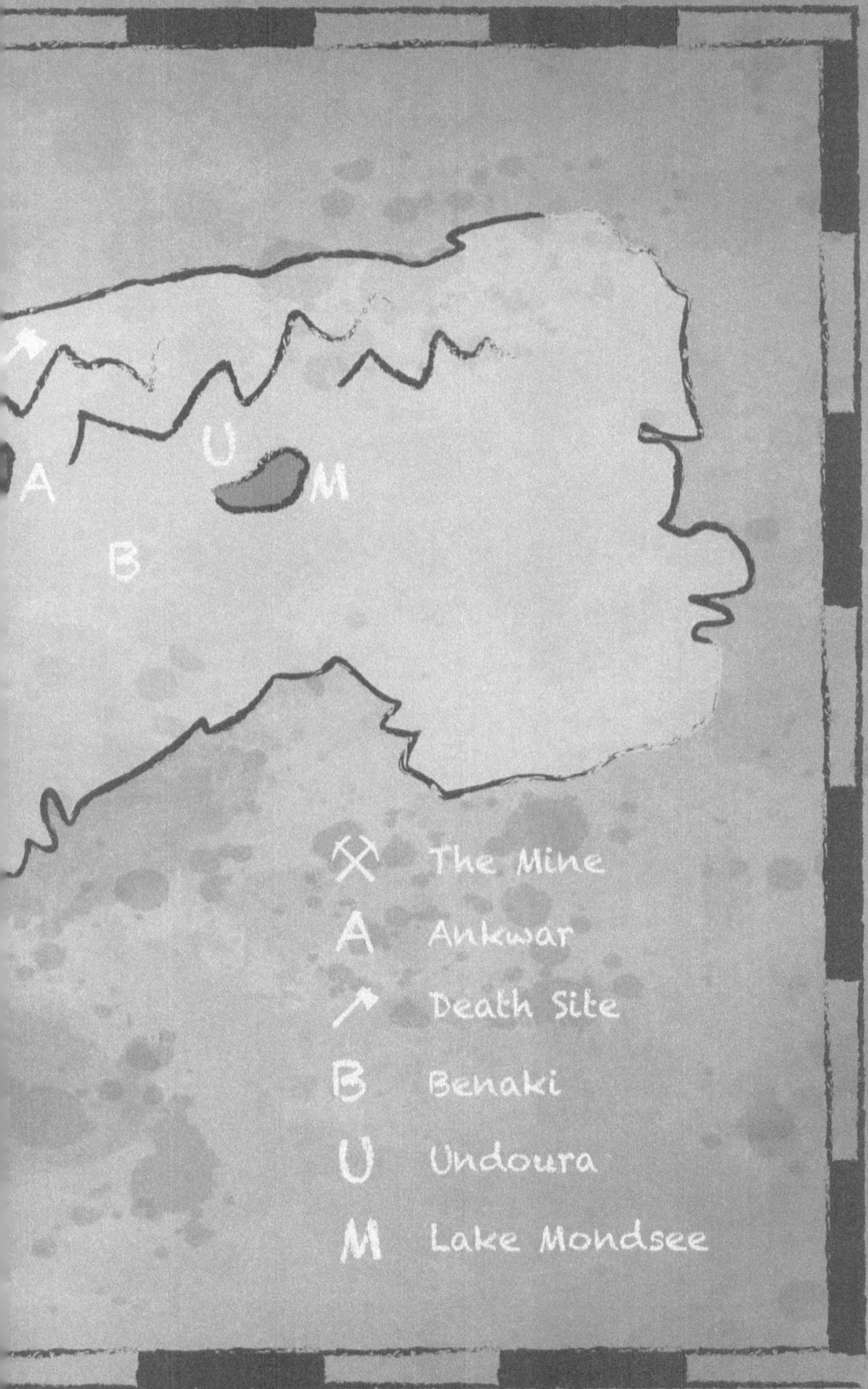

X   The Mine

A   Ankwar

↗   Death Site

B   Benaki

U   Undoura

M   Lake Mondsee

# FOREWORD

The email message that reached me unexpectedly in 2020 came from Virginia, USA. My address was given by a reporter from Austria to a school teacher named Sharon Krasny, who found the discovery of the man in the ice very interesting and wanted to get more information from an archaeology expert at the University of Innsbruck. I was used to this type of request because the whole world was fascinated by the discovery of the Iceman, and I often had to answer such inquiries. I usually did this over the phone, but Sharon was different. She wanted to write a book about the Iceman and his time! I asked her whether she might not have taken on too much and pointed out to her that this project would probably not succeed without the necessary scientific background. The author took this wake-up call very seriously, and we subsequently exchanged letters for years.

Sharon went from being a teacher to a diligent student and did all the tasks very well. She was not only tireless in her literary research. She also wanted to really get to the bottom of the subject by taking on the hardships of a long journey to Europe to seek out the original habitat of the Stone Age Iceman.

She ventured into dangerous glacier regions in the worst weather conditions and followed the paths that Ötzi must have once taken. This made her more aware than ever of the conditions under which people spent their everyday lives in the Alps back then. And it was precisely this experience that helped the author write her story as authentically as possible. It was equally important to see the original equipment, the clothing, and the mummy of the man in the ice in the museum in Bolzano. Only then was the author able to get a true picture of Ötzi's character, and I am sure that at that moment she was able to identify with him and, for a moment, put herself back in his time. These were all important components that contributed to the success of the book, *Shroud of Ice*.

Congratulations, Sharon! You did it!

Dr. Walter Leitner

# AUTHOR'S NOTE

Five years ago, *Iceman Awakens* Book 1 was published. Since that time, more understanding has been revealed about Ötzi. Turns out he was bald and of Turkish descent with his mummy correctly indicating the pigmentation of his skin. Since the release of book one, I was a recipient of Fauquier County's Excellence in Education grant, I had the honor of traveling to Austria and Italy to find Ötzi's story. The people we met were more than kind and generous. The events that happened significantly altered the story I was writing. Here's a brief retelling of that journey.

On July 23, 2023, I had the pleasure of meeting Dr. Walter Leitner in person. We had only previously met via email where Dr. Leitner answered my questions and provided insights and knowledge of the research as my expert advisor. He was a tremendous host, escorting us to Ötzal Dorf and giving us a private tour of the reenactment village based on archeological findings from 5000 years ago. I sampled fresh bread baked on a heated rock, saw the housing techniques, together with barns and animals from the agricultural aspects of the society, and a burial site. He drove us to Vent, Austria, and introduced us to our wonderful hosts at Alt Vent Tyrol hotel and showed us the primitive hunting rock together with findings that his archeological students recovered from the rock, including the tiniest arrowhead carved out of a beautiful, white stone. He pointed us on our way as we said our farewells.

July 24, 2023, we began our climb up the path of the Similaun mountain. It was raining on and off all morning. In fact, it had been storming on the mountain for three weeks prior to our arrival. We left shortly after 8 a.m. and made it to the Martin Busch hütte for soup at 2 p.m. We still had over an hour to go to arrive at the Similaun hütte that would shelter us for the night.

We came to the split in the path that Dr. Leitner had told us to watch for. To the right, we would see where Ötzi was found. Straight ahead, we would reach the hutte. Since we were wet and carrying all our supplies on our backs, we aimed for the hutte. I am very thankful for that decision. The mountain had plans to show me her strength. Storms opened as we proceeded above the tree line up the rocky slope. I speak about this experience on my TEDx Talk, so let me just say that had we gone first to Ötzi's finding place, I might not have made it as hypothermia began setting in when we were about 200 yards from the hutte. I now intimately know that the mountain certainly challenged Ötzi covered in glacier snows and ice.

July 25, 2023, after spending a night listening to the thunder shake our hutte, we woke to a brief snowstorm. We were over 9000 feet above sea level. Anything can happen when up in the clouds. We began our descent, foregoing traveling to the finding spot, and we headed down the mountain. As we approached the tree line, we passed marmots whistling before their descent out of sight, we passed cows grazing on the hillsides, and we saw flocks of sheep moving over the passes. Most importantly, we began to walk upon the space that Ötzi walked 5000 years earlier. How did we know this? The mosses on and in his body revealed the path he took. As I saw the green waters of the lake, breathed the pine-scented air, and touched the boulders, I found the ending of the story I had previously been struggling to complete.

On July 27, 2023, I enjoyed a private tour with Nico Aldegani at the South Tyrol Museum of Archeology. Mr. Aldegani thoughtfully shared this experience with me as I met the man from the ice in repose. The museum was empty except for us, and I had the opportunity to ask a plethora of questions and take tons of photos with the exception of Ötzi himself. Returning home from this impactful journey, I edited and finished my draft putting into place the ending I believe honored the story needing to be told.

Part of the challenge of writing Ötzi's story, or Gaspare as I call him, was to address the facts that added to the mysteries surrounding his final days. For example, five different hemoglobin were found on his coat. These could be from battle, or even just him wiping his knife on his coat after eating meat. How the blood got there is not known, but scientists can identify five different sources of blood on his coat. He had bracken in his stomach – it's toxic, so why did he digest the fern? Many questions surround the oldest cold case and are woven into the threads of the story.

My entire purpose for writing *Iceman Awakens* and *Shroud of Ice* was not to be 100% an authority on what happened to Ötzi. The fact remains, we will never be certain. This is historical fiction. My purpose was simply to restore dignity to a widely studied and little-understood man, who has taught us so much about ourselves. What I found instead was the gift of my voice as a writer. As I worked to open the human condition that the facts around Ötzi suggested, I found words that resonated in the universal and timeless story of what it means to be alive. We seek love. We seek to be remembered. We seek to know our purpose. Please enjoy this final chapter of an amazing archeological find of the 20th century. Thank you for joining me on this prehistoric travel to the possibilities of the Iceman's world.

A new heart I will give you, and a new spirit I will put within you;
and I will remove from your body the heart of stone
and give you a heart of flesh.
(Ezekiel 36:26)

# CHAPTER 1

# THE MINE

The darkness moved in the stillness. Silhouettes seized at the shapes of madness in my imagination as they shuffle in front of me. Four layers under the earth, four layers deep within the copper mine, the stale air suffocated the many voices to mere groans; young men carrying baskets of debris, walking in line, seeking the coming light from the tunnel's mouth. Yet the only light to pierce the depths was from the lard spluttering oil on the stone by my feet. The shadows danced erratically around the eyes downcast over sunken cheeks, some nervously glancing up as they pass by. Most bodies vacantly stared at the load in front of them. I have no power to save or destroy, but I represent Malek, who does. In this mine, Malek has no need for weakness, no care for more than an increased haul of copper. My role ensures the work presses deeper.

The air down here weighs heavily on my decency. Orders barked; mercy withheld; what is out of sight is easily justified. I repeat my name, "Gaspare, Gas-par-e," praying the darkness won't banish what goodness might remain. With a figure stumbling near me, I shouted the usual orders, feeling Malek's venom cross my tongue yet again. I licked the sweat off my lip and snarled the words, "Get back in line." I moved away from the light. Darkness so thick, so alive, covered the cavern. Shuffling feet sounded through the narrow corridor. Scritches, ticks, and thuds came from the bone tools wedged against the clammy walls, working to extract the magnesium streaked with copper ore. I watched the light flicker, the lard splutter, and the empty faces pass me as I stayed pressed against a wall. *Was there any breath of life that I could own?*

Coming toward me in the blackness, a wheeze announced one laborer and a wracking cough another. An empty thud announced a fallen soul. Two boys pulled a body to an appendix of the tunnel. The boy's body could stay preserved in a dark sleep, his suffering ended,

1

his light gone, and his little legs finally relaxed and tucked under him. No prayers, no wails, no memory remained. He simply vanished from life. The slightest whisper tried to purge my heart, "Gaspare . . . Gaspare . . . please."

When not in the mine, I paid close attention. The little freedom I had gained from hauling rocks to moving the lines came only from how useful Malek found me. Copper meant status, which meant mobility. I watched the interactions of the traders, or the men from different tribes as they talked and negotiated what they wanted. I needed to learn. Just seeing visions wouldn't save me in the life surrounding the mines. Malek knew cruelty. The gift I had, the one of visions, had seen his prophetic fire thrust its way up from a black heart and burn to his mind and through his acts. I had predicted his role would change from slave of the pits to ruler over them. His prophecy came true—whether through fate or by his own hand, I'm unsure, but he was promoted from hauling rocks on his back as a slave to condemning others as slaves. Now, nine springs later, Malek, the most feared slave master of the pits, kept me near like a lucky talisman or a pressed-worry stone. He asked me to soothsay for him. For some extra water, or scraps of meat, I attended to his needs. Malek found me useful. Nothing more. But he knew.

As I gathered supplies at the end of the day, I listened. I spoke with a man from one tribe. Blending words and gestures like a bird's mating dance, I found my way to communicate a need. My next trade, negotiating goods, created the same dance with a different tribesman. Language took shape in my mind. I kept my ears open. The traders' reach brought treasures such as amber from the far northeast along with different races of several unknown tongues. Detangling word order created webs and puzzles to keep my mind focused. Malek needed my gift of languages even more than my gift of prophecy or medicinal healing. Words hold power.

Once a boy had been hauling copper and dropped his load because he had tripped. Malek rendered him unconscious as a result, but Malek's whip only penetrated so far. His fierce, inner fire produced only blackened ash. Fear merely inspired chattel. Fear does not bond within an individual. Words, a man's language and way of sharing ideas, history, and traditions, penetrated the heart and mind. Malek could break a man's body, but I could connect with the little pride and hope that remained. Those meager connections were tendons holding me from extinction. Could a man change? Could a greater purpose be salvaged, or had my village sacrificed me for mere ash?

Dreams, however, have ideas of their own. Dreams hold the boundaries of the heart. Both horrific and pure, a dream's song calls to a deeper sense of purpose. Daring to dream did not possess me, but a small spark can exist even in dying embers. A bit of tinder and gentle blowing can ignite the belief into hope. All that's needed is one believer. But I was not that one.

# CHAPTER 2

## THE TORTOISE'S TRAIL

Nine starlit points made the sacred bird's shape sent to pull down water from the skies. Father had taught me to read the stars using the Raven, a cross of stars flying toward Telio's River of Stars. The full, bonemeal moon spread luminously through the vast richness of colors found in the shadows. The darkness tingled. I stood alone, empty, and isolated from the marrow of life around me. Gazing again at the stars pulled questions echoing from the corners of my mind. Who else might be seeing the Raven and maybe thinking of me?

A chill brushed my cheek. The night sky was the same that had covered me back when I had found Chealana as a pup. She had been so little, hardly the beautiful wolf I watched her become. Her fur, saturated from birthing, had been dark in my hand. I searched the stars overhead and found the bluish one I had named after her. I wished her spirit once more to the highest point on the Raven's wing.

Night, the comforter of madness, took my feet down the same worn path to the lake. My mind felt its way back home, fingering the torn corners of forgotten faces of family, friends, and Mara.

Kneeling to the lake, I cupped water to my mouth, quietly sipped, then covered my hair with cool droplets running into my eyes and down my neck. A slight rustling sound near my feet shuffled through brown, rotting leaves. A little more movement revealed the shape of a rounded shell dragging toward the undergrowth of a nearby tree. Head erect, legs stiffly stamping the moss, she made her pilgrimage under the cover of darkness. The tortoise's legs lumbered slowly forward, pulling the weight of the sixty bones she carried on her back. She stopped when she saw me. We both knew her options. The tortoise's blank, round eye looked at me and evaluated her way. The legs disappeared, and the head began a quick tuck back into herself.

My belly told me to crush the shell and cut off the head of the tortoise. I felt hungry. Yet her hesitation and my confused thoughts of home brought only my last sight of Mara's body sprawled on the ground from my brother's public shaming: her dark hair viciously twisted in his hands as he dragged her, his foot finding the soft spot in her belly. I shook my head, suffocating the lie that there was nothing I could have done. A knot in my stomach multiplied my fault, so I tucked deeper inside. I pulled a makeshift dagger from my belt and felt the dulling edge of the blade against my thumb. My movement solidified the tortoise's decision: sealing herself away became her best safety. I rose from my perch near the water, reached down, and lifted the shell. Poking the tip of my dagger into the edge around a foot hole, I turned the sealed shell around, looking for the best opening. None existed. Moonlight cast shadows in her shell's ridges. She had disappeared and shut out the world, but she had not escaped. She could not escape. The shell, made up of three times the number of bones in my own hand, is the tortoise—a spine stitched into her back. Woven into her very being as was my own cowardice that I wore. I ran my dagger in a tickling line down her belly and returned the pilgrim to her path.

My cowardly shame stitched neatly to a sense of who I was; I could not escape either. The bones of bitter memory held me safely inside my humiliation. Mara couldn't love me. I had proven myself unworthy. Sensing her reprieve, the tortoise lumbered a bit quicker, shuffling into the shadows of the dead leaves to cover her path into the night. The moon's milky trail slid over the water with the ripples a fish made.

A cracking sound from behind told me Haliam could not sleep.

"Our pull of copper since the new moon has been lower," Haliam said.

"How much lower?"

"Enough for Malek to be angry," he answered.

Haliam's eyes stared across the lake.

Throwing a stone four skips, I replied, "Malek is always angry. He's never satisfied."

"True, but the backs of the boys take that anger, not ours," he said.

"Not anymore," I answered. "What do you want of me?" I turned to look at Haliam before bending to pick up another stone. Even in the moonlight, the forklike scar marked his jaw.

He seemed to wrestle with his thoughts. "I don't know."

"You can just say what's bothering you, Haliam. What does it matter? I cannot do anything, so speak." I selected another smooth stone, discarding two before I found a skipper.

"The moon is full. The third full moon since the last delivery," Haliam said. "The traders should come soon: Anak and the others. We could have . . . how do you call it . . . our luck?"

"Luck? There is nothing lucky here."

"So, not luck. How do you call it when a time comes for you to take?"

"I don't know . . . maybe a chance?" I guessed.

"Yes, that's it. We could have our chance, as you say," Haliam answered.

"A chance for what?"

"Why don't we go with them?" he asked.

"Why? Do you think a trader like Anak is going to invite us?" I asked. "Perhaps Malek will give us a bundle each with supplies for the journey?"

"Anak knows the way."

"Why should I go? Do I want to be impaled? You see what they do to those who try to escape." The slave-built walls of the compound were not just around the perimeter. I launched another stone over the water. The stone only skipped across the water once, with a heavy plunk. "Why do you keep asking? It cannot be done. We're better off here."

"Are we?" Haliam asked. "I get tired of stepping around men made of bones, and the children . . ."

"I don't see them anymore."

"You're . . . how do you say . . . satisfied here?" Haliam asked.

"I didn't say that."

The silence of the lake pulled our gaze out across the waters to the far edge. The wave's lapping sounds blended with the frogs' mating calls. Fear buzzed behind my eardrums.

"Don't you want to go home?" Haliam asked.

Displaced anger threw down my reply. "Why? What's there? There's nothing left for me. Do you understand? Nothing . . . *nuk* is what you say, right? *Nuk.*" My sharp reply tasted like acid.

No one missed me because no one had come. When my legs had felt like breaking on the mountain's rocks, the only thing to pick me up had been the pull of the rope tied to another slave. No one came to help me. Why should I want to go home? They were better off. The old village cries of "cursed one" from my memory joined the fear buzzing—death had marked me.

The flutter of a bat's wings scuttled overhead. Smacking the mosquitos one last time, I shifted to leave.

Haliam stopped me. "An old tale from my village tells of a great man who died and stood before the greatest god. The man thought his greatness enough to have earned passage to the god's presence. The deity looked him over and commanded the dead man to show him his wounds. There were no scars, of course, because he hadn't done anything great. The god sent him back till he found something worth fighting for." Haliam let his words linger. A frog sang louder; puffing his chest, he repeated his call, desperate for a mate in the dark.

"Where is that boy from the well who fell trying to give me food all those springs ago?" he asked. "That boy would want more than this place."

Scoffing, I turned away from him and the moon. My head shook. "That boy fell off a cliff and died," I said.

"I don't believe that. I won't. Only one with a heart of courage would have pushed through the crowd to help me. That courage cannot be gone. The heart of the eagle lies inside you, Gaspare," Haliam said, making a fist and pounding his chest.

"I failed. You never got my food," I said.

Haliam quickly reached for my shoulder. With the hoarsest whisper, he said, "I feasted on more than food. All those people, all that hostility and anger that surrounded me, were defeated each time I remembered your courage. I made the trek across mountains here because your kindness reminded me good still existed." Haliam looked at me, willing that boy from the past at my village's well to stand in my place.

Shrugging my shoulder loose, I dropped to my knees and poked a stick into the sandy edge. "This place is my punishment for all of the lives I've sacrificed," I said. The self-pity in my reply tasted dry.

"This isn't your punishment, Gaspare; this is your choosing. We can do this. We can leave this place behind and find our . . . how do you say . . . our . . . destiny written in those stars. For all your visions, you can't seem to see you were meant for more. You are . . . *pastikale*." Haliam's voice softened. Chealana's star looked down, twinkling as in agreement. That bluish glow of Chealana's star flickered more than the other stars.

I scoffed. "*Pastikale* . . . full of potential. You've got it all wrong. You're the dreamer in this place." His bold words slid back into the cradle of slavery that I couldn't fight against.

"Think about it, Gaspare. That's all I ask. Just think about it. *Mensura?* Promise me?"

I appeased him with a slight nod.

"*Mensura?*" Haliam pressed, extending his hand.

"Sure, *mensura*, Haliam, *mensura*. I promise."

"Thank you, Brother," he said. He turned to head back to the hut. "Let me know your answer in five suns. The moon will be lessening. We should still have time before Anak's team comes."

The steady lapping of the water eating the edges of the shore continued. Night darkened a little more. Silence was broken by a swat of my hand against my leg. The mosquito buzzed away. Toward the mountain, a wolf howled. *Chealana's call*, I thought. Another mosquito's bite resulted in a quick smack to my cheek. As I drew my hand back, I felt the subtle stickiness of the bug's body mingled with my blood. The water softly covered my feet, then pulled back again. Leaving and coming, leaving and coming, the water's rhythm called me to notice the shadows' vast depths and colors. As I wiped the bug on my tunic, hunger began to gnaw inside.

# CHAPTER 3

## HUNGER'S HOPE

Malek walked down into the great cavern to survey the progress of the newer middle mine, only three levels deep. The morning sun had not yet stretched as far as usual for his visits. The air twisted in tension from looks of surprise quickly masked by backs bending deeper and steps quickening. The workers leaned into the strain of being behind. He walked through the bodies walking in a line, a scowl deepening across his brow. His being there caused chaos in my brain. Something in his mood today didn't sit right.

The rays of light didn't reach this far underground in the mine. Only the flicker of the flames dancing on lard illuminated the blackness, the curling, black, snake-like smoke demanding a share of the oxygen.

He stopped with his hands on his hips. "Where are we in the haul?" Malek asked.

"We . . . we . . ." I stuttered. My hesitation had not gone unnoticed.

"What's the problem?" Malek barked.

"They've hit rock," I began.

"That's what they're supposed to be doing. How are rocks a problem?" His cold voice burned with anger. Sterilized of traits of human compassion, Malek stiffened, readying himself to strike. I felt the whip of words and got the sense his mood wasn't about production. Back on the surface, the smelter's fires sent black tendrils into the sky. The workers had gotten a late start with the fire. Rain, snow, or fog never seemed to be a factor to Malek. Twice already this morning he had met delay.

"I'm sure they will get around the block. They just need more ti—"

He held up his hand.

Walking over to the guard, Malek moved into position. He did not survey the area. He did not hurry his step. He reached for the guard's bow, threaded an arrow into the site, and waited briefly for the next to step out of the narrow hole. The randomness of his assault matched his reasoning. He simply desired fear. Pulling back the arrow, he let fly his message and intent across the cavern. His mark didn't hit one old or sickly, nor did he drop one strong and able to regain strength. His arrow plunged through a small, thin chest.

The boy had come in on the last trader's line. I had noticed him. He couldn't have had more than eight, maybe nine springs to him. He never smiled, never spoke. He stayed quiet within his own space. The arrow's mark dropped him like an apple from a tree. He rolled slightly to his side. Silence came from his open mouth. He looked like a fish gasping in the poisonous air.

Malek handed back the bow, turned to me, and said, "No more problems. If they slack again, keep back their food." Then he walked away.

Many men had died in my presence. Old, young, strong . . . I had seen so many. None of them bothered me like this one. The boy's thick wavy hair stirred something inside me. A nagging nudge questioned my memory; something felt familiar. Discreetly, I neared the hole till my feet nearly touched the little body with hair evoking the color of a summer field. I turned the boy over to see his face. In his dying, I saw my first vision of hope. The eyes, a rich-honeyed brown with flecks of gold, twisted my stomach with familiar excitement. Their shape, the long lashes, the curve of his eyebrows, the rise of his cheekbones, I knew the structure of this face. This young boy's face resembled Mara's. As I touched his shoulder, an intimacy of home surged through my hands. An internal fire burned, its smoky curls teasing my memories awake: the hearth I had sat at so many times sorting beans and lentils warmed through my arms. The boy took three more gasps, the feathers of the arrow protruding through his broken chest. His breathing slowed. I placed a hand on his shoulder to reassure him. His eyes fluttered and went silent.

Could this boy be from Ankwar? His features looked so much like hers. I hurriedly searched his tunic. I only had one light near me, but I needed to see. The tunic he wore must have the weave of my father's house, anything. Something from home. The legs of other passing miners bumped into me, jarring my balance, and knocking me onto the boy. I brought the light closer. I needed to find the pattern. Red threads would be difficult to see in normal light, but his tunic was crusted and frayed. I strained to see the thin zigzag weave and any threads that might be left. As I scratched at the dirt, a few lines of little red threads, appeared. The red pattern from the house of Tandor, the house of my father, lay in my hands. How had I not seen this before? How did he find himself in Anak's line? What had happened in his village . . . my village. . . to his mother . . . my Mara?

The nails on his small, encrusted hand were torn. Picking up the slender hand, the same hand that had held his mother's, I gently fit his hand into mine. It was still warm. I brought the tender fingers to my cheek. Had his father ever held his hand and showed him how to fish or shoot a bow? Had his father carved his first knife? Had Aroden done a better job as a father than a brother?

Another miner's leg bumped my shoulder, knocking me forward. The copper pits didn't offer room for my grief. His head fell back limply when I scooped him into my arms. He felt hollow in my arms, light like a sparrow.

Two slaves came to me. One motioned to take the boy from me.

"*Nekala, nekala,*" I said, shaking my head.

The slave dropped his eyes quickly and left. I could feel the warmth still on the edge of the boy's skin, cooling. This mine wouldn't suffice as a tomb. The mine's depth of three layers deep was too new and the work was still ongoing. I needed my mine: the mine's shaft I had dug when I arrived here.

On the other side of the lower mine, where the old pit gaped at the sky, I walked with Mara's son. I would lay him to rest in one of the finger caves seven levels below; one I knew well. Disbelief mixed with possibilities. My grief pushed through a door long forgotten. His frame, light from malnourishment, still became heavy as I crossed the last rise to the mine. I took him past the reach of sunlight, where the dark air dried on my tongue, dank from a mine grown dead.

I knew the finger extension where I would place him. Without needing to think of where I went, my feet followed the old path into the depths. I wouldn't be able to go all the way back. Before the shadows deepened into one, I laid the boy on the ground and looked for the lamp that marked the entrance to the once-great room. Had the last slave of this mine responsible for oil left a light behind?

The lamp sat on the rocky shelf; the flint strikes beside the bowl waiting patiently for miners to return. Twelve hits and I caught a spark on the tinder. Cupping my hands around the tiniest of light, I gently blew the cinders to glow white then orange. No wind would scatter and threaten my efforts. I blew controlled breaths on the tinder causing the glow to spread and little threads of red travelled down the tinder. A few more breaths and the red strands caught the old, yellow twine popping into a small, white flame. The strength of light collected and issued forward to push back the cold weight of dampness. Hoisting the boy on my left shoulder and holding the light in my right hand, I struggled to continue deeper.

Lower down, water coated the walls. His weight pulled me low enough to avoid scraping my head. We had stopped working this hole three full springs ago. Malek believed the copper to be bled dry; the obsidian-like streaks of copper hadn't caught enough light to merit wasting more time here. He had us move to a new location, but not before five men had been shot by his random arrows to convince him production was done. No one would venture into this cave again. I could give Mara's son the burial of our people.

The musky smell of cold air weighed heavily on my back. The abandoned ground filled my nostrils with dust. This had been my hole where the prophecies began. Here in the dark, my hand had bumped into different men while grabbing a bucket or a stone. Not every time, but sometimes a picture came to me from that brief connection. In the dark, I learned how to see. I learned how to interpret. This hole is where I saw Malek as a burning tree; I saw the heat of anger he held inside.

Decay's acrid scent lingered in the chill's clamminess. How many times had my feet pressed smooth this dirt? How much copper had I, myself, brought from the bowels of this mine?

Two more lengths of the larger rooms and we would be deep enough. Passing the stacked rocks of former hammers, I counted the closed-off paths. No more copper had been found beyond this pile of rocks. I risked squeezing back a bit farther than intended; the steady temperature would preserve his body.

I moved aside the rocks. Laying his back gently down, I arranged his limbs carefully, having him rest on his side. He couldn't feel anymore, but feeling began returning in me.

This cave would have to serve as both the council room of my elders and the Apu-ah hole for the boy's spirit to descend back to the earth. He had no belongings to trade as our custom required. Nor did I. Both of us slaves, far from anything that identified our lives as men, we had nothing. My village honored the dead by trading one of his possessions with each man in the village. We recognized and honored what the dead man had brought to our tribe through the acts of his belongings. And we wished the dead safely into the darkness with a gift from our own character. Here in this cave, the only item of value the boy owned was on his body. I couldn't use his tunic as an offering and leave him naked down here in the dark. I tore off a piece of the tunic, rubbing the soiled weave between my fingers. Had Mara woven this for her son, or did this handiwork belong to Kaiya's fingers? The dirt embedded into the fibers buried any scent but Earth's. Burning tears in my eyes blurred the pattern of the red lines within the brown weft. In my pouch, I found a smooth stone from the lake. This trade would do. I lay the flat, gray stone in his hand, covering the token with my hand.

There was no burial cloth for his face, no women wailing outside, but the forgotten words of my tribe came through me as a song echoing off the walls. The light danced in shadows. The color left his lips. His blood had left, seeking the way back to his shattered heart. I sang the words carrying him back to the earth. My eyes closed against the stone walls of the mine. Instead, I looked into my memory. The rhythm of home rocked me slowly back and forth.

Words of the distant lands from under a younger sun washed and cleansed me as the shadows danced and my body rocked. The dead gave birth to life. My face bore the stream of tears, as the words of blessing turned to silent wails. I could no longer sing. I shook from silent screams. I knelt in the nightmare of my failure with one, final prayer. Meant to skip, this stone would remain here in grief's lake, pulling me through the loneliness to a place of longing.

What had happened to Grandfather's blessing? Had Mother's vision of me from that day at the hearth with the spilled lentils been a mistake? She had seen me as a holy man. Had the gods declared me unworthy of this role? My life did not tell the story of great things. A flat, gray rock summarized what I had achieved in life. I wanted to take the stone back, but instead, I struggled to sing the ceremonial words. As I rocked and chanted over the boy, my grief stoked the coals inside my heart. Kneeling beside a younger me, I felt all the potential I had seep back into this hole. Daily obscurity had chased away any color I had felt. This couldn't be what I was meant to do. Mother didn't sacrifice for me to stay in this fragmented existence.

The walls pushed the sounds back to me, amplifying the mourned loss of youth. Through clenched teeth and stinging eyes, the cry of whys arched my back as I leaned into my heels, fists beating my thighs. No answer came. I rocked. I wept. I chanted. My cry came through quivering lips. As I found strength to sing, I lifted my one voice to be joined by a chorus of my echoes. How could the wisdom of Grandfather and Mother have been so wrong? I found no answer in the ritual's undying words. I fell to my side, holding my arms tight, feeling isolation cover me. Too much of nothing meant no room to take anymore. The darkness called. I just needed to let go.

A spluttering of the oil's wick brought my answer. The fuel, almost gone, meant if I stayed much longer, I would be buried here with this boy. At that exact moment, I knew what I wanted. Resting my hand on the smooth stone, I said the final words of a prayer, grabbed the lamp, and went as swiftly as the low passages would allow me. My thoughts focused as the flame flickered lower. Soon there would be nothing to see. Darkness would win.

The finger cave opened to the first larger room before continuing up the levels to the daylight. The green dust of copper layered the floor. Water trickling down the walls moistened the green to black ribbons running through the sides. Streaks of copper still ran through this mine. The copper was always so close, yet what value did copper hold if I died in this mine for not finding my way out? I felt the beating pulse in my ears. Everything looked the same in this blackness. That sameness created the scariest idea, but to focus on that fear now would be to sacrifice my chance to escape. With lungs burning, legs straining, and mind empty except for one thing, I pushed for the light.

The heavy cold touched my spine and wrapped a cloud around my head. The lamp gave a final flicker as I crossed the final great room and entered the passage to the surface. Returning shadows suffocated the last of the lamplight with a splutter. I dropped the lamp, and the bowl's clatter matched my heartbeats. I moved toward the wall and patted my way along the sides, keeping my eyes on thoughts of Mara. She could guide me. I knew my direction. The shortened ceiling of the passage scraped my head. I bent more into my escape. Panic, like dry dust, seized my throat as darkness pressed all around me. I could drown in this night. My lungs heaved for the light of the sun. Mara's memory lit my hope. Desperation strained into desire. I could feel home in the scrap of cloth in my hand.

Fifty more steps and the air's weight changed. Anxiety tried to show me distractions. The darkness felt permanent. My perception became a reality. I was too far down. I wanted to quit. I wanted to slide down the wall and crumple on the floor. Instead, I blinked harder, focused more on Mara, and kept my feet moving. Twenty more steps and I saw the soft, distant glow from the surface. A new sense of urgency replaced a dull roar of nothingness. Daylight could be seen, and I ran. Not looking anymore where I was going, I tripped on a rock and fell, sprawling into the edge of sunlight.

The fresh air cleansed my lungs as I gulped as much as possible. Rolling onto my back, I faced heavenward and the sun's blinding light. Feelings of being alive pounded in my head. More fresh air filled my lungs. No one ever loved the shore so much as a sinking man. Every muscle in my body pulled. I carried more than just myself to the surface. I felt new. I wanted more than anything to live. I craved more. So, this is what it felt to be alive. The near touch of death made my grasp on existence stronger. Smells sharpened, sounds amplified, life awakened. What I wanted more than anything, what I desired from deep within me, came as the purest truth.

I wanted freedom.

*Focus, Gaspare, focus.* Life waited for my embrace. Hope played in my mind and heart. I wrapped Mara's fabric around the palm of my hand. My new anticipation created a change. The change sparked faith. Freedom kindled the belief that I was meant for more. And so, I believed.

# CHAPTER 4

## THE DECISION

Instead of seeking stones, I stooped to the water of the lake and squeezed dirt from the boy's tunic. Threads so carefully dyed and spun, released a brownish ribbon across the water's surface. Ripples spread the ribbon into a cloud, carrying the soil of the mine away. My fingers worked, pushing the water in and out of the woven weft. The pressure between my forehead and ears pushed harder. Squeeze, rinse, inspect. Squeeze, rinse, inspect. The sun gave way to the moon's waning slice into the night sky.

Haliam would come for my answer. With each rinse, the fabric's threads darkened, swollen with droplets, their texture familiar between my thumb and forefinger. I remembered the pot Mother had kept in the house. She had traded seven of her finest pieces of pottery for those exoskeletons, the ones used to make the precious dye. A sense of pride blossomed in my chest as I squeezed the last drops of water out. Each crusty bug shell I had found climbing the oaks had been added to Mother's jar. Father's position in the village had allowed for this tiny luxury of color. Just a handful of strands could be dyed this purplish-red hue in our family cloth.

I wiped the day's dust from my eyes and nose, keeping the memory in place. I gave the scrap of tunic a final rinsing, sniffing to ensure the pungent mud couldn't be distinguished anymore. The smell of dirt had lessened, but not entirely. There was no escaping the filth of this place. The fabric felt heavy and swollen from water. One more time, I squeezed out excess water.

Mother's secret blend of madder root combined with magnesium made her weavings from the house of Tandor unparalleled. While I looked out over the lake's reflection of the sky, words from the song of Salir drifted between my memories. I sang the words I remembered. The other words scattered into line fragments that I hummed with the lapping water's rhythm. It was the same song I had sung to Chealana all those springs past. Forgotten words, hidden from a happier time.

Hanging the dripping length over a branch, I returned to my endless search: hunting a smooth stone. I scudded a gray stone across the water's surface and felt for a second one. The center of the lake did not reveal a vision of the young woman from Salir's song. No fair woman would take me to the bottom of the waters. I reached down, letting the waves rub up against my fingers. I imagined Salir's woman would look something like Mara, if only she would call me. The water would close over my head and let me sleep in her arms. My hand dipped farther into the lake, feeling the cool promises from below.

Haliam came to stand beside me. Silence stayed between us, interrupted only by the frogs chirping. I slowly stood. Haliam started to say something, caught his breath, and waited. The desperate frog chirped louder.

"Yes, Brother, you were saying?" I asked.

"I didn't say anything," replied Haliam.

"But you want to."

"You are really going to make me ask?" Haliam glanced sideways before skipping his stone two heavy hops across the lake.

"You threw too soon." Picking up another stone, I wanted to show Haliam how best to skip a stone. I bent to throw this one—a nice four skips before the rock plunked below the surface. "You try."

Patiently playing along, Haliam picked another stone. I reached to stop his hand. "You must find the right stone," I said. "The one that fits smoothly in your hand—much like the surface of the lake itself. That's how the stone skips. When the stone has run far enough, it pushes its shape into the surface, making ripples with the path of its life."

I gave him a smooth, well-weighted stone. Haliam turned the rock over in his hand, looking for the fit. He tucked the points between his forefinger and thumb, bent to better see the surface of the lake, and with a flick of his wrist, he cast his stone—one, two, three, four, five hops before the droplets opened to carry the stone below with a plunk.

"Not bad, not bad for a mountain dweller." I laughed, adding, "The secret is all in your breathing." *Breathe, Gaspare, breathe . . .* Gabor's words awakened in me. I shuddered.

Haliam waited for me again in the space between us. His dark eyes focused straight ahead under thick eyebrows. Silence by his side. "Is the lake holding up one of your thoughts?" Haliam asked.

"Maybe so," I answered.

I pulled the scrap of tunic from the branch. The cloth's dampness tightened around my grip. I looked at the stars. The moon's shape pulled toward the earth as a bow. His cutting light curved, preparing to show his full face once more. The moon's arch shimmered, reminding me of the weight of my old bow. Before Haliam could ask again, the softest whisper of words found a voice, "I want to go home."

Home. I had lived here almost as long as back in Ankwar. This should be my home. So many betrayals at Ankwar, so much shame to bury, yet roots bearing seeds grew in my confession, causing the sunflower of my thoughts to turn toward home.

"This is good news, Brother," Haliam replied. "Good news indeed."

The night air absorbed our questions except one.

"How?" I whispered. "How will we get out? Anak is no fool. If he sees us, he'll sell us somewhere else or bring us back. I won't go back to the mines."

Haliam nodded.

Once the idea of leaving settled in, my thoughts would not release the hope of seeing my valley again. "We could cause a distraction," I offered, "but that means getting help from others."

"No, we cannot trust anyone," Haliam decided. "What if we left the night before, and hid along the path or took to hiding in the chieftain's village? When Anak's group leaves in the morning, we pick up the trail."

"We would have to travel far to avoid being seen by the camp. The villagers would surely report us. Anak never leaves straight away. He stays at the mine for two nights before heading back, so we would be missed," I said. "If we fail to find him, we will be lost."

"If we stay, we are already lost, my friend," Haliam replied.

He was right. My growing sense of freedom told me staying meant giving up entirely. I looked up. Chealana's star flickered. Could she help me? She would be shifting upward soon. Our trip would take more moon cycles than we could plan. Had I mapped the stars well enough?

"How?" I whispered to the sky. "How? If we kill Malek, there are men above him and guards all around. If we get every single slave to rise up—"

"No, the better plan is to go unseen with little reason to follow us," Haliam reminded me. "No more blood on our heads."

The lake lapped at our feet, licking our toes. In the quiet of our thoughts, the water calmed and called me.

"Haliam, what if we take the water's edge?" I asked. "This has to come from a mountain river somewhere."

"We don't know where."

"Does it matter where? We need to leave, and the water will hide our trail."

"There has to be another way."

"I can't think of any."

The silence returned. Haliam fidgeted and kicked at a few stones.

Haliam looked at me. "Brother, you *do* want to leave, don't you?" I asked.

A chill came up my neck. Salir's song called in my heart with a vision of freedom.

Haliam turned and searched the trees, anything to replace my plan. "Yes, I want to go, but not by way of the lake." He dropped his head and muttered, "I can't swim."

The words seemed ridiculous, but no humor seemed to fit the moment. The moon's bow shimmered like my woman's hair across the lake's surface, luring me. I ran my hand through my hair. I tried to think of a way.

"I can't swim. The one time I did try to do more than bathe myself, I almost drowned." Once shared, Haliam's fear took shape.

"That does create a problem. I can't risk you flailing about, drawing attention with your drowning."

Neither of us laughed. The lake seemed like our only hope. Haliam continued, "I have hidden some of the smelted copper. We could trade the minerals for some shelter or food."

"First, we would need to find someone to trade with. We need to go in the opposite direction from Malek and the chieftain's village. How much could we carry?" The bright future dulled under the obstacles. I remembered the water touching my toes. The coldness meant the sun of spring hadn't yet warmed the depths of the lake. Her cold hands upon our chest in the water's depth would steal our breath. With Haliam unable to swim, we wouldn't make very good progress, if any at all.

Anak's line should be here possibly before the next full moon. He would seek his payment of copper and goods. Leaving, he would travel faster. Would his path lead straight back the way he had come? Did Anak have other journeys he made along the way? *Think. Gaspare, think!*

It hit me like lightning: we had come to this mine tied as slaves and we would leave tied as well. "Haliam, we need rope."

"I can get some," Haliam answered. "How much do you need?"

"Enough that you don't get lost in the water following me."

"The rope is always kept near the smelting pots or on the legs of the newer slaves," Haliam said.

"We will meet here again with tomorrow's moon. By then, his light will only be a slim crescent to hide us," I said. "I'll try to bring some food." Patting my pouch, I could feel the edge of the flint. We had one necessity.

"And I'll bring the copper and rope," Haliam confirmed. "So, we have a plan then?"

"No, not exactly, but we have an idea and a list. That's more than nothing."

Haliam crossed his arms, looking satisfied with the progress of the night's conversation. He knelt to feel in the water's edge. When he found what he wanted, he stood, placing a smooth, black stone in my palm.

"This is for you. One day you will find the right hand to fit this stone. She's waiting. Go far, far, far from this place before letting the water seize you. Find your woman and hold her in your hand."

I flipped the stone in my palm. The weight of it was comparable to the stone I had left in the mine with Mara's son. I wrapped the dark stone in the fragment of the tunic. Slipping the tunic into my pouch reminded me of another stone that I needed before I could leave. I will have to add one more thing to my list tomorrow.

Haliam seemed content. He had been ready to spend more time convincing me that we needed to go. Now he needed to convince himself the water would not kill him. He stretched his toes forward, touching the surface.

Looking back at Chealana's star, seeing her blue coolness overhead, I felt we might have a chance. No plan, no real knowledge of where we were or where we needed to go other than into the mountains, following the trail more north than east, allowing the sun's setting to straighten our direction till the evening star and Chealana's star could help us. The shimmer on the lake reminded me of Salir and his forbidden love. If my love of freedom was forbidden, then let me be taken down to the depths to be forever in her arms. Salir's story had not ended in death at the bottom, and something told me neither would mine.

# CHAPTER 5

# A NEW DAWN

The smelter's fire cracked, licking the air. Charcoal chunks, deep in the fire's center, pulsed an orange glow from blackened cores. Clay pots containing malachite ore sat nestled in the flames. Six blowers held clay pipes attached to long, hollow branches, pushing more air onto the coals, keeping the pots fiercely hot. Their faces glistened and were swollen red, but they didn't stop. Inside the pots, the malachite's green markings released into the air, revealing copper's spirit. The metal's color matched the fire from which she was born.

This batch of smelted copper would be used to trade with the routes that came to the mine. The raw malachite would be crushed into sacks, but this refined copper lay waiting for any special bargaining Malek needed. On a table near the cooling pots, two flint lighters and the fire paddles were lying the same way they had earlier. The men tended the fire. They each blew through their clay pipe in sequence. The air warped around them. Their sweat dripped down from their brows into their eyes surrounded by ruddy, parched skin. While they worked against the push of heat, I worked closer to the table. The rhythm of their breathing moved in heartbeats around the living fire. Keeping cadence with the efforts of the men, I placed my hand upon the two flint lighters. Tucking one of them into my palm, I left the table. The men continued to blow on the flames; they never considered me. Surviving our journey required fire and tools.

The strong smoke smell from neighboring fire pits ladened the space with the heavy scent of burning birch oil into tar. The tar would be invaluable. Pieces of cured birch tar lay in a basket under a table. I grabbed two pieces and popped them in my cheek, quickly shuffled through the basket for two more, and went back for just one more little bit. Glancing around, I tried to hide any traces my greed might have stirred. The hard tack met immediate resistance under my teeth. My body heat warmed the tar to a nice gum consistency. My tongue slid the softening wad to the back corner pocket of my cheek.

Someone returned to check the fire. Quickly I scanned other goods on the table for a piece of antler I could take. Pushing aside a few broken remnants of stone, my tightening stomach muscles let me know I lingered too long. No horn or antler tips were left lying around the smelters. I needed to go before anyone asked why my search for herbs brought me so close to the fires.

Getting a goat stomach was my biggest challenge. Today, a white-haired man was watching over the goats. The way he stood reminded me of Grandfather, and I prayed this old man would be blind like him as well.

"Ho there," I called.

"What is it?" the scratchy voice asked.

"I need to fetch some milk for Malek's woman," I answered, hoping she hadn't already come.

"Why doesn't she come?" he asked with no real desire to know.

"Malek doesn't feel good. She asked me to come." Lies came much easier when kept short.

"Where's her bowl?" he asked, still not moved to help me.

"She asked for a bladder of milk," I answered. "Listen, old man, I need milk for Malek."

Eyes slit into a face of stone scanned me for any signs of treason. White wisps danced gently in the breeze above his bushy eyebrows. This old man's age gave testament that he knew how to go unnoticed. He knew how to survive. I meant nothing to him. He'd turn me in quicker than a hawk snags a mouse. The old man's hand strayed to rub his lower back where the stiffness lived. That back wouldn't survive dragging a haul of rocks to the surface anymore.

He pointed with the craggy end of a stick at the wooden spoon on the table. "You can find one over there," he said.

Instead of hurrying through the pile, my fingers lingered and seemed to consider the sides and weight of each vessel.

"Take one and be gone," growled the old man. He didn't like anyone remembering he was with the goats. His perfect hiding spot extended his time to see another blue sky.

I selected one stretched stomach, ladled milk into the pouch, and said farewell to a grunted reply. As I turned to go, a small whistle carved from a buck's antler caught my attention. The size of the whistle fit nicely in my palm. I had everything. Someone looked out for us on my end. Hopefully Haliam will be able to find rope.

We didn't have the luxury of a pack to help us support any supplies. Looking down at my wrapped feet, I could see thin spots in the pelt's covering. The journey would be long. The mountains would still have snow on top. Crossing the mountains the first time, my shoes contained the proper layers of grass and furs to protect and insulate me from the mountain's bite. Now I would have to find some good pine branches to make do until we came upon more suitable materials. Salir's song from the moonlit lake didn't offer comfort here in the daylight, surrounded by so many questions. Last night the darkness hid the stupidity of this plan. Now doubt found lots of places to poke holes.

The bladder of milk kept me from walking among the slaves. They would swarm me like flies on a rotting carcass. Making my path along the outer ridge of the camp, I found where the new younger slaves clustered. A group of them surrounded a smaller boy. One of the bigger boys kept reaching over and smacking the little boy's head. Then another boy joined in and kicked. Just like the chickens destroying a weak or injured hen, these boys systematically took turns increasing their hits. The smaller child would shrink into himself, become sick, and before winter he'd be dead, a crow sitting on his belly. The taunts from the other boys told me their language came from the same region. The small boy said nothing. I kept walking. Our plan required not involving anyone else.

But the sound of a whack followed by a stifled whimper stopped me.

"Hoi!" I yelled. I could tell which boy was the attacker: he wore a satisfied smirk under the look of intrigued curiosity at the damage inflicted. He stood a head taller than the others. The other boys, scared by the power they had witnessed, bumped into each other trying to run away. The last to leave was the attacker, dropping his bloodied stone.

The small boy lay on the ground whimpering, his lower lip quivering, and his hand reaching for his forehead. I turned to go. Our plan didn't include a little boy. I recognized a mostly silent cry, knowing he fought for air between the realizations of his lost mother and home. He was learning to suffocate his cries. This wasn't part of my list. I turned for a moment and saw what they had done to him. Red trickled through his hair and down over his right eye. He wouldn't make the summer, let alone winter, with that group of boys. Malek would weed the weak. His small fingers made him valuable to the mine, but not if he couldn't bring what he dug back out.

I bent to help the boy sit up. He flinched at my touch. Blood now trickled down from his nose. How had he ever survived the journey from where he had come?

"*Kula, kula,*" I said. I slowed my reach for the boy's shoulders and instead allowed my hand to gently rest on his tight, brown curls. Dark eyes wide with pain looked up at me. "*Kula,* easy boy, *kula,*" I repeated. Reaching slowly for the bladder, I added, "Come take some drink." I tipped it back, allowing a little milk to touch him. He hesitated but took the sip.

"*Kula . . . kula.*" I gave him another sip. Feeling the fresh, white taste of milk, the boy's hunger gave him courage, and he reached to hold the bladder. He finished and coughed with a thin, white drip from the corner of his mouth. I brought the bladder to his lips again. As his belly filled, the tension in his eyes relaxed a little. His shoulders still shuddered. I didn't want shock to set in and waste the dinner that I had given him. This time the boy drank, but a bit slower.

"What's your name?" I asked. "What's your name, *nadek?*" I tried using a word from a southern tribe. He remained silent. I pointed to my chest and said, "Gaspare," then pointed to him. "Name, *nadek?*" I repeated this five times until finally, I got a weak answer.

"Kimree."

"Gaspare,"—I pointed to myself—"Kimree"—I pointed to the boy. Three repeats. The boy seemed to focus. "Gaspare . . . name, *nadek*. Kimree . . . name, *nadek*," I said, pointing each time.

From the swelling lips came a shy, "Gaspare?" His voice sounded lost. I smiled and nodded. The gift of language created a thread of trust between us. Looking at Kimree, I saw hope begin to warm him. More than the milk, hope could sustain him.

Standing, I held out my hand and said, "Kimree, come, *putay*, come."

Never dropping eye contact, Kimree slowly reached out his good hand. I tucked the bladder under my other arm, and we made our way back to the goats. An older woman had been tanning a hide near the old goat keeper. When we approached her hut, she was outside with a clam shell shaving fur off a hide; tufts of it floated away like dandelion puffs. Glancing over, she saw Kimree; she put down the shell and walked to meet Kimree. No words were needed. She had seen this before. She took him over to her water and dabbed a damp cloth over his forehead, cleaning as she went. On the ground next to her stool, the sun caught the smooth shine where two sharpened antler tips lay. My good deed had led me to the last item. I left Kimree with her clucking around him, one tip still on the ground. My list complete, I headed back through the camp feeling lighter than I could remember.

The bladder, much lighter now, no longer created a challenge to hide. My stomach growled just a little in reply. Kindness sparked promise within me. Kimree had awakened a side of me I had tried to forget. Maybe my whispered prayers in the mine had been heard. I felt a subtle shift—compassion, here in this land of rock and endless pain, meant maybe I could find the man I should be.

In the thick, green moss grew a cluster of seven delicate, pale-blue flowers. The simple, unexpected beauty here at my feet evoked pleasure. Stooping to pick them, my hand decided not to. Four little blue petals were dancing in the air, suspended on invisible stems. A gentle wind bobbed their little heads ever so slightly. I brushed the tops with the tips of my fingers. It was enough.

# CHAPTER 6

# THE ANCIENT OAK

"Hoi," a voice cried. "Why don't you be of some use? Fetch some more water from the well."

Grateful for the distraction, I took the bucket and fetched water. Taking some gulps for my own thirst, I caught the reflection of movement from a large shadow passing overhead. I looked up. The wind softly rustled between the long, brown flight feathers. An eagle whose powerful wings made for swift, silent flight flew over. If I stretched myself out, I wouldn't match the span of this great beast. It was low enough that I could see the eye. This bird defined strength, and his eye contained no questions. Pure focus in flight. Following his direction, I saw the mountains waiting: the very mountains I needed to cross with Haliam.

I watched the wings. This creature was free. He could fly away from this place and go where he wanted. As I watched him, I knew I wanted more, too. Deeply breathing in the same air, he flew on I closed my eyes enough for me to see my old valley green with spring and the children running toward the mountain to find berries. The rhythm of their feet and the song of their laughter came back to me. Behind my eyes, the feeling of home and the longing to leave brushed my anticipation. Of all the fires started by my hand, none warmed me more than this flame.

Looking up again, I traced the path of the mighty bird. Tomorrow's chance would come. If I had to chew off my own foot, I would save whatever ideals tied me to humanity. I was going home, but not without my birthright. As the sun stretched her way to the other side, I found my way back to the giant oak. The width of this tree required two men reaching around to barely touch fingers. Her size saved her from an axe; her meat would be too heavy and require too much effort to use. Instead, her boughs had become sacred. Standing under the strong branches and feeling the cool grass underfoot felt right.

Like my village's menhir stone, the gray bark felt as smooth as the ridges of the hills. The veins in the bark gave a path for my fingers to follow down to the hollow. I scanned the arms overhead. This tree had grown stronger since I was last here. One bough . . . I just needed to find my one bough.

My fingers felt the cool bumps as I walked around the trunk, scanning the heights. Nine springs had stretched the branches higher. The new green leaves had begun to sprout. Winter's coppery-brown clusters of leaves still clung to the branches, making certainty difficult. But a slight breeze lifted them again briefly, showing me the bend in the branch where I had cut and tied my marker.

Positioned under that bend, I walked away from the trunk the number of steps I had walked before. A young sapling stood barring my way. Lying a little closer than before, I found the spot. The crag of a large, half-buried rock jutted through crunchy leaves. Poking the leaves with a stick, I listened for the rattle of hidden creatures. Venom's warning didn't come. The stick pushed aside layers of leaves, heavy, soggy stacks of black compression returning into the earth.

After digging in the unyielding dirt, the stick broke. I threw it away and tried my chisel; the chisel didn't move the dirt fast enough. I dug with my fingers. I wanted to feel what I had left behind. It had to be here. I traced my way along the uncovered rock's edge till I saw the shape of a flattened string. The string stood out from the soil. I pulled till a slightly larger, black bump resisted from farther under the dirt. Picking up my chisel once again, I pried under the bottom of the string at the top of the bump. Easing the lump from the ground, I felt the soil release my pouch. Brushing off the dirt, I held my treasure again.

The leather, blackened beyond recognition, slowly opened. Holding my breath, I thrust my finger inside, groping to feel the stone. My finger bumped into the smoothed edge. After all this time, it was there, the piece of gaspar Grandfather had given me. The familiar dip in the side of the stone felt natural. The stone hadn't changed. The little pouch still had the strength to hold the necessities from my list: pieces of birch bark, the antler tip, and the black stone from Haliam. The flint strikers went in also. I could easily weave some long grasses to construct a new cord for the pouch.

Near me grew a feathery cluster of caraway. Numerous white buds full of sweet, dense flavor stood erect among the softness of the greenery. I broke off a sprig. The land would provide us many tinctures, salves, and nutrients along the way. The moist smell of the pouch now held the rich spores of decay. The seeds from memories stirred. Nine springs ago I had dug this hole—my hands, bruised from fighting, hurriedly scraping to find the safest depth. The oldest boy of sixteen had sized me up as small, easy to control, much like Kimree's attacker. He had wanted my gaspar stone.

That older boy had watched me absentmindedly rubbing my pouch when I first arrived. He had decided my pouch was easily his. Once taken, he had proudly worn my birth stone around his neck, evidence of his rule. A black eye, a busted lip, and soreness for days rewarded my efforts to regain my inheritance. He trusted his greed too much. I hadn't fought a bear and lain near death for him to hurt me now. Regaining my stone from the boy required an intermingling of patience and cowardice. One moonless night came, and a sharpened flint meant the boy didn't wake. Then I'd dug the hole and bent the branch, leaving my pouch and past waiting in the ground.

The sun now touched the top of the tree line. Off to the left, a slight movement shifted in the light among the rocks on the slope. The texture and stiff curve of long horns contrasted with the still rocks. The gray coat on its back blended perfectly with the landscape; only the horns betrayed the grazing ibex. The length of the horns indicated the age of this alpha of a sizeable herd. Seeing the goat's surety among the rocks contrasted my fears of that night and mingled with the guilt of the buried pouch now around my wrist.

The ibex's horns bobbed farther up the side of the rocks. I tightened my hold on the bladder. Questions of our journey bounced in my head as the goat claimed a higher position on the rock. Haliam just needed confidence. If I could just get him through this first length of the journey, we would be all right. The ibex bobbed behind some rocks. The reddish-orange cast of the sun sank into the arms of the tree line. The ibex stopped. Possibly we could make our way without Anak's directions. Likely not though. I lost sight of the ibex's path. That older boy had been like my brother, Aroden. Like the oak's strength, jealousy grows deep between siblings. Unlike the older boy, I wasn't returning to kill Aroden. I wasn't sure I could even claim what was mine. What was I hurrying home for? My stone and my secret had lain waiting here in the ground near the roots of that old tree. So many layers hid the answers I sought.

# CHAPTER 7

# WATER'S FLIGHT

The two guards who stood near the lake would no longer be standing when they finished the fermented juices stolen from Malek's party with Anak. Bretasko, the head guard, never allowed the men to drink on watch. His fierce eyes always watched for the weak link among the sentries. A man's life would be shortened if Bretasko caught him off task and not focused on the borders. Tonight, however, their secret sipping would cover our escape. Added valerian root seeping into the berries helped ensure heaviness of eyes and a slumbering spirit.

Breaking through the tree branches, I found Haliam staring at the stars. "Come now, Brother," I whispered, "did you think I wouldn't be here?"

"Maybe a little," he admitted, but the way he eyed the water told me he feared more than my absence.

"Haliam, look to the star on the left. Do you see the one that is part of the line?"

Haliam studied the stars and asked, pointing, "The bright one, there?"

"No, three over and up a bit," I said, extending my arm to guide him.

"Yes, I see it."

"Keep that star and her eight sisters always on your right and pointing in the direction you walk," I said. "No matter what happens to me or to us on this trip, keep those stars on your right side."

Haliam nodded. No jokes or nervous chatter. Only starlight gave us something bright to believe in. That belief would guide us into the hills and hopefully home.

"Here, blow this up," I said, handing him the bladder.

Taking a breath to blow in the bladder, Haliam stopped and gagged. "Couldn't you have washed this out?" he asked.

"Hush now, get that thing blown up," I replied.

I tied the rope around my waist and waded slowly into the lake. Cold water burned my feet and legs, rejuvenating my senses. My toes found a smooth rock to wrap around. I stood there till the cold subsided.

"Tie that bladder around your neck," I said. "It's in case you slip."

Haliam did exactly as I said, but when I turned back to look at him, I could only drop my head. To laugh would mean he'd take the bladder off. Maybe the nerves of the moment proved too much, maybe the exhaustion from not sleeping finally caught up, but I had to pull the corners of my mouth down, pinching the laughter that threatened to expose us. My shoulders jerked with the laughter my mouth could not express.

Haliam shifted uneasily. "If I die looking like this, at least I have the consolation that my blue, bloated face will haunt your dreams," he stated.

Haliam tied the other end of the rope to his waist and began to enter the water. The chill forced him to take a quick intake of breath. He had been concentrating on so many other things, he didn't think about how cold the first part of our journey would be. If staying didn't mean certain death, Haliam might have quit, thrown off the bladder, and gone back to his mat for sleep. We had, however, no way back. Only forward. The crime of drugging the guards would be understood for what we had intended; we could no longer stay.

The water gradually came to be like the deep snow on a mountaintop rather than a powerful wind knocking our breath down. As the surface came above our waists and then to our chests, we raised our hands to the sky, holding the few supplies we carried as an offering to the crescent moon. The moon's low angle created a single slice of reflection on the surface. No light could penetrate the lake's surface, so we felt our way with our toes, careful not to step in a drop-off. When my toes didn't touch the bottom, we backed up a few feet and I redirected us to the left. Haliam's short quick breaths sounded from behind. His body would only continue getting cold if he didn't slow his rate.

"Like this, Haliam, deep breath in . . . hold two, three . . . release."

"I can-n-n-n't ca-ca-catch my air," he stuttered.

His shivering indicated he would not make the length of the lake if we didn't stop. Turning, I said, "Haliam, look at me, Brother, look at me."

The whites in his eyes shone with fear. I went on: "With me, Haliam, with me." Together we breathed in, tried to hold a little, and breathed out. As we repeated this, the holds became longer, and the panic lessened. Haliam began to allow slow, deep, rolling breaths to calm his lungs and his heart. Shivering lessened its hold on his shoulders.

"Focus on brother moon," I said and began telling him about Salir's journey in small bits.

Haliam assured me he was ready. I put one finger to my lips. I heard faint sounds of commotion coming from the direction where the guards slept.

"We must move," I whispered.

Gentle ripples lapped off our bodies as we pushed our way into the dark, leaving sight of the shore behind. The water carried the sounds of our breathing. I stepped forward quicker than I had been going and smashed my toe into the side of a rock. The pain knocked me off balance.

"Grab the rope," Haliam whispered. "Grab the rope." The breathing had steadied him, and now his turn had come to help me.

By grabbing the rope, my feet could touch solid ground. The rope, meant to help Haliam, saved me. Water's amplifying talent seemed to reveal our pounding hearts. Haliam reached to finish steadying me. Glancing to the shore, we couldn't see any guards yet. The excitement had filled our ears, so I waited a moment to gauge where they were. Luck shielded us; still, no torches shone on the shore.

Haliam smiled and said, "I'm warm now."

Another deliberate smile made its way to my lips as I looked at him and raised an eyebrow.

Together we began moving forward again. Slow as before. What good was speed if we created noise alerting everyone? Not risking going farther out, we edged our way northwest following the shore toward the hills.

A bend in the lake came soon, as did the first torchlight bobbing along the shore. We crouched lower into the water. The moon stayed silent and small. We came nearer the bend as the sound of men shouting to each other drifted across the water. My head pulsed from the numbing cold and tension of carrying out our plan. We dared not even whisper for fear the water would tell on us. Three torch lights came to rest at the place of our escape. Their flames flickered and bounced a little before one torch left. The second torch seemed to speak with the third torch and bobbed off in the direction it had come. The last torch came to the lake's edge. Haliam and I froze. Nothing moved except the fish and currents below. The slight pull from the undercurrent swirled around our knees. We were close to the river that fed this lake, so close to being free to follow its run up into the mountains. The torch still stood. We still crouched. The torch waited. We prayed. The water licking our ears was the only sound.

Finally, the third torch followed the other torches bobbing back into the woods. We dared nothing more than a sigh and looked to the stars. The Raven had kept our secret, and Chealana's star brightly shone. She was on my right side, pointing the way home.

# CHAPTER 8

## THE TRAIL

Rocks, chipped and jagged, gripped the shore like teeth sinking into the leg of land where I stood. The water's rush ignored the rocks, bashing and bubbling downstream. Anak's trail lay uphill above the river. We had made enough distance from the camp and the trail to ensure no one would see us. The fading moon arced overhead and would shortly give way to his sister's golden warmth. Determined to take our chances near the river, we settled near a tree cluster. The water's chatter would mute the crunchy leaves around us.

I went to the river rocks, hoping to feel a trout hiding, and pulled the speckled body up to the surface. Haliam's eyes widened in surprise. The fish became our first taste of freedom. I held the body to the sky as a thanksgiving tribute to Shal, the god of water. The fish's mouth gaped wide, and the body twitched before I broke its back upon a rock. Fire couldn't be risked no matter how small. I used the little pieces of flint I'd stolen to separate the spine, pulling out most of the bones. Wet, tightly packed white flesh became our first bites of liberty.

After eating, Haliam sat with a stick quietly poking at the ground. I chose a long drink from the river rather than sitting. Each gulp brought no answers to our dilemma. I poured a handful of cold water over my hair and wiped my face. Maybe the words would come as we prepared to sleep. Only the quiet of frogs chirping greeted me as I returned to our camp with pine boughs. I spread the fragrant needles over a mossy outcropping and kept some boughs for a blanket. A fire would help so much. The fresh smell of pine filled my nose. Sticky sap wouldn't coat much with the short time till light. Soon, shadows and sleep began to take hold. In the sunset of my energy, I heard Haliam decide to speak.

As I rolled back into my mind, sleep drowned out anything he might have said. My eyes just needed a little bit of quiet from decisions and darkness.

\* \* \*

Too soon the sun lifted the last of the night air. A cooling fog hovered over the river. We would need to move into position before Anak's group passed. I scanned our little enclosure. I couldn't see Haliam. The pine boughs prepared for him were left aside where I had placed them. The sounds around me were spoken by birds, not my friend. I jerked to my feet, trying to remember what he said. The cool fingers of dawn touched my nakedness.

"Haliam?" I walked over to the path. "Haliam?" I took a few quicker steps in the other direction. "Haliam?" A hoarse whisper was the most I dared.

Branches moved to my left. Out from the brush stepped Haliam, hair freshly wet.

"Good morning, Brother," he said.

"Good morning," I replied. "How long have you been up?"

"I never slept," he said. "Here, try these." Haliam handed me some dandelion greens and garlic roots that had been freshly dug and washed.

"I thought you had left," I said, taking a bite.

"I thought about it."

"What stopped you?"

"We left in the dark, and I couldn't see. When the sun came up, I realized I was free. I have you to thank for that," he said, pointing the green tip of the garlic my way.

Shaking my head, I dressed. "I cannot make this trip alone. You know that?"

"Yes, I know," Haliam answered looking down.

"I mean I wouldn't make this trip alone. "

Haliam only repeated, "I know."

We made our way farther up the river's edge, keeping in line with the mountain pass. Gnarled tree roots and mossy stones braced the river. A small grove of low-growing willows created an ideal hiding place. When the wind blew, the leaves lifted, revealing a whitened belly. This color change and movement hopefully would create camouflage for us.

From up the hill came the murmur of distant conversations. A flock of small birds took to the air as the voices came closer. We took our place among the willows.

Anak's voice came first. He only had five men to command, but his orders rose as if addressing the village council. His voice's familiar scratchy quality stiffened my spine. Haliam and I crouched lower into the willow leaves. The men's spirits, lighter due to their load of copper, gave swiftness to their way.

One man in the rear seemed to carry the most. He tried to stop the procession, yelling, "Hoi! I'm hungry!"

"So, stay and eat," yelled the reply from the front.

"We all should stop," came the request somewhere in the middle.

"What, so Malek's men can find us?" Anak said, turning toward his crew. His voice echoed off the water and trees. "Once they learn what's in your pack . . ." Anak gave a look daring discussion as he pointed to the heavy sag in the sack the last man carried. The man dropped his gaze and shifted the pack's center. Hunger would wait. They moved on.

Anak pushed them farther along the path past where we lay. We waited longer, staying beneath the branches, ensuring a snapped stick or shifted branch would not betray us. Our chests were as still as we could keep them. With the last sight of the rear man, we left our hiding spot and worked our own path just off the trail. Keeping their voices near, we stayed low and close to the river.

We all walked on: Anak and his men, then Haliam and I far below. As the sun began her descent toward the treetops, a noise from behind us alerted Haliam. He quietly motioned me back down behind a large tree just as the face of a guard from the mine cleared the top of the trail's hill. Without a sound, the guard pulled an arrow from his quiver as two more guards came into view and threaded arrows as well. When all six guards had canted bows aimed at Anak's men, the assault began. Before Anak even heard the cry of his men, two arrows pierced through his own back. Arrows volleyed down, and Anak received another blow, dropping him to his knees. His men turned to throw their spears, but in the speed of the attack, not one spear left its hand. The woods were filled with the swish of arrows swimming through the air. The men dropped to their knees, their last breaths on their lips. The sagging pack pulled its owner backward, sprawling him awkwardly across the path.

Three guards came up and walked among the fallen men. Bretasko was one of them. Some men use violence to prove themselves strong. Some watch the mangled results with fascinated relief that they had not been the victim. Bretasko was neither of these men. He moved in the surge of strength knowing the destruction he would cause and sending a message of fear to any survivor holding out hope of escape. He knew his will would be wrought through the acts of his men. Bretasko did not negotiate. He did not take captives. He did not waver in his path. The bows were lowered, but daggers were out. Anak lay twisted on his back, one hand on his chest. His breath rattled. Haliam and I pulled farther down into the undergrowth, praying the cover was thicker. We watched the first guard look through the packs. The sagging pack Anak had indicated caught his attention. The guard kicked the body of the rear man over to cut off the pack. Pulling out something I had seen on the smelter's tables, he motioned to the other guards, lifting the item. The guards collected the stolen tools and daggers traded from the Eastern tribes. I had seen the smelters making copies of these advanced tools. Bretasko's massive shoulders pushed through the first two guards. He did not hurry. He did not need to. His steps echoed thunder from the mountain's peaks: reverberating, full of warning, and very present, his eyes focused and sharp, assessing as he moved. He knelt near the stash of retrieved goods, fingering a few pieces. Anak stole prototypes of tools and weapons cast from copper; a weight more than he had earned.

Bretasko nodded to the first guard. The guard walked over to Anak's dying body, bent down, and blinded him, making sure Anak's spirit couldn't see its way into the next land. Anak's dying screams echoed in the trees. With his dagger pointed into the joint, the guard removed Anak's right thumb as the body slumped further into the ground from its writhing position. He wiped his dagger on Anak's coat and tossed the scrap of a thumb inside the pack with the stolen goods. After a quick exchange with Bretasko, two guards left with the pack's contents, back in the direction of the camp. The other four guards continued looking through packs. Anak's greed had sealed his fate. The rest of the contents seemed to just be the usual copper payment. As quickly as the guards came, they left, with Bretasko being the last to go, his sharp eyes scanning the trail and undergrowth around the path. All the guards left except for the two men Bretasko had indicated to stay behind. Those two guards knew if they returned prematurely, there would be consequences. They spread out to search the trail surrounding the dead men. With that, the fierceness of Malek's head guard disappeared back toward the mine.

When the sun had shifted significantly, and the willow branches seemed a darker shade of green, Haliam and I made our way to the clearing where the bodies lay. Even in the cool spring air, flies had begun to collect on the bloodied lips and noses of the dead. The woods were far from quiet, but no one mourned these traders. Malek must have suspected Anak of taking more than his gain for some time to send six guards like this.

Stepping around the bodies, we looked for anything that might remain. None of their food or water had been taken by the guards. Keeping one eye on the trail and picking through the fallen men's clothes, we each claimed a dagger. I selected a couple of the best arrows from various quivers. This stash saved us a lot of work and resources. Without these tools, our journey would have been short-lived. Now we had a means of protection and a way to get more food.

Haliam picked up a spear dropped near the hand of one of the men. I headed for Anak's body. There beside him lay what once had been mine. Taking my old staff in hand, I could feel the light weight of the ash wood my brother Gabor had carefully chosen. The sheen of the wood had weathered well from the oil of Anak's hand. Still strapped to the top was the bear's baculum smoothly curved. Running my hand along the length, I thought of the day Gabor had given me the staff. He had declared the bear a great beast and me a bear hunter. There had been admiration in his eyes.

"Gaspare, I thought they had come for us," said Haliam.

I turned my staff in my hands, wondering how many backs Anak had beaten. Absently, I replied "Yes, it seems we are not as valuable. Maybe we haven't been missed yet." Even while saying this, I knew Malek would eventually need me. He would ask for me. He needed my languages.

I looked up at Haliam with realization. "You saved my life, you know?" I said. "I hadn't seen or heard those men. I would have been a captured bonus to the goods they were sent to retrieve."

Haliam nodded his understanding with a slow smile and said, "This could only be from the gods."

"This is from Anak's greed," I corrected him. "He cheated Malek one too many times."

We looked around the path, waiting for an idea of what to do next.

"Without Anak's group to follow, we've lost our guide for when the trail divides," Haliam continued. He suddenly seemed less eager to dismiss the gods intervening on our behalf.

I rubbed the staff in my hands. "We'll find the way," I answered. For the first time since I tied that rope around my waist at the lake, I believed what I said to be true. I had my staff, my stone, and my friend.

"We had better get back down to the river in case those two guards come back," Haliam said.

Checking the trail behind us, I nodded in agreement. We didn't know the extent of what the guards were after. Possibly they were still looking for us. The sun cut through the trees. The light behind us made the trail look inviting. A small animal skittered above in the leaves.

The agitated caw of a black crow came from a nearby branch. Soon, Anak and his men would be carrion for the vultures and other birds answering that call. We headed back down to the river, the leaves deep around our feet.

This river would have to be our guide through the rolling hills up into the mountains. We would have to trust her to lead us true. The problem with water is that her determination to incessantly move makes her a force that could drown a man. Haliam had cleared one lake, but rivers had more undercurrents and hidden traps with stacked rocks and shifting bottoms. We both needed to depend on Shal's generosity.

Shal, however, wasn't known as a god of mercy.

# CHAPTER 9

# THE RIVER

The river widened, splitting the mountains and carrying the sky upon her back. Restrained with rocks and exposed roots of trees daring to hold to her shores, she pulsed forward, never looking back. To do so would drain her soul dry. The silver sheen on her surface, so much like Chealana's fur, belied a soft texture she did not have. Her waters captured the expression of motion's still life silently working her way, gathering insignificant sediment and sand. In little inlets, limestone particles resting on the floor of the river reflected a hypnotic turquoise blue. Gray rocks, partially submerged, jutted evidence of the river's persistent toil, always pushing tiny, irrelevant particles from surfaces till they no longer stood tall. With our path lost above, we needed to trust her power and focus to lead us home.

I stood a moment longer on the outcropping, allowing our decision time to settle. Below me, grasses erect like little hairs indicated a cold we would have to face. Behind me, Haliam waited on the damp shore.

"Brother," he called, "what are we waiting for?"

"Not really sure," I said. "Maybe deciding how brave I feel," I muttered more to the river below.

I turned to look at Haliam. He nibbled on a thin reed, which bobbed as he said, "Can't say that I'm eager to face her cold embrace either, but what choice do we have?"

I turned back to face the river, and he answered himself, "None."

So many times, I thought I had become a man. This river had another lesson I needed to learn. Haliam seemed emboldened by the near-death encounter with Malek's guards. Now risk rose to meet us once again.

I sighed. "I just wish I knew what lay beyond that bend up there."

"Probably more of what's here and equally cold," said Haliam.

Small stones were clustered in the water at my feet. Their true colors revealed mottled browns with gray or pure whiteness; I selected one with a red vein on green. The smooth, small ridges felt cool. This rock would mark my journey. Rubbing it for luck, I slipped the stone into my pouch.

"Are you ready?"

"After you," Haliam smiled.

"We can try the shore farther up to see if a deer trail is there."

Haliam shook his head. "I'm not too eager to meet Malek's men when they follow those trails to refill their own water."

"Then we'll look for a place to cross here, and then a trail on the other shore."

"I can't imagine she gets narrower farther down."

"I've never noticed this negative perspective of yours." I laughed. "Neither can I, but maybe we'll be lucky, and the god Hekor will have pity on us and give us a fallen tree or path, something, anything he believes we can hold on to," I said. "Those waters can be shallow or deep, but they are definitely swift."

Little whitecaps of water spoke in swirls of movement as they worked their way around the boulders. Leaves rustling behind us caused us both to jump. We traced the sound to a squirrel darting up a tree.

"We've stayed too long," said Haliam.

Haliam's idea was to take his rope, tie one end around his waist, and hand me the other end.

"Right, now where's your bladder?" I asked.

"I'm not wearing that thing."

"Would you rather drown?"

"Absolutely," he answered.

I tightened my end of the rope before we turned and made our way out into the morning sun. The water stayed at knee depth. As little fish darted out of our path, the river's bottom stirred the water a light brown tint, clouding our way. The depth continued past our knees and then thighs. I felt the rope tying us together lose slack; looking behind me, I saw Haliam slowing even more, his wide eyes staring at the water, trying to penetrate the brown ripples for a safe step. We were getting deeper. Turning back around, I noticed something below the current felt funny.

The smooth surface of a hidden rock covered by a thick sheen of green moss caught my foot. The sheen was living and not just moss. It pivoted under my weight, biting my toe. Had I been facing forward, my balance would have been enough to keep me upright. Being caught in a turn meant I already had no balance. Distracted by the sudden pain in my toe, I lost control and fell in. Like plummeting into snow, the cold river stung, taking my breath. Just as the water shut out the sky above, I felt the rope tighten. Pressure from the river closed around me, her force deafening. She closed over me embracing me with her fingers of currents pulling and pushing me down.

I saw the underside of bubbles while my feet danced to find solid ground. My arms and legs hit against the surface of the rocks below, but I could not stand. Haliam's tight hold on the rope gave me a focal point. Icy cold shot straight to my brain. My left hand reached back to hold the rope while my right pushed against the surge to level myself upright. The river wanted to move me like the many particles in her way. My feet floundered sideways. The weight I carried pulled me in the direction of the current. We didn't have much, and I couldn't let go of what we did have, but the fight to regain footing increased the river's hold on my back. Some arrows worked their way free of the quiver. The bobbing sticks aimlessly pointed the arrowheads downstream before disappearing. Water splashed into my eyes.

From the other end, Haliam shortened the rope until he stood close enough to extend a hand to me. Noise from the outside world garbled into rushing bubbles. Once more I struggled to stand and my right ankle, the same fated foot, caught the jagged edge of a rock, adding to the bites of the hidden monster and the cold. Haliam's strong hand steadied my shoulder. Trying to reorient myself, I stood amid the rapids, gagging, coughing, gasping, doing anything to breathe clean air.

Without warning, an arrow pierced through the water to the right of us with precision. Another arrow struck a rock on our left. We turned to scan the shore and saw one of the guards stringing another arrow. I had given us away. The guard fired a third arrow, grazing closer. He turned and called to another guard.

We crouched in the water. "Haliam, can you help me cross?"

Looking over his shoulder, Haliam assessed the guard's range. Seeming to forget his fear, Haliam tugged my arm over his shoulder and plunged forward. He pushed through the water's resistance, aiming for a jutting rock on the other shore. The river was determined to push us back, down, or sideways; we focused harder. Another arrow flew into the water before being joined by a second. Grunting, straining, crossing the open space amidst arrows, rocks, and current, we pushed through the water's eddies and foam. The morning sun danced across the surface with radiance. Blinding light made tears blur our vision. Were both Shal and Hekor trying to kill us today?

The breeze picked up, lifting little ripples of water into little white caps of waves. Together with the sun's fire, the river turned into a dazzling cloth, sparkling white with crystals. The guards on the shore could no longer reach us. They would have to venture into the water if they were going to catch us. Realizing the cease in arrows, we stood taller, making one last great effort. Running and floundering through the river, we finally reached a sandy bar of white limestone. The blueish-green waters were a welcome relief, but we couldn't stop. Even though we had picked the narrowest part for crossing, the river still stretched before us, making the opposite shore seem just as unreachable as it had at the beginning. Haliam held my shoulder tight. We used my staff as an anchor, drawing on the bear's strength as we clawed our way across. There was no time to carefully avoid more hidden rocks or their treacheries.

Eventually, tall grasses came within reach. The depth of the water lowered, and the shadow of the trees came out to cover us. Once on shore, we allowed ourselves a moment to breathe and to look back. The guards on the other side were looking for a way down the slope. The incline was too steep. For now, they would not be able to follow. But they would find a way.

Looking over at Haliam, I noticed a stick coming from the back of his left arm. He seemed unaware until the numbing cold began to wear off. He had been hit. Tossing him my staff, I suggested we keep moving. That arrow would need more than a quick break. We limped as quickly as we could to the nearest path and vanished into the brush.

Once cleared from immediate sight, we assessed our own conditions. My right foot was fat, swollen skin stretched across toes as thick as sausages. As air reached the cut, blood began to pool at the tip of my whitened toe. Whatever had been on that rock decided it didn't want me standing on top. My ankle also had a cut, and blood now dripped into a tiny stream. Haliam reached for my foot but jerked back. The arrow shaft prevented him from straightening his arm. The pulsing pain of the arrow growing in his arm became our focus. He felt the straight lines of the shaft coming from the back of his arm and the black tip of an arrowhead protruding out the front of his arm.

"He was aiming for your lungs or heart with that shot. You're a lucky man," I said.

"Looks like we both can't really go far now," he said, wincing when I touched around the exit wound.

"Nonsense, this arrow isn't in bone, just muscle. It wants to come out. The icy water helped keep you ignorant of it, most likely."

"I'm beginning to notice it now," he said as he held his wound. "Exactly how will we ever outrun them once they make up their minds to cross after us?"

"We need to get that flint out of your arm. Then I'll pack your wound with some herbs to hold the cut till we find a place to build a fire."

Looking back across the river, Haliam noticed the guards looking over the river trying to determine their next move before turning back to the trees. "We won't have time for a fire now," Haliam said. "The guards will be here sooner or later."

"The more we drag through this brush, the easier our trail will be to follow. We need another way."

"Should we try heading back to the river?"

"That's a bold choice, but probably our best. If we stay low and are careful, we might go undetected."

Haliam considered my answer. I leaned back and looked up at the trees. Despite the pressing danger, the air felt free, and my lungs stretched to take in excess. The canopy far overhead felt full of possibilities. True, the guards now could confirm our escape. Maybe other guards would soon come looking for us. Malek's men would not be so easily appeased. Rest would not comfort us for some time.

Gently twisting the arrow's shaft, I eased the flint tip closer to the edge of the skin, bulging and pushing further through his arm where the stone worked. The head of the arrow appeared to be rather small, more for shooting a small game than a moose or man. A quick knick with my dagger and I could reach the shaft behind the head of the arrow. Haliam's yell didn't give our position away. I had already done that.

"Brother, I need to break the shaft from behind," I said.

Haliam didn't answer. He clenched his teeth and braced his feet against a stone in front of him. Careful not to jerk his arm, I sawed at the shaft with my dagger. A moan followed by another made the next decision easy. A snap from the breaking twig sounded. Haliam turned to the side, gagging. Once enough of the stone had emerged, I grabbed it tightly and tried to pull and push from both sides. Haliam's face whitened. His face was covered in a sheen. The widest part of the arrowhead passed through. The size was little more than a thumbnail. A final tug brought the shaft out. Haliam gasped for breath. He began to shiver. I pressed my leather pouch to the wound. Haliam's shortened breaths became shallower. His face was white as limestone, and his blue lips from the cold began to pale to a green color. Shock would soon take over. He held the bloody arrowhead and dropped his head between his knees. His back spasmed as his stomach relieved itself. Laying him back down, his head aiming down the slope, I covered him with anything I could to warm him. Daring a visit to the river, I filled the bladder. I packed grass in his wound till we could find proper herbs.

The sun's warmth reached down to his body. The breeze seemed to stop, allowing the rays to focus. Asking him anything, begging him to focus and drink, I prayed. I couldn't let sleep take him. Slowly his eyes began to focus. Some color returned to his skin. The packing of his wound looked good. He would need a change soon, but I didn't want to risk touching the tender area. I dug through the pack we had taken from Anak. I pulled out a package and found dried meat. *He could definitely use some smoked jerky for the salt and protein.* His lips regained some color with every bite of the meat.

He slowly sat up. "Our chances of survival just increased," he said.

"Why do you say that?"

"Both Hekor and Shal have tested us, and we walked away."

"You won't be walking anywhere soon," I said.

"We can't stay here waiting for those guards."

"Don't worry. I have a feeling about this. Just give me a little more time to change your wound's dressing." Leaving Haliam propped against a rock for warmth, I walked among the wildflowers just a bit from the shore. There, the feathery stems of yarrow grew. Further away some more stems and roots from plants that looked like centaury caught my eye. The pinkish blooms were not ready to show yet, so I couldn't be certain; Mother had shown me as a boy how to make the tonic in the summer when the flowers of both plants were visible. But the plants seemed right, and the remedy would stop the blood and lower the inflammation for both of us. When we could make a fire, I would prepare the herbs better and seal the wound with the fire. Now, I didn't wish to go too far away. I needed to get his wound packed. We would need to move.

Lifting the packed grasses from Haliam's arm, I could see the irritated, red holes. I repacked the grasses, adding some spit and the buds, risking some of the rope to tie his poultice in place. He drank some more and tried to stand. A wave of dizziness swept his head. I grabbed him to lower him, but he stopped me.

"I'm okay. We must take this slowly."

As we gathered up our packs, the air around us filled with dreams of how our journey would evolve—dreams filled with lofty hope mingled with the current despair till we had created a fragile state of confidence. I talked of how we would set traps for rabbits and grouse and eat from our own banquet every day. Each night we would sleep with a world of stars above us. We would keep heading in the path of the sun. Anak's path was lost. The way home would not be easily found. We didn't have our guide. We did, however, have our freedom. That new possibility pulled us toward the northernmost star, directing our path to the mountains and what we hoped would be home.

# CHAPTER 10

# LOSING SIGHT

The river was a true guide. She led us forward into her rolling hills and up to the mountains. Her moods changed quickly, from pushing through narrow gorges to sprawling lazily in the sun with little islands and white rocks, to waterfalls of varied heights. She was the mistress of the land, and she knew her powerful beauty. After another moon's face, her shores began to be rockier with fewer trees. The distance across became wider. Her body had spread; the depth and currents pulled deeper into her belly. This river revealed even more power.

My toe was doing well enough; the swelling had gone down. Only two little punctures and an angry gash remained. Haliam's arm needed rest, but no infection had set in. The fire we made had helped sear the wound closed. The climbing on rocky terrain pounded our joints and required balance of both arms. Our choices were shifting away from following the river to finding help. A small village had to be somewhere nearby.

The sun brought more rocks to our path. The sound of many winds filled the space ahead, echoing off the rocks' hard surfaces. On such a clear day, that could only mean one thing: the river was falling. By the time the sun had pulled her light to the middle of the sky, roars from below rose like yelling workers in the mine when a cave-in had occurred.

"She's angry and ready for blood," Haliam said, tossing the twig he had been twisting.

"Yes, froth is forming on her rapids. She would smash anyone upon those rocks, breaking bones for bread." We watched the water dip and lean into the rocks.

"Why did we cross to this side?" asked Haliam.

"Doesn't matter now."

"Do you think they made it across?"

The pounding of the river took the place of any answer. Looking away, I picked up my bag off the rocks and began to head toward the edge. We had passed several places they could use to cross over.

"Without a doubt, they will follow," I replied. "Malek will have his control. Our heads upon a pike will ensure that no one else tries to escape. Didn't you see Anak's hand?"

"Maybe the river will narrow again."

"Maybe . . . and maybe she'll continue to widen."

"Then she will need to teach us a better way," Haliam said. "I refuse to believe the gods won't help us." The scar on Haliam's jaw reddened.

"If we continue to follow her, she'll push us out into the valleys. We need the mountains. No, we must cross again," I said. "How is your arm?"

Haliam turned his arm with a little shrug. The wound was still packed with a poultice, so I let it be. No excessive redness or angry red lines seemed to surround the area.

Looking over the edge of the rocks, we saw a small patch of sand jutting out.

"There must be a path down to the river. Look there." A narrow way between boulders cut from many springs of high-water erosion took us to the edge. No room to move except forward. Crevices on the rock's surface helped to brace our feet. The river's raging rapids made me step back once we got to the bottom. The small alcove at our feet seemed mild enough, but the rapids waited. We looked around. Not much there except a few logs that had broken loose from upstream.

Haliam's eyes widened as he exclaimed, "Shal be praised! He provided us a way over his mistress."

"What? How?" I asked.

"We ride these cedars down."

"You're crazy," I said.

"They will float. Looks like they've been drying here on this shore for a season plus."

Following him to the fallen trees, I nudged the bark with my foot. "You might be right."

"Of course, I'm right." He glanced at me with a serious smirk. "I rode a goat once as a boy. We can make this log here a goat," Haliam said, going toward the one mostly exposed in the pile of three.

"You rode a goat as a boy?" I asked.

"Yes, no time for that now," he replied. "Help me loosen this big one from the other two."

"We're going to throw ourselves on the mercy of Shal because you rode a goat once?"

His raised eyebrow challenged me to find a better solution. Nothing came. After breaking off as many top branches as we could, Haliam's idea found us straddled on a log with our packs tied to the top. Broken branches jutted out enough for us to take hold. The river's greedy fingers grabbed hold of our log, bobbing us downstream like a duck. The little bumps in the water felt like we were the skipping stones bouncing along the surface till the river decided to pull us below. We were at her mercy. The water led where she desired.

The first boulder came. Not tremendously big, but big enough to crack a branch and for the back current to pull at our log and begin to twist us sideways. The next hit shattered another extended branch.

"You were right, Haliam, you were right!" I shouted back to him.

"If only we had a way to steer," he said. Our log headed straight for exposed rocks lower downriver.

"Tuck your feet! Nothing sticking out!" he shouted over the water.

Skimming along, going faster and even faster, the water rushed downward. We bobbed along on top. The sun warmed our backs while the waters below pierced our legs with needles of cold. White foam and clear splashes of water danced around us. The bumps were picking up again as the rapids approached.

An arrow flew from behind me and wedged into the log in front of me. Swiveling quickly, I saw Malek's two guards along the shore. They loaded more arrows into the bows aimed at us.

With no choice or time, we slipped off the side into the water. Grabbing desperately to the trunk before our ride floated away, we tucked close to the side. Our packs, still strapped on, helped to shield us a little. The rocks ahead or the arrows behind meant taking chances with death either way. Maneuvering to hold the log in our armpit, we submerged ourselves keeping only our heads out. The river's power pushed our log and pulled our legs backward as we moved even faster. It was useless to fight the current. The front of the log bumped off rocks. Splashes covered us as we were pummeled into a tighter passage between rocks. Each jarring made us cling tighter, pulling everything we could closer to the tree. A muffled moan from behind told me Haliam wouldn't take the water's beating much longer. Daring a glance behind, I noticed Haliam's poultice sagging on his arm. My hope for him was that the chill of the water masked the pain. Water pushed down our throats and into our eyes, showing no mercy. Nothing but her voice was in our ears. White wave caps lifted our log, tossing us further down course. As the log darted between boulders and around the swirls, I began to understand what she was saying: today was not the day we would die, or at least not this way.

The pounding of the rapids came on stronger. Our lightened log careened off the surface of half-hidden rocks. Cracks could be heard each time a larger boulder blocked the way. Bruises accumulated on our legs. Only the sound of roaring filled my ears. My eyes tried to focus straight ahead. Three more cracks, each one shaking our hold. Dry spit coated my mouth.

The rapids dropped straight down. The log followed, lifting my stomach. Three other rapids poured into the same drop, creating a wash of power. One final crack against another rock at the bottom pulled tension in my neck. Pain loosened my hold. I let go.

Thrown back from the momentum, I surfaced away from the log. I needed to ride this river or break upon the rocks failing. I tried to aim my feet downstream; my body shot along the currents, catching up with the log and Haliam. The drops in the rapids washed over my head, wanting to simultaneously push me down and pull me forward. The water tried to submerge me again. Another rapid pushed Haliam's log to hit a boulder, and the log splintered. Haliam had to make shore with only one pack tied to him. As I came rushing along, he stabilized, and I grabbed hold of his leg so I wouldn't pass him by. Once in the calm shallows near the shore, we threw ourselves down in disbelief that we had lived.

The intensity of the river had relaxed, and the shore flattened. We could walk this section near the shore. Lower branches extending over the river made good holds. Before long, we emptied out into the calming shallows. Coughing out the excess water, I climbed up to the shore. My toes squished into cool mud and warm, sandy dirt. The breeze felt good along my face. We had just survived the worst Shal had sent us. All parts of enjoying being alive washed over us.

"I think she likes us," he said.

"Who, the river?"

"Yes, I think she likes us. Otherwise, she would have killed us."

"She sure tried. A goat?"

"We made it, didn't we?"

Shaking my head, I focused on how blue the sky looked. "I don't think I've tended any goat with that much spite."

"Oh, she's a feisty woman, all right, but she saved us more than once from Malek's men."

"True—they won't cross here, but we're still on the wrong side."

The white wisps of clouds lazily flowed over the stream of the sky. Lying there, I could almost feel the ground beneath me turn. My pack was gone, along with my staff—necessary sacrifices to be safely ashore. I felt my chest and found the pouch still there. There would be more bears in my future, I was certain, but only one stone from Grandfather.

"How's your arm?" I asked, seeing the poultice was gone.

Before Haliam could tell me, an arrow pierced the air and landed uncomfortably close. A second arrow closed the range to its target.

We scrambled into the branches for cover like hares and hid behind the great rocks. Malek's men wouldn't give up. I could see them talking, regrouping, pointing. They would track from that side of the river till another chance came to cross.

Mountains reached to hold up the sky on both the east and west sides of where we hid. The path of Anak didn't matter anymore. We would need to make our own way and pray for the best. Maybe Shal had shown favor to us. Maybe Malek's men would catch us another day. Clutching our one pack, and pushing farther into the brush, adrenaline pumping into my ears replaced the pulses of the river. Birds flushed up to the heavens as we walked too close. The blue sky above filled our lungs with an abundance of life: full and enough.

If I died today, I wouldn't die complete, but I would rest satisfied knowing this feeling of contentment. The graying profile of the mountains stretched wall-like in the direction the sun headed. One of those peaks meant our way home. Just one, but which one?

# CHAPTER 11

# THE WAY

With the morning sun's arrival on the third day since Haliam's wound, I noticed reddening beginning with some cloudy drainage from the site. We needed a thermal hot spring. Back at the mines, Malek and the officials would travel each full moon to a thermal spring nearby for treatments. Mud like that would bring healing strength to Haliam's arm and our sore muscles. With Malek's men on the other side, we followed the river, heading a bit south in hopes of finding our warm bath along the way.

A little dormouse ahead in the grass caught the attention of a perched red kite sitting high in a tree. Wings bent back and tucked, then opening in time to glide in, she landed heavily on the mouse, piercing its neck with a sharp talon, hopping once to make sure the mouse was stunned and knocked out, and then carrying the little crumpled fur up to her nest, a messy collection of leaves and sticks high above our heads. Spring meant babies and a new life. Food was needed to keep life thriving. We were no exception. We needed to eat. We also needed to rest.

"Let's walk a little farther before stopping to make a fire," I said.

Haliam didn't complain, but his footsteps were slow. With back bent, his body looked heavy. He kept walking in stride with me, but his breathing had changed. His unusual quiet indicated the arm needed tending. As good tidings from Hekor, a mineral smell wafted on the air.

"Let's head to those rocks," I said, pointing to the right. White and gray jutting formations created a small channel toward the spring. The smell soothed and carried warmth to us just before we could hear the busy sound of little bubbles disrupting the surface. As I squeezed through the tightening path between the rocks, I saw it: a small reservoir lay waiting.

"Come, Haliam; let's take time to rest."

We walked into the water. The soothing spirit calmed us with a welcomed relief. I cupped water in my hand. The water tasted sweet. Haliam rested against one of the smoother rocks, his wound fully submerged, his eyes closed. I could feel the same lethargy coming over me, but if we were going to survive, I needed to act more like that red kite and less like the dormouse. Leaving him to rest, I took the bow we had been working on. It was not smooth and finished, but the yew wood we had found was a stroke of luck, and the way was long, allowing for many opportunities for me to whittle and shape the branch to create the desired curve.

Returning later with a small rabbit and more leaves and blossoms for a new poultice, I set to making a small fire. Haliam stirred a little when he heard me. He was the image of the lake: smooth and clear with no need to hurry anywhere.

"Haliam, maybe you should come out. I've brought some food for us here."

He half-opened one eye, blew some air out of his mouth, and moved his hand over his face, stretching his jaw down as he did.

"Reach down there and bring me up some of that mud you are soaking in," I said. A dripping handful of grayish, mineral-rich clay would make an excellent patch to dry and heal the spreading sickness, to ensure the red line stopped running up his arm. I lathered his arm, sealing everything, even into his armpit, returning to the spring more than twice to get enough mud to coat his torso. As we ate the little meat from the rabbit, color relaxed back into Haliam's features. He was healing more on the inside. Seeing a normal color return to his cheeks, I felt confident of his ability.

"Haliam, before sleeping, go back and soak a bit more in the spring. The water can wash away the mud." I set to prepare a new poultice. He nodded and headed to the water's edge. He didn't look back. He let the water rise and cover up to his chin and closed his eyes again. The shadow of sickness had not yet entered his eyes, although he already looked thinner from our time running from the guards. The secrets of the water were drawing out the poison of our escape. We could continue our journey not like scared prey darting for holes and hiding places, but as men walking into the valley and hills.

# CHAPTER 12

# NATURE'S CLAIM

Spring in the forest became summer on the mountainside. Walking down the hills, we heard the wind rushing overhead through the trees like waves of water. Nature's elements mimicked each other's sounds when surrounded only by her beauty. Crackling fire sounds resembled trickling water or snapping branches that spoke with the bird's song. The smells further up the hill felt open and fresh, but the smells further down towards the start of the smaller streams were heavier and damp with spores, moss, and pine.

The land was full, rich with enchantment. Mountains unable to contain all her goodness erupted with water falling from crevices, the sound like heavy rains with a clear sky. Waterfalls were abundant: hiding in caverns where the strong, stern, gray-chiseled rocks leaned into the delicate fall of white waters that twisted on their surface, thinning the stream to reveal a blueish quality to the water before spilling into the green waters. Some waterfalls split around giant boulders, resembling milk spilling from a bowl. Our favorite fall we named *Bokti*, meaning "young fleece." We could see this majestic fall from a great distance. Powering over the mountain, Bokti shouted a healthy welcome to us from afar. As we neared her basin, the strength of Shal was pounding from the height of an eagle's flight, yet Bokti's hair spilled all the while like the threads in Kaiya's loom back home.

The valley and mountain's beauty slowed us a bit with delicate flowers that grasped the rocks tightly. Tiny stems held particles within the crack while pale yellow and peachy petals bobbed above, luring bees with star-shaped stamen. Other stonebreaker flowers covered the surface of the rocks like moss producing the tiniest of blooms. A tree, in the middle of the river, grew exposed from a boulder. The tree raised her branches like the antlers of a legendary stag, her lower roots entwining around the rock like a mollusk. Life had found a way to do more than survive. Powerful examples encompassed our every move with determination, motion, and dignity that laid claim to the right not just to exist, but to thrive. Daily we walked through a display that taught us to stand taller, to look farther, and to breathe deeper.

We followed the sun by morning and camped under the light of the Raven by night. Each full moon brought a glow and softness, healing the fears that we would be caught and taken back. Surrounded by pure goodness of balance in all growing things, we began to forget, to relax. Yet even in paradise, a crucible is formed, filled with worry over thoughts that didn't happen. We hadn't seen Malek's men till we came near the first village on our trail. They had found a way to cross. Staying hidden, we watched them with the villagers. That had been three full moons ago. An older man in the village had pointed them in one direction. We pursued the other.

The villages began coming closer. Where there are villages, there are trade routes of flint, cattle, and slaves. We were finding our way. Some nights we stole a chicken or eggs. Haliam found some einkorn hanging to dry, so we harvested supplies and crept back into the darkness unseen. Worry, however, followed us. I didn't like taking from the livelihood of these people. There was always a way to justify our taste for civilized food. Secretly though, we desired the community of others, and the luxury afforded to those living near the help of their families.

A small fire heated a smooth stone, and Haliam cooked eggs while I ground the einkorn and made a small bread paste. Haliam tried to calm my worries by saying, "Tomorrow these little eggs and bread we are feasting on shall carry us to the next village. We'll soon find our way back. You'll see."

Not convinced, I turned the little bread pastes on the stone with a grunt.

"The gods have brought us this far, and that's not for nothing. The gods will direct our path home. I feel it in my bones."

"Your bones, huh?" I asked.

"Yes, my very bones," Haliam replied as he sat back to knap a piece of flint into an arrowhead. My skepticism at my own role as a holy man wouldn't allow me his belief in the divine intervening to guide us. I whittled the piece of wood to finish making an arrow shaft.

Our silence nudged me to say, "Do you know why Malek's men seek us?"

"Hhhmm," came the only reply with rhythmic tapping on the stone.

"He's never going to let me go, Haliam."

Haliam's tapping slowed. "But he did let you go. We just need to avoid him."

"For how much longer?" The words reeked of pity we couldn't afford. My stone's stroke on the arrow shaft pushed in too hard, snapping the end. The tapping stopped altogether.

"So, we continue making our way along the edges of these small villages. We do what we must do."

I focused my attention on the rough-cut end of the branch. I needed to turn my tool to carve out the tender meat of the shaft. Then I could sit the arrowhead. The sun's light had begun to shorten. Leaves found their colors of yellow and red. Neither of us believed the gods wanted us to push through the mountains in winter.

Haliam rose to add a little more wood to the fire. A chill had begun to settle on the nights.

After a bit, he broke the silence. "I'm no fool, Gaspare. I know we need to find a single location to stay and make proper clothing and equipment to survive the cold. We can't when we constantly are hiding and on the run from Malek's men. But I am not going to stop believing we will make it."

I sat quietly, taking my punishment. My brothers, Gabor and Esteban, would have cuffed me already. Haliam struggled to stay positive, but the tapping didn't begin again for the night. He took some water and made his place to sleep.

"How about in the morning, we collect what we need to boil down birch tar so we can glue these arrows together?" I asked.

Haliam took the bait and said, "Certainly, Brother. I have three arrowheads finished. I can strip some sinew and gather some birch bark."

"We can stay here a few more nights then," I said. "We've covered a good amount of distance these past four or so moons."

"Yes, but we need to stop stealing from the village," Haliam answered.

"Why? They won't catch us," I boasted.

"Sure they will. They will only believe so many eggs have gone missing. Besides, I am hungry for meat."

"Well let's hope these arrowheads of yours are sharp enough."

"Let's hope this bow of yours is strong enough."

In answer to his statement, I held the yew branch out, balancing it on my fingers. The length shone smoothly in the fire. The curves that I had carved out a little at a time bent nicely.

"I just need a good stone to tighten the fibers." I pivoted the bow, admiring the work. "Then I'll get you some meat."

Leaning back, I couldn't help but agree with Haliam: it would be good to stop and rest. The land here could provide all we needed if we stayed. The animals were plentiful even without the farmers from the village. The craggy mountain, streaked white with limestone, established views in every direction, impressing a sense of the abiding strength dwelling within us. But the river's pulsing that pushed through the valley kept us restless and moving with her. No matter the temptation or desire to put in roots, there was unfinished business at home. Things I needed to address. People I needed to face. If I didn't return, how would I know the answer to my biggest question?

# CHAPTER 13

## ESCAPE

Mountains grew into more mountains. Boulders weighed heavy, pressing all forms of fossils deep within the stones below. These mountains were our way home. Our legs had grown stronger since leaving the mines. Our pace should have been quicker, but not combined with the mountains, ignorance of our location, and being prey for Malek's men.

Some parts of our trail took us through narrow gorges cut through the rock by shifting earth. Other parts took us on ledges the width of our feet where little stones scuttled below. Storms came, chilling us deeply till we found shelter in a cave. Sun scorched the weight of our packs into our backs on other days. With lungs strengthened and legs sturdier, the climb became easier, but not the way.

Stopping to camp under the remaining yellowing leaves, we set about gathering twigs for our fire. I left with my bow to find food. Haliam went a different direction to gather birch bark for our needs. We would stay here for two suns making new birch bark carriers, melting the tar for gluing, and finishing any repairs we could. Our supplies needed restocking.

I knelt in the high tufts of grass behind the rocks. Cheala's breeze pulled on the tassels of summer's last seeds as she crossed over. A small herd of three ibex stood near a bush farther up the hill. The mother had birthed two kids that spring. Old enough not to play at her teats anymore, young enough not to stray far, the two youths grazed near. She stretched her neck to pull more leaves from the inner branches of the bush. The mother's short horns would be useful for making the carving tools we would need as winter approached, but she was not the one I had sights on. I moved a little closer to the edge of the rocks. Glancing over my shoulder, I could see a sharp drop behind me. To avoid falling, I lowered myself to be closer to the ground.

The smaller of the two kids was slower moving than the other. The little goat didn't jump up the rocks but stayed rather still and quiet while its sibling jumped and kicked up the sides of two large boulders, looking for more leaves to nibble. I moved a little bit closer. Some loose pebbles rolled under my foot. I just needed a better angle. The slow kid would bring the bigger herd down and be caught either now by me or by another predator before the winter moon reached a full cycle.

I brought myself to full height. Quietly, I pulled the string up to the bow's notch. My thumb ran across the smoothness, feeling the tension within the wood. I positioned my back away from the cliff's wall, daring a space closer to the rim, my feet parallel to each other and the edge. Looking further up, the rest of the herd was visible grazing above. The arrow lay upon the riser just above the curved wood where my hand balanced the bow, the flint head sharpened last night, was ready to find its mark. Cheala blew a little more, lifting the hair on my head. My breathing enlarged and slowed, clearing my mind. The length of the arrow focused on the space behind the little kid's front leg.

I tightened the string, feeling the moment, readying my release, securing my anchor hold. The shot should bring him down. The taut strain from waiting triggered the wood's flaw within. The tension in the bow snapped, creating an explosive boom in my hand. Shards of wood filled the air around me as splinters spun out.

Immediately the mother and two kids darted up the side of the cliff, landing on the smallest ledge and bounding to the next. They rejoined the rest of the herd. The last tail bobbed out of sight and was gone before I could stop myself skidding down the ledge. Knocked off balance, I slid down the side of the mountain. Seeing the cliff's edge that I slid toward, I snatched at anything as an anchor. Loose dirt carried my grip away. My feet scrambled, sliding further apart, the void waiting below. I lowered my center, knocking the arrow out of my way. The arrow scuttled over the edge. Lying on my belly, I reached for a branch growing out of a crag. Stretching, my fingers lightly touched the tip. I needed just a bit more reach. Fingers searched to hold on. Nothing secured my grip.

One of the broken pieces of my bow slid off the ledge, taking more pebbles over. The string caught behind a larger rock, stopping the bow fragment. I pulled the end testing how secure. The string held me for a moment, long enough for me to shift my weight, and then the string loosened, slipping further. I had to let go. My raw fingers dug into any crevice, fingertips searching desperately for a hold. They pulled hard on the small rocks jutting from the narrow ground. Stone pressed my chest from outside. Fear pressed my chest from within. Gasped air dirtied my mouth. Flying spittle wet the dirt. Blood trickled from my hands. My ears rang with the noise of shattering wood. The blood pulsed heavily. The sounds of my panic suffocating. I must try.

I dug in with my ribs and stretched, yearning for the feel of the little tree in my fingers. It was just beyond my reach. I grabbed at the needles once, twice, but they just tickled my fingers bouncing up and away. Cheala did not help. She chose to be aloof. I lurched one last time. Grunts powered my last effort. My fingers grabbed hold of enough pine needles, just enough to push with my other hand and grab a little higher. The little branch, growing on this unforgiving surface, held me. Finally, I could place my hand flat on the rock's stable surface. My left foot found grace on some raised nub of the rock. The cliffs below would have to wait.

My muscles began to exhaust. I could feel a prickling sense of near escape together with splinters from the bow. As I straightened and regained my stance on the rock, my chest heaving and burning in pain, I looked up . . . straight into the feet of Malek's man.

He stood on the ledge above me, sneering. My display of survival must have been ironically amusing to him. Not much space between us to plan. Not much room to move. He felt confident his journey was successful. I felt certain my time had ended.

He threaded his bow, took aim, and focused entirely on me. Disgrace would not stain my last thoughts. I would not die begging or dodging fruitlessly on the side of this mountain. My spine lengthened and my lungs filled, taking in the precious air, savoring the last, long release. My eyes steadied, and I could see him anchor his pull hand on his cheek, a position he had practiced many times.

A slight movement on the side didn't make us take our eyes off each other. From that movement came an impact that sent Malek's man falling over my head and down the cliffs of the mountain. His cries rolled and bounced, ending below with a thud. I looked with wonder at Haliam standing above me, bracing himself from following the man below. Haliam's hand reached to pull me up. When I climbed to his ledge, we both looked over to see the twisted form of our stalker lying broken below.

Hearing another noise, we looked to the end of the passage and saw the second guard. He had heard the cry. He came too late. A gap of silence filled the distance between us. All of us calculated our options. No one saw a way clear. He sized us up and considered the air and terrain. He had weapons, but only time for one of us. His chances of being the only one to walk away were divided. We stayed tense, not moving. I didn't think our chances were very good.

The guard chose his action first. Never breaking eye contact, he looked at Haliam, gave a slow nod, then considered me, repeating the nod. He waited. We both in turn nodded in reply. The guard lowered his bow, backed away in the passage, and went off into the mountain. His form changed from alert predator to a free man.

Haliam and I waited a bit longer without moving and without celebrating. The many moons of being hunted and hiding had ended. We were left trying to recognize our good fate. We looked at each other, considered the moment sacred, and turned to find food and our way back home.

# CHAPTER 14

# WINTER'S HOME

When the sky grayed and released the first flakes, we took that as a warning and made our way lower into the valley and the next water source. Continuing to move with the sun, we heard an axe chopping a tree—no other sounds, just the thud of a tool hitting wood. Another yellow leaf fell in front of us as we stopped to listen. The odds of the man being dangerous were less than our need for food and rest. We stayed north and downwind from the sound and continued down the slope.

We crouched as we approached the clearing, anticipating where the echoes rang out. Crawling a bit closer to the rhythmic knocking, stillness, and quiet was our cover behind the long grasses and rocks. Cresting the little hill, we saw the source of the noise and the last of fall's display: seven rams competed for mating status. Rut season had begun.

Two powerful males' heads heavy with curled horns, raised on their back feet for leverage, the muscles in the rams' legs then rippling upon impact with the ground. Running forward, they tipped their heads. Then another hit. Two more males squared off, lifting their sizable weight on just their hind feet before crashing into their opponent's horns. A third ram butted one of the competitors in the rump. They went on like this, oblivious to us. Hunting them would be easy enough. To approach the body to clean and gut was less certain. Those rams each outweighed us by double. We watched the magnificent futility of what females did to these powerful brutes.

Haliam pointed at one of the smaller males toward the back. This season would not be his champion season. He would be lucky to mate at all in this herd. The competition was too steep. I nodded and crawled on my belly, the high grass camouflaging my approach. I parted the stalks before me with my new bow. With this grouping, I would need to drop the ram and wait till he bled out. I couldn't risk him taking off or walking openly among them. If I aimed just right, he would stagger and fall unnoticed.

The male I targeted presented me with his rump. It was up to me to come closer, more to the south of the group. The snow falling had increased steadily. The thicker flakes covered more of the ground. I was close enough now to see the whiteness of snow staying on his back. His hide would warm us, as would the soup we could make while cleaning. I notched the arrow and moved a bit more for a better presentation. The male shifted and once again, I had a rump in my sites. To my left, a small rabbit hopped by. He would make nice gloves, but we needed more. Still, I took aim, and the arrow meant for the ram struck the rabbit. The kill was clean and instant. The rams didn't notice. The head-butting continued. Hekor's bounty was opening to Haliam and me.

As if sensing my gratitude, the ram turned slightly. No longer a poor shot, but not a perfect one. I waited just a little longer. The cold burned my cheeks and nose. That rabbit meant so much, but I had to wait. He wasn't enough. The big rams raised up for another dance. The reverberations shook the air. They hammered on. One of them got closer to my young ram, forcing him to step back. There it was. The shot I longed for. He would be down and a blessing to our great need. I rose up once again from the grass, kneeling on the hillside. I felt the strength in my spine hold me. Snow fell on my outstretched hand, numbing my fingers. I would need to shoot before the chill became too much.

Just as the biggest male reared up, my arrow struck hard, precisely where I wanted. Offering up a prayer of thanksgiving for the ram's sacrifice, I quietly reached for my rabbit and returned in the same manner I had approached: on my belly and out of sight, but greatly warmed by our good fortune.

Haliam celebrated with a firm smack on my shoulder and a ruffling of my hair. He was proud. We found shelter from the snow in a grove of pine and made a fire from dried needles and pinecones, the fragrance adding to our celebration. We would need to stay safe for a couple of suns if we were going to fully process the gifts the ram would provide.

When the thudding stopped, we looked back up the hill and saw the males had moved on, except my ram. He lay a little way off from where the arrow had struck. We both said our prayer of thanksgiving to the animal for his sacrifice, and I finished his time with a song I remembered.

Upon the rise of the third sun, we continued with packs filled and sufficient warmth to get us to a village. From there we followed the narrow path that widened into a trail, bringing us to the edge of a village. The first huts we saw were typical rounded shelters with thatched roofs. This village, however, was larger than most. Toward the center, we found larger dwellings formed from stacked stones. These homes seemed to have different purposes. Not all belonged to families. One great hall looked to be twice the size of our council meeting room back home. Hopefully, in a village this size, we could blend in and find a place before spring brought a safer passage.

We had arrived as the sun was beginning to finish her journey across the sky. A white haze lay in the air with a chill that indicated we were due for a storm, the clouds heavy and gray. The smell of snow wet the air. A few children saw us and tipped their heads in curiosity, watching. The tallest one picked up a rock. He never took his eyes off us. The other children looked to him and back at us. We couldn't afford this village to be hostile. We stopped to face the children. A little one in the back hedged a bit, weighing the wisdom of running off. Adults would soon come. We needed this to work.

Haliam and I both showed our hands as empty. The tall child stood still and watched us. He didn't drop his rock. We took a few more steps toward them. He spread his feet into a stance, pulling his arm back in warning.

"We need your help," I said.

The boy watched us, so I repeated, "We need help."

He said something I recognized. He spoke one of the languages I had learned at the mine. Relief eased my shoulders a little. I called to him in the tongue I knew. The boy ignored my request. His wariness increased, and he began giving the other children commands. He spoke quickly to the youngest, who ran off. Finally, he lowered his stone and replied, "You wait." He put up a hand indicating he wanted us to stay there. The boy, no more than eleven springs, turned to the others. On his word they spread out, making a line so we couldn't pass.

By this time, the first child's alarm had gathered a couple of mothers. The little boy hid behind them as they cautiously approached. The young woman, who seemed to be his mother, nudged him, and he ran on to one of the buildings. The mother spoke with the tallest boy, and he pointed toward us. The first mother was small but had wise brown eyes. She stood silent, thinking. We did the same.

I smiled, but her sharp eyes said she was not weak. I proceeded with respect. Behind her came three men from the village, a little boy leading them. The men were older than Haliam and I. They came with confidence. The oldest boy met the men, and the first man jerked his head, indicating the boys to stand down. They formed their wall behind the men. The first man was my height, short stature, but stood with strength of bearing. He knew his place and directed his questions at me. As we spoke, I could feel the small woman weighing my words. Haliam stood straight and tall, only looking forward out of deference to the men. I finished telling of our journey east and our need to rest; the man listened. The ram's horn tied to my belt raised the man's eyebrows, but only a little. I extended my hand with the horn and nodded for him to take the horn. The man's narrow, dark eyes took in everything about us.

"We are making our way to Ankwar village. Do you know it?" I asked.

Looking once more at our feet and lack of belongings, he shook his head. "Come, the snow is about to fill our village. The mountain will be difficult to cross." He turned to the small woman and said, "Manara, go. Ask Denjaka to place two more bowls of stew on my table."

Manara nodded and left. The boys stayed close, pleased to be part of the men. Our host introduced himself. "My name is Krenden. I am the chief of this village, Benaki."

"My name is Gaspare, and this is my traveling companion, Haliam." I motioned to Haliam, and he nodded in reply.

Krenden reached for my gift, accepting the horn saying, "You must forgive our doubt. Lately, thieves violate our borders."

"You have a good guard with your group of children," I pointed toward the tallest boy with a nod and smile.

"Yes, Friand would have led an assault against you if given cause."

"I thought he might," I concluded.

Krenden spoke little as he led us through the village. Something was giving Krenden cause for concern. I saw him glance toward the west of the mountains multiple times. Krenden soon entered what appeared to be the largest dwelling and showed us to the table. There we saw Manara and another woman.

"Denjaka, here are two hungry vessels for you to fill," Krenden said with a hearty tone.

Denjaka motioned for us to sit at the end of the table near Krenden, our backs to the door. The smell of roasted meats and einkorn bread turned a growl from Haliam's stomach. Krenden laughed and handed him a leg of mutton. The women did not join us. Village men came two at a time or alone. They took places at the table. When the table filled, I noticed two men standing on either side of the door behind us. Denjaka and Manara brought bread cakes and meat to the table. As the men ate, their questions determined our motives. I kept my history quiet. We were refugees. Krenden didn't need to know about the mines. Instead, I focused on my village, Ankwar, and what little I remembered of its politics. We, too, had a few raids before I left. I suspected them to be connected to Aroden, but didn't mention it.

Instead, I chose to say, "Haliam and I went on a journey to find allies to help us stand against those who wish to do harm to other villages." This lie felt comfortable; however, with all lies, the longer the lie the easier it is to spot the falseness. My betrayal came in my ability to talk even somewhat crudely in a language close to Krenden's. I hadn't considered this to be a flaw till now.

Krenden listened, nodding his head slowly. "Your village language is not known to us here, yet I understand your words. How is it you learned our language?"

Panic squeezed my throat. I looked around and noticed an axe like the one Sulvak had shown me. It had belonged to the holy man of Ankwar. Krenden had one in his house now. Reaching out, I hoped to land on some truth with a lie.

"I spent time at the temple in the village of Undoura near Mondsee. That's where I met Haliam. I also met others speaking a similar tongue as you."

Krenden grunted as he took another bite of his meat. "You are a *chenkra* then . . . a holy man?"

The necessity of our situation dictated a confession I did not believe. "Yes, I am." I lowered my head. I camouflaged the rising heat by taking another bite of meat. The men at the table shifted a little. They watched Krenden for a signal. Had I stepped too far in my lie?

I turned to Haliam, looking for a way to say sorry.

Krenden instead asked, "Is that where you got your *mentak*?"

I didn't know what he meant by mentak. Panic squeezed tighter. How could I get out of the lie if I didn't even understand his question?

Krenden repeated *mentak* three times and finally pointed to the charcoal prints on my arm.

"Ah, my tattoos?" Relieved to finally be able to tell the truth, I answered, "No, that was from my Mennatti. My rite as a man."

Krenden leaned back in his chair. He regarded me with interest. "What does your tribe require of its boys to earn being a man?"

He motioned to Manara to come and bring more meat and drink.

"I had the challenge of four gods: Cheala, the goddess of the air; San, the god of fire; Shal, the god of water; and Akeala, the goddess of the earth. The last came in the form of a mighty bear. We fell together from a cliff. He almost killed me." I didn't look up. No one had ever asked. My joints ached from our mountain trek. They ached in the various weather we encountered; each a reminder of Akeala's price. I shifted my legs under the table and reached for my drink.

Krenden seemed to question my hesitation. "But you didn't die," he said. "You must be no ordinary chenkra to wield power over such a beast." He nodded, and the men around us eased back into a more relaxed position in their chairs. On his signal, the two men at the door came and accepted food from Denjaka. The room relaxed. We had passed the first test.

We finished our dinner, drank from the store of mead, and fought back the sleep threatening to shame us at our host's table. Denjaka noticed our struggles and whispered in her husband's ear. Laughing, he brushed her aside, but she said one more thing and he nodded in agreement. "You are right . . . again, woman, you are right." He turned to us. "Denjaka believes you are trapped in the clutches of sleep and that I should end your fight for the night. Stay with us tonight, and tomorrow we shall see what we will do."

"Thank you, Krenden," I said. Haliam understood enough to know the offer we desired had been made, and he hesitantly mimicked the words I repeated. Denjaka and Manara showed us to a place farther into the home. There were furs and blankets to welcome our tired bodies. Before darkness closed our eyes, I saw a retreating candle while visions of home took me into dreaming.

# CHAPTER 15

# WINTER'S REPRIEVE

One night at Krenden's became a second, and then a full moon's face came and went. Haliam employed his skills of carpentry, and I helped with the herds that needed feeding and breeding. The old shepherding skills naturally took me back to my roots. Warmth could be found in routine and purpose. Life could bring mercy in the depths of winter's reprieve.

One morning, a sheep limped out of the pen to graze. I noticed her hiding an injury, but the ewe couldn't hide a faint smell coming from her back end. Manara was outside pulling some water from the well when I called her over.

"Manara, do you know anything about this sheep?" I asked.

Looking at the ear nick, "Seems she was a new ewe this last lambing."

"She's limping and I smell infection." I bent to see her rear leg pushing through the thick wool. I had been out in a distant field the day before, but I didn't remember her. "Does she usually graze with the herd?"

Manara looked closer at her leg. "She must be one of the two the dogs were chasing. I heard the boys talking about it but didn't think much more."

"She won't make the winter if we can't get her healed." I probed the wool and found only one gash. I remembered that Haliam and I had collected some birch mushrooms as we were hiking through the last forest. "I might have something that could help her in my pack."

"Normally, we would just eat her."

"She's rather small, but her fiber is strong. She'd be a good stock."

I turned and went to the house, greeting Denjaka. In my pack, I found the mushrooms. I took the biggest pieces back to Manara.

"If we can make a poultice, confine her to limited movement, and tie this to her leg maybe she will have a chance to heal," I said.

Manara saw the state of the mushroom and broke off a little piece to try. "Ah you mean *brechen gomba*. I have some dried that we could use." Manara left while I took some water to wash the leg. The sheep sidestepped, trying to avoid my hands. Manara returned, carrying some nice strips of dried mushroom together with some dried ferns whose delicate fronds still held the spore's underneath.

"Typically, we wouldn't waste this treatment on a single beast," she said.

"I can see that," I answered. "She is still quite young. How many lambs did she drop?"

"She had two healthy lambs," Manara replied.

"One meal or many more lambs? To me she is worth repairing," I said.

Manara deftly applied the treatment to the sheep's leg, and I tore strips of fabric she had brought to secure her work. "You're very good at that," I said. My sleeve fell back and revealed some of the tattoos set by Chal, Ankwar's holy man. She glanced as I pulled my arm back. If she had seen them, she didn't say.

Manara smiled. "My husband was the *chenkra* for our village. I learned from him."

"You speak of your husband as if he is dead, and yet I ate dinner with him the first night."

Manara stood up straight and looked at me with a heavy dignity. "Krenden is not my husband," she answered. "He was the brother of my husband."

"So that was your husband's axe I saw at Krenden's table."

"Yes. Hanlen died on his last trip to the temple. I was hoping you might have known him."

"Your husband was at the temple when he died? That doesn't sound right," I said, the words coming out louder than intended.

"None of it sounds right. I had thought maybe you had known him . . . when we touched—"

"You *did* feel that! I didn't know what kind of seer you were." I became fascinated with Manara's story. If I wasn't careful, she could undo all of the trust Haliam and I had earned by drawing out of me too much I hadn't said.

"Yes, I knew you for a good man. That is what I told Krenden."

"Thank you."

"Only if I see good will I say so."

I nodded but turned my attention to the sheep.

Manara continued. "The light around you was pure. You have the fire of Amal. I believe you to be the *chenkra* you say you are."

Not able to face Manara, I looked off to the mountains. A memory of Mother looking up at me from spilt lentils surprised me. A cold breeze blew about my face. My eyes tightened. I had thought the pure light to be Mother's vision. How could both women have seen the same thing?

Manara broke the silence when she said, "I should go. Denjaka will need the water I was supposed to bring. Many men are coming to dinner again tonight. We have much to do."

Clicking and leading, I moved the sheep back into the shelter, filled hay in front of her, and left to take the rest of the herd out to graze. Manara had already reached the roundhouse with the water. She didn't look behind, her back straight and head level. I gave a sharp whistle. The sheep moved toward the field on my command.

The isolation of the field is a place to ponder. Today my thoughts wove back and forth around questions of the past. The gentle movements of the sheep, and the sway of grasses on top of the snow, all worked to lull away the morning. A boy from the house brought me a bladder of warm soup and some smoked meat. His was the only company I saw till the time came to shepherd the sheep.

Whistling again, I began moving the older ewes with my staff, gently nudging them. The whistle turned into an old tune once the bleating pointed in the right direction. I hummed and saw the flute in the hand of Taran, my old friend, who used to play that song for his sheep. The memories felt warm and pleasant. I leaned on the staff and looked to the mountains. Krenden had said there were about three of these ranges between this village and the temple village of Undoura. If we made our way there, someone would know the direction to Ankwar from Undoura. It would be good to see Taran again.

But life had begun to feel normal under Krenden's roof. This work I knew; I understood. Ankwar was only something I remembered. As a cold wind blew around my legs and back, I began considering the warmth of the known here as opposed to the fears of the past in Ankwar. Maybe Haliam and I could leave in the spring, but what would be the harm in staying longer?

The sheep returned to the pens where Haliam waited for me. He had been quiet lately. A snowflake fell on my cheek. I noticed the gray sky. Everything felt like we were in for a storm.

"Hoi, Haliam!" I shouted. I lifted my staff, and he shifted his weight to open the gate. The first ewes passed by him as they gladly returned to the shelter. We worked together refilling hay and water for the many animals. Words were sparse. When he had stopped himself from asking twice, he finally said, "I would like to know, Brother, what is your intention with Manara?" Haliam looked me hard in the eyes.

"Well, I just learned she is not married. She's a widow," I began. My answer did not seem to appease him.

"She is a widow. This I know."

"How do you know?"

"One of the men I work with told me," he answered flatly.

My friend's silence began to speak. He looked hurt by the idea of my intentions.

"I have absolutely no romantic inclinations at all toward Manara," I said, backing away and shaking my head.

"You don't have feelings toward her? The two of you are always talking and together."

My friend's agony was not something I would be responsible for this time. I leaned back on the pillar of the gate.

"Manara is a seer. She's like me."

Haliam shifted. "What do you mean?"

"At the table on the first night, when she took my staff to Krenden, our hands touched. I saw something."

"What does that mean? Are you bound by fate to each other?" Haliam asked.

I shook my head at the idea and shrugged. "In a way yes, I suppose we are, but not in the way you mean."

"Then what, Brother? Speak quickly, for this torture is too much."

"Her husband was the *chenkra* for this village—"

"So, you are to replace him," Haliam interrupted, ready to believe his heart breaking.

"No, that is not it at all."

"Then what is it between you two?"

"She sees in me what I thought died long ago. She sees me as a *chenkra*, a holy man."

Haliam still had trouble hearing what my words meant. For the first time in almost ten springs, I had to admit out loud what I previously denied: I had been promised to the path of the chenkra.

"Haliam, there can only be one who holds my heart. Manara is not the one."

"She is not?" Haliam asked again.

"No, Manara is not. I wish you all the happiness in the world. She's a good woman."

Haliam leaned on the fencing, relieved, a faraway look in his eyes. He stood up a little taller as he breathed in deeply. "Time to go find me a woman." He smiled, and we walked together toward the house.

Manara did not hold my heart; the thought of Mara lingered. Her eyes guided me as sure as Chealana's star. Remembering Mara pulled at my earlier thought to make a home here, but at least here I couldn't hurt her. Every morning that Haliam and I continued to stay and not return to my village would delay seeing Mara again. I didn't know if I could face her. The memory of her hurt by Aroden . . . I paid the price for my cowardice. Still, the thought of those eyes with the golden flecks . . . .

This time I didn't try to make the memory disappear.

# CHAPTER 16

# SPRING'S ARRIVAL

Heavy snow covered the mountain trail that night, laying a soft stillness across the land. The next day's snow worked to close the mountain pass until Krenden's decision of what to do with us extended for another full moon. During those long, dark days, Haliam and I made ourselves useful in multiple ways. We spotted the wood that needed hauling before the hearth grew cold. We noted the animals that would need to be put down from age. We found ways to be useful.

During a village slaughter, we worked steadily through the series of squeals from each animal. Wherever a hand was needed, Haliam and I offered ours. We helped by stunning the animal before the main vein was cut; pumping the front leg, removing the blood from the sliced jugular; stirring to keep the blood from coagulating before the soup and sausage could be made; hanging the hides to remove the hairs; or cutting the fat into cubes to be heated down, extracting lard needed for lamps, cooking, and sealing the meats in pots all to survive the cold the mountains would bring down.

Jellies were made from joint fluid to preserve the meat. The ice helped to do the rest. Bones and hooves would be used for soap and smaller tools. Every part of the animal was viewed as a gift; the sacrifice honored by everyone using everything with no waste. The animal joined in the work of keeping the village alive. The work was honest, clean, and necessary for all involved. The spirit of thanksgiving was evident in the tasks that continued through the night till all was done. The village would be fed and cared for over another winter's wait. No one complained. Instead, a hum of working happiness and fulfillment warmed our cheeks and kept our hands moving.

Bellies and lamps full, everyone's efforts turned to celebration. The drums and flutes were arranged together near a large fire. The older men, foreheads painted white, began the dances with steps they had worked together for many winters: arms raised, old legs lifted. The women swayed, humming, listening to the elder men's voices vibrating the throat singing that echoed the ages and called in chants. Together, their swirling songs evoked Earth's ancient ways. The women danced with eyes closed to better focus the prayers elevating the music and momentum. Gray heads bent back on shuffling feet left the center, signaling the drums to swell from noble to a powerful pounding of honor as the younger men took to the circle, their dance designed to demonstrate prowess in youth and strength in body. Stripped to the waist, they leapt, spun, and lifted their bodies up off the ground using the core of their beings. With the sheen of sweat covering lean backs, the night's intoxicating rhythm pulsed through the hearts of the village. Faces shown with hope this winter's end would bear them to another spring.

Krenden sat in his place, smoking and enjoying the mood of the people. His eyes held the twinkle of the fire. The ruddy cheeks made him look younger while the shadows hid the inherent depth of his vitality. He was joined by two of his closest councilmen and elders too old for the dance. Instead they drank. Surrounded by the potency of the men, Krenden relaxed. Looking over, he caught Denjaka's eye. His chest swelled in anticipation of his wife.

Denjaka went to the fire circle, and the women followed. She stood straight and looked ahead, stepping the patterns she knew well. Her beads shimmered in the light, and the lower hem of her outfit swayed in a rhythmic swish. The other older ladies stayed in step with Denjaka with their hands behind their backs held straight, emphasizing their shapes as they stepped. Denjaka raised her arms, showing the curve of her bosom as she leaned and turned. The younger girls came in among the older. They dropped their eyes down with long, dark lashes as they stepped, hair neatly braided, reflecting an arch of the fire's light like white flowers contrasting with the blackened sheen of their hair. Together they created a crown of womanly dignity, which filled Denjaka's circle as she presented the grace of the tribe's women.

Krenden wasn't the only one captured under the night's mood. Haliam noticed the smiling lips of a young girl dancing with two others. He drank some more and realized she had seen him as well. Haliam leaned over to me and said, "Gaspare, isn't it time we got a woman?"

I shrugged a little. "What of your desire for Manara?"

"She is set in her ways as a widow." He braved a point in the young girl's direction and said, "More like that one, over there, with the long, dark hair?"

"Which one? There are three."

"The one with the beautiful lips and eyes that shine like stars."

The stars are far away and cold. I grabbed some more walnuts and broke open the hard shell with my dagger along the seam. The tender white flesh inside flaked out on the tip.

"What if she is someone's girl?"

"What if she's not?" Haliam was not to be distracted so easily. The night's moods and honey mead bred confidence and that begat foolish notions.

"Haliam, we are foreigners in this village. Each morning our existence here is weighed in Krenden's decision of what to do with us. We have no rights here."

"I have every right as a man. I have every right."

"Brother, this village is not ours to claim."

Haliam darkened. A cloud covered his previously optimistic presence. To continue to carry the mark of a slave was a heavy burden to shoulder. We were both young. We should have wives and titles in our own villages. To have been free in our previous communities, we would be producing sons, growing crops, and offering our own goats for the village slaughter. We had nothing but borrowed moments from someone else's lives.

"I work hard. I work hard and I want to make a way for a family." Haliam said. "That girl over there is nothing. But I want to hope. I want to . . . ." The words tumbled off into a hollow place filled with questions.

"Haliam, we can't face that mountain alone, not now, not with winter still heavy upon her face. I'm just asking you not to go after that girl without knowing if she can be given to you."

Haliam stood, sobered by sorrow, his focus strengthened by questions, pregnant and sagging around us.

"When will I have my place?" he asked. "When we reach Ankwar? When we make it to your village?" He grew tense; the tightness in his jaw flickered around his reddening forked scar as he finished with, "Even if we make it, Ankwar is not my home. I have no home," and walked away past the fire's light. A quick look over at the girl and her companions cloaked guilt over me. Haliam was right. Was Ankwar even going to consider me welcome?

\* \* \*

Shepherding the sheep out on the fields allowed me the first glimpses of winter's end. Each day I would bring back a small cluster of the delicate white flower drops or the tiny cups of flowers in purple and yellow. Denjaka always thanked me, so happy to see the promise of spring. The hardy flowers broke through the frozen land, much like the people who had settled here. The day's light came earlier and stayed longer. Chickens gave their eggs once again with the lengthening sunlight. The mountain was waking. Life returned with warmth in her arms and dew in her hair. The mountains would soon be safer to pass. The lambing day would arrive before the next full moon's face. The time to leave was coming.

Haliam finished whitling the whistle he was working on. He blew in it once to hear his angles. The horn tip was hollowed nicely, and he was able to get a good pitch. He wrapped it in a small piece of cloth on a leather cord. Tucking the whistle into his pocket meant the trinket would find its way to a girl's neck later in the day. I prepared to go and tend to the flock. Krenden noticed that we were settling, but also were never quite settled. We had worked equal to any man but had never claimed a space for ourselves. We ate what we needed and provided our strength for chores and endless repairs.

Yet with spring came newness that turned life rosy. Spring made the difference in our resolve. He came to me before I left for the field.

"Will you take last spring's lambs to feed?" he asked.

"Yes, I offered to go. I want to spend time in the fields."

Krenden looked at me from under bushy brows before turning to read the skyline.

"I used to tend the sheep at home, in Ankwar."

"Hm," he replied, nodding his understanding. "You miss it then, Ankwar?"

A nod indicated my hesitation.

Krenden never spoke of the plans he had for us. Our first few moons with him, he would say his decision would come the next morning, but snow or bitter winds came instead, pounding on the doors of the village. He didn't cast us out. He was not cruel. I didn't know how our rejection would be taken if he offered a life here and we chose to leave instead.

I searched the dirt with my foot for my answer. "I have been anxious to get on with my training. . . to be a *chenkra*." Saying holy man with foreign words felt less emotional, not personal. I couldn't claim my role while feeling my failure's weight. Krenden remained silent, listening.

"Manara has been teaching me some of the medicines and poultices. I'm excited to learn more."

"Manara is good."

His shorter replies affected my hurry to find more words.

"She has great wisdom as your *chenkri*. I've learned much from watching her."

"Then it's decided. Stay and she will teach more." Krenden rocked back on his heels as he said this, believing he had found the solution.

"I am afraid we have taken your hospitality for too long. I need to return home to help my brothers."

Krenden's frown reached his brow. "What of Haliam, your friend? Is he longing to return to Ankwar with you? He doesn't look like you. He doesn't seem to be from the same land you grew up in. I see him talking and looking at a young girl. He has other plans for sure."

"Haliam is free. He may choose as he wishes. I thought the girl was to be given to Halen."

"Maybe Halen, maybe Haliam . . . there are many girls in my village. He can find one."

"I would miss him. We've been through much."

"The path is too difficult for one to go alone without knowledge of where to go."

"If Haliam stays, I will wait and ask to join a trader's group on their way." There it was. My plan was exposed. Krenden had only suspected. Now he knew.

"I had hoped that you and Haliam might stay on with us, possibly help set our spring seeds for the harvest."

Silence was my best answer. It would be an offense to continue pushing my position. By saying nothing, I seceded the victory to Krenden—only for the moment, till I could find a better way to leave, even if it meant going out in the dark once again. Haliam was free to stay, but I was also free to go.

Later that day, when I brought the sheep back to the shelter, Haliam broke away from three of the village children, who were enjoying tossing a ball with him. He looked happy. I couldn't take that from him.

"Gaspare, there you are," Haliam greeted me. There was an openness in his gate that hadn't been there before. This village had been a place of healing for him. He strode up with relaxed shoulders and open palms.

"I just returned from the fields. What do you have for me?"

Haliam extended the rope he had been carrying. He had been working on braiding the grass with the children; they had good, fast little fingers and could catch the pieces of grass tightly in the loops.

"What do you think of my rope? It's much better than the one we had when we left the mine." He stretched out a length and tugged to demonstrate the taut weave.

I closed the entrance to the sheep's enclosure. "I see you enlisted some help. Maybe that's why it is better." I looked at him. "Krenden asked me our plans for staying."

Haliam dropped some water for the sheep.

"Tell me, does your girl like her whistle?" I continued.

"I haven't given it to her yet," he replied.

"What are you waiting for?"

Haliam put his hands on his hips and breathed deeply. The sense of the village and all that had come to him was taken in with that breath.

"I am waiting to give it to her when we leave."

My brow furrowed. He continued with, "It's what we've planned. The mountains are opening, and the time to continue is here."

"Haliam, I cannot ask this of you."

"You're not asking anything of me. This is the plan. We stay with the plan."

"You are happy here. I see it on you. This village has room for you."

"I cannot let you cross those mountains alone. Besides, I would like to finish this way we have started."

"Brother, this path is mine to travel. You do not need to force it upon yourself. Haliam, you could have a family here. I can take up with a trader. I'll be all right."

"Gaspare, I'm not letting you take this from me. I pledged to you at the lake we would see Ankwar and we both shall."

"What of the girl? You like her?"

"I can come back once I know the way. Besides, she's a woman. You, Gaspare, are my brother." He put his hand on my shoulder. For me to not accept his gift would be foolishness.

"Thank you, Haliam. Thank you."

"So, we should speak with Krenden together. He's a hard man to say no to."

"Yes, he is," I said, smiling at the thought of him.

"Three more suns?" Haliam asked.

Laughing now, we walked back for dinner. "Yes, three more suns will be good."

# CHAPTER 17

# A FAMILIAR FIRE

Spring's cooler mornings slipped from winter's hardness as Haliam and I finished our passage through the mountains. Ahead, we could see the gray arms of smoke reaching for the skies like a grove of mountain pines. The hills rolled and knelt around a placid lake. Here in this mountain place of caves and forests waited my delayed destiny.

Soon, there was no doubt: we had arrived at the village of Undoura, the village of the holy men. Anticipation swelled as we passed into the midst of clustered homes. Men appeared wizened. Women walked as swans swimming, their long hair falling like feathers around their shoulders. Here, under the moon's shining and the sun's blessing, I longed to learn the ways of the village. Everyone worked. Everyone meditated. Everyone slept.

In the hotter parts of the sun's trail, we went into the forests. Part of our training was meant to notice the insignificant works of nature. Digging into the tiniest crevices, we retrieved clumps of little bristly moss packed in on crumbs of dirt fallen between the rocks. Thin tendrils like wisps of hair contained enough life in this moss's greenness to support the seeds of a tree, allowing the roots to sprout. The moss held the tiny sapling anchored to the rocks. Alive, the moss's nutrients softened and protected the harsh habitat provided by the rock. The inconsequential moss allowed the tree to stand facing the fiercest life up against a rock, naked in the elements with very little foundation for roots. We meditated on life's simplistic lesson on rugged endurance during the midday fast.

We looked for fern rhizomes and were taught to count the leaves identifying bracken. Bracken, when taken in early spring, could be used to purge the irritation of worms building in someone's system. When taken late in the summer, however, bracken could blind a sheep or bleed a cow. This lesson of poison's potent healing became another day's meditation. I nibbled on the tiniest bracken leaflet, testing fate with a greater desire to ease my discomforts. While the bitter juices of the fern slipped over my tongue, thoughts of Ankwar's poison churned inside me. Timing would be everything.

Each day, I watched a woman who seemed more and more familiar. Her movements like a shadow developed my curiosity. Daily, she walked in the corners of the sunlight. She moved to make herself invisible. The more she worked to be unseen, the more my mind worked to see her. Regularly she and a young woman were quietly together, seldom interacting with the villagers. When she came near, a nagging thought lingered. I couldn't place how or why, but when she served me soup after our einkorn harvest, the way her hands moved sparked a familiar sense that I should know.

Once, as the ripened fruits of summer leaned into the browning branches of fall, I saw her at the stream with the younger woman. They were gathering water and other medicinal herbs. I moved close enough for her to hear me.

"Help me with these herbs?" I asked. She glanced at me, so I asked again: "Help me with these herbs?"

"What do you wish to do with them?" she replied.

"I need a poultice for my friend. He's hot around his head and looking flushed."

"Then you do not want those herbs." She turned.

"Wait. Won't you help me?" I asked.

"I will find you the plants you need. Not these. Other plants help fever."

I followed the pair of women back to the village. She went to where the drying clusters of sage and yarrow hung, deftly took an assortment of the leaves and handed the bundle to me.

"Boil these into broth. Give a drink to your friend. He should sleep and will feel better when he wakes." The words came with a recognizable accent. As she finished explaining, I heard words from home mixed with the dialect of the Undoura tribe.

"You are not from here, are you?" I asked.

A shake of her head.

"You speak as one from Ankwar. How do I know you?"

At the mention of Ankwar, her eyes widened for a moment. "I wouldn't know how you know me," she said. "I must finish with my work now." She turned to the younger woman. "Natika, we must hurry and finish gathering back at the river."

"Mother, I will go back and finish the work there. I don't mind," said Natika.

"Natika," I repeated. "That means sorrowful. You must be from Ankwar, but how do I not recognize you?"

The woman stopped and looked at me for the first time. Her eyes narrowed. After a moment, she tilted her head and gazed at my face.

"What is your name?" she asked.

"I am Gaspare, son of Tandor from Ankwar."

Whether the gasp came first or the dropped basket, I couldn't say. Fear seemed to mingle with disbelief as the look of a spirit crossed her face. As one searching the stars, she searched my eyes.

"Show me your arm," she said. "Quickly, show me." She grabbed my arm. Her fingers immediately uncovered the tattoos from my great fall. Whispered wonder came quietly from her lips as she gently traced the lines. She spoke of gaspar, the treasure, the nurturer, reaching up to touch my face. Her muttering hesitated, but then she brushed my brow, feeling the slight bump that had always been there.

"Gaspare?" She looked deeper, wanting to believe the ghost before her.

"Yes, I am Gaspare. Who are you?"

Snapped from her trance, she turned to flee, but I grabbed her wrist and pulled her back.

"Please, tell me who you are."

Glancing at my grip, she answered, "My name is Zuka. I worked with Chal."

"You are Zuka? It was you . . . you gave me these tattoos."

She pulled away. "I must go. I have too much to do before this day sleeps."

She turned, and I let go. Watching her walk away, I wondered what had happened back in Ankwar for her to leave. Would she tell me news of my brothers or Mara? I tried to see Zuka again, but she managed to avoid me each time. A few mornings later, I saw Natika alone in the village, sheltering under a tree from the high sun. Her hands were busy separating long strands of grass. Haliam walked along with me as I approached the young woman sitting.

"You are Natika, right?"

She looked at me, shrugged, and began braiding her grass lengths. Looking at her, I saw that her mother's secretive life as the outcast of Ankwar had taught Nakita to keep to herself. She had carried the shame of her fatherless childhood.

"I saw you once as a little girl. You would not remember me."

She didn't look up but kept her fingers twisting right over left and under, lengthening the grass into rope.

Haliam sensed my failure and slid beside her, picking up more blades of grass and separating them into sections for her to use. They sat quietly creating the braid. Haliam understood best. Trust requires patience to grow. I joined them on the ground and sat knapping my dagger. My tools had been neglected. I would need to take time to see the village smith for a cleaner sharpening.

When her length of braid was to satisfaction, Natika nodded at Haliam. Taking the full length, I watched her beginning the deft, knotting and looping, weaving the rope into a tip and then a triangular pattern. Not a word passed among us. When it was finished, she placed a sturdy, woven sheath on the ground next to me. Standing to leave, she said, "I remember you."

I picked up the sheath. Natika's gift showed her excellence in the trade. She had woven a sheath fit for an elder complete with the loop for tying around my waist.

When she had left, Haliam smiled. "Let me see that," he said.

I handed him the sheath; he turned the gift around, examining the tight corners and the precise angle of Natika's work. His smile seemed to reach deep into his thoughts. He grabbed a remnant of grass Natika had left. He nibbled the juice from the stem and looked up at the trees. The seeds at the end bobbed and bounced as his tongue shifted the stalk in his mouth.

"I will need to fix my dagger so it's worthy of being displayed in this fine pouch."

Haliam smiled. "Let's put that newly sharpened blade to use."

"What do you need?"

"Your dagger is not the only item needing something woven. I have a task I would like Natika's help making."

Haliam's vision led us to the groves of young linden trees. We bent and cut the lengths of the pliable trunks. Haliam removed smaller branches with a flick of his dagger while I cut another sapling.

"How many more do we need?" I asked him.

"Two more should be sufficient," he replied.

Our branches gathered, and we stripped the bark, peeling down the outer layer like skinning a rabbit. We made the tree vulnerable to find the essence of the living length of bast that fed the tree. Once soaked, the tree's arteries would provide the desired tenacity and flexibility to cushion and support. The linden tree was a staple during our training at Undoura. Drying the flowers and seed pods provided relief from many ailments: sleeplessness, inflammation, and even skin rashes. These strips would provide strength and protection.

Satisfied, Haliam took his bundles and sat near Natika under the same tree. He began tearing the strips into even smaller, narrower strips and then started braiding. Natika looked at Haliam, shook her head, and took the strips from his hands. She held her hands so he could easily watch and learn. She didn't smile. He leaned closer, observing her swift, steady rhythm, twisting back and forth, over and under. The strips stretched past Haliam's arm span. She motioned for him to take the rope. Haliam gently pushed her hands back, smiling, and pointed at his feet. Natika smiled this time. A small smile, and stood up saying, "In the morning, I can make you both a pair, but you need to find more materials if you want good boots."

As she left, I glanced at the distant look on Haliam's face. He watched her walk away and lifted the plaited strips to smell. He rolled back on the ground, quite satisfied, with hands clasped together and raised to the sky.

"That's the woman I want with me."

I tossed some extra strips at him and went to go check on the sheep.

With the coming of the new sun, Haliam woke and took his gathered materials to where Natika sat. He arranged the required deer hide, calf leather, moss, and long grass. Next to the supplies he placed the braided linden bark. Natika approached, looking pleased to see Haliam in her place. She sat beside him, inspecting his prize, tsked a little as a hen searching for the tiny bug, and smiled. Natika marked the length of my foot in the dirt, and then I left those two, sitting there under the tree; Natika forming a mesh weave from the linden strips and Haliam stitching the calf leather on the toe. When I returned much later, they were finishing the second pair of woven boots. Natika's slender fingers had tightly packed the moss in with the grass. The boots would certainly protect us from the mountain's inevitable snow.

* * *

The tree leaves above were yellower now. They shook when the wind blew. A few broke off and sailed softly to the ground, twisting through the air. Winter will soon push the light to the horizon quicker. Our decision would need to be made to press on or wait another season before the final trek to Ankwar.

The moon's fullness had just finished when Zuka came to find me. She had noticed Haliam and Natika growing closer. She knew. When she approached, she held out a cut of smoked meat. She had taken a strip down from the drying place, choosing the fatty meat of the leg.

"Will you be traveling back to Ankwar soon?" she asked directly.

"I believe so, yes."

"Natika cannot go."

We both paused. I had no voice in this situation, nor did she.

"Ankwar was not kind to her."

The tension in my legs burned from squatting. I leaned back on my heels and moved the stick I was holding in the fire with the venison. I glanced up to gauge if she would continue without prompting. The fat on the meat sizzled, popping over the fire.

"Ankwar was not kind to me, either," I answered.

Zuka replied quickly, "She was just a child. They shouldn't have taken their vengeance out on her."

I shifted my weight and tested the heat of the meat.

"I won't go back," she said quietly. "I won't, but I can't keep her here if Haliam takes her."

I tore a chunk of the meat off the stick and offered it to her. She shook her head. "No, you eat. You need thickening to survive the snow's deep cold."

The sound of squishing meat between my teeth and the taste of hot, bloodied juice warmed my throat. "Zuka, what do I return to in Ankwar?" I asked her. "What of my brothers?"

Her sigh escaped long and fatigued as if driven from her lungs by the high winds on the mountain pass. Zuka looked into the night sky. The black clouds crossing contrasted with the fading moon's light. Chealana's star cluster had moved, but her blueness still radiated comfort.

"Esteban and Aleya are well. She was able to keep a baby, finally. Gabor and Kaiya have two sons from what I know. They have raised the twins alongside their own." I smiled at the thought of Kaiya and her flock of children. The look of little Zaria in my arms was my only memory of the twins. She must be ten springs now.

"The village decided to keep Mother's twins. That's good," I concluded. "That's good."

Zuka paused and watched me carefully. "With you being sent on the trader's path, the village turned even more internal, arguing and disagreeing," she said.

"Sulvak, Chal, the elders . . . What happened to them?"

"They brought guilt and shame upon the younger men supporting . . . Aroden."

And there came the bitter taste I thought I could control. His name spoken reignited his treachery. I stopped chewing. The rich taste became a chewy lump of meat bereft of any pleasure.

"And what of Aroden?" I finally asked.

Zuka's clear discomfort indicated his part in her exile. She paused with the length of darkness between us.

"He stirred great discord among the leaders," she finally went on. "At first his meetings were only in secret. His words entered the council room on the lips of others. But Sulvak and Chal, along with some of the other elders, convinced the council of the dangerous choices they made. A late freeze that spring snapped the sprouts, followed by a drought later in the heat of the growing season. The crops didn't recover well. They feared a curse would stay on them. They couldn't admit their wrongdoing. Aroden wouldn't let them."

I stayed silent, remembering the crowd and hearing the jostled yelling of the damage to crops they ascribed to me as a cursed one.

"Your banishment saved the twins," she said finally. "Fear or regret, maybe both, caused them to set aside any risk of angering the gods."

The reply of *that's good,* stuck in my throat as I swallowed. The fleece of a scapegoat was mine to wear.

My stick pried the smoldering end of a log. Air allowed underneath breathed fire back into flame, licking the blackened crevices. Sparks cracked and rose on the heat to the darkness. When I let the log drop, the light of numerous fireflies sparked brilliant orange, and the ashes deepened in powdery gray depths. Smoke shifted in the breeze.

"What of Mara?" The question I had carried from the mines throughout our trek over the mountains sought the necessary oxygen to ignite embers deep inside. Dryness coated my tongue.

Zuka turned partially away. "Mara was well last I saw her."

"Zuka, did Mara have a son? He would have been born after I left."

Soft as whistling dove's wings in morning light came her reply: "Yes."

The last of the summer's crickets chirped. A bat darted in the dark. "Could he have ended up on the trader's rope?"

Softer still as the ripple on the water came her final, "Yes."

"How? How could Mara let her son go? How could Aroden let his son face that shame, and the danger of the way?" Even as I spoke the words, I knew how.

"He had been born mute," Zuka began. "He couldn't speak, and eventually we learned he couldn't hear. Aroden couldn't stand the reminder."

"What reminder? What could he possibly feel to send his own son on Anak's line?"

"Jealousy."

"Of what?"

"You."

"Me? I was gone slaving in the depths of those mines. How could I have threatened him from where he had sent me?"

"He was convinced the boy was yours. He saw him as part of the curse."

Zuka's final words struck me across the face with the cold reality.

"I never . . . I never even . . ." I had only held her hand. My inadequacies to protect Mara reared up before me, striking from the ashes. The smoke slowly danced like a snake curling upward, charming the air. I reached for the ground behind me. The pain in my legs tightened, the muscles never right since my fall.

Zuka handed me a skin of water. "Mara came to me asking for help. When you . . . left, Aroden had beaten her. He had kicked her stomach. She had been pregnant. She carried the child for seven more moon cycles. The boy came early. He was so small."

"What was his name?"

"Balick, the child's name was Balick. Aroden couldn't stand the sight of him. He let his hatred be known. When the child was found to neither speak nor hear, he convinced everyone your curse was carried through your seed." Zuka paused, weighing whether to continue.

"Please." I reached my hand towards her. "What of Mara?"

"He tried to have both Mara and me burned at the menhir. The council stopped him, but not without him getting some compensation for his trouble."

"What do you mean?"

"They banished me. Said I was working darkness on Mara's mind to betray her husband. That I had given her herbs to force the baby to come early."

"Had you?" I asked.

A silent nod was her only reply. Zuka sat with her face toward the fire, shoulders back and chin set. "Natika and I escaped that night." She had reasons of her own to hate Aroden. I could see how the shadows had hardened her.

"But Natika was young. The village would not remember."

"I doubt they would remember."

"Zuka, I will speak with Haliam. I cannot promise the answer you seek, but I can offer you my promise that I will personally see no harm comes to your daughter."

Her faraway look came back to the circle. Zuka's dark eyes considered me. Placing a hand on my left arm, she exposed one of the tattoos imprinted there. "Taran, your friend, did this one. You still have those who have missed you in Ankwar." Turning to go, she spoke over her shoulder, "When will you know if you are leaving?"

"We go before the moon disappears. I have my ceremonial rite to complete. Afterward, we will head to the mountains."

"See me before you leave. I will prepare some extra supplies for your survival." Zuka walked into the darkness.

I sat alone by the fire. A breeze shifted. The smoke twisted, bulging its sides, hiding the tendrils. The fire sat back down into the log's cracks, dimming the lights, and bringing focus to the depth of blackness filling in among the trees. Chealana's star, now covered behind a drifting cloud, left an empty hole. The air belonged to the night, and the night always moved. Morning felt a long way off.

# CHAPTER 18

# TRUE RITES

The skies pressed deep, holding the final rain of autumn as we headed to the sacrificial atonement stone. Remnants of seeds and a little dried sinew from the harvest offering remained on the smooth surface. I knelt naked, head bowed, my palms on the altar, waiting. The head of all holy men, Attioc, stood before me. He handed me three tied branches of rosemary, each the length of my arm. I beat the herbs onto my shoulders, the sticky leaves breaking the scent of remembrance upon me. Pieces of the rosemary flew into my hair and on the stone around me. The red marks from the pattern of the branches started.

Attioc, the eldest holy man, proceeded, arranging three special pots. The containers were of the finest craftsmanship the trade lines could bring. One contained a small quantity of frankincense, tears from the sacred father of trees. One held precious myrrh, plucked from the thorny bushes, whose pain soothed the disease's decay. The third one had galbanum, extracted from stems with the woody scent of a forest floor. All three of these resins had traveled great distances on the trade routes, each sacred sap crushed and dried, then crushed and dried once more in ceremonial preparation. Today, on the stone altar, I would apply the final pressing of these three purging essentials, presenting to Attioc my offering. I took out my pestle stone and this time when I ground, I would grind them together as one, chanting the ancient words taught me here in Undoura.

My left hand pushed the pestle, working to touch the base of the mortar's cup. Crunching grit rubbed like sand, smoothing the rough edges I held inside myself. With my right hand, I protected the delicate dust from the winds. Each sensation of grinding crushed through layers of past thoughts—wrongs that had been done, doubts I couldn't control, fear I could never be good enough—each thought a sacrifice of my inadequacies. I could feel the coming chill move up my spine, and I leaned into the bowl, protecting the contents with my body.

The grinding strength in my hands rendered the rarest tears of sacred trees to dust. Beginning with frankincense's healing attributes, my circular rhythms began crushing the shiny golden dust into grains so fine. Rocking, I sang from deep in my throat and pushed the stone mortar, offering up scents to tickle my nostrils. I added the darker brown of myrrh crystals and slowed my efforts, concentrating on keeping the two powders in the bowl. The ceremony of pressing reinforced lessons a holy man would need when seeking answers: discipline, healing, faith.

The rocking slowed to more of a back-and-forth, setting the rhythm of wailing in my back and shoulders. Undying ancestral words invoked sounds from my childhood. Through the movement, memories of grieving widows made anger surface inside me. Father's death shrouded my perceptions. I hadn't made my peace with Aroden. Attioc had told me where I stumbled, that is where I needed to begin digging. Zuka's words taunted memories left for dead. Aroden had killed his son. Hatred distracted me from the focus I tried to maintain. This ceremony had worked to the surface a festering sore with roots deep inside.

I pushed the pestle down harder. The scratching sound of the sand-like powder reminded me of the wind swishing through tufts of high grasses growing along the river. The bowls of lit lard struggled to keep the flame aright in the increasing wind. A large flock of sparrows fluttered in a shadow of flight curving and riding Cheala's currents. The field we were in lacked shelter if the storm should open. We did not hurry.

As I added the final resin of galbanum, my shoulders ached, my back burned, and my tightened legs began quivering. The rocking deepened, and from a place hidden within, a chanting cry called the ancestors who walked with the stars. The cry came forward from my core beliefs in all my grandfather had taught me, offering the sacrifices of my past self. The cry formed a river of the ages washing over my voice, which sounded foreign to my ears. The cry, like an animal lost in the darkness, lingered on the wings of the sparrows as they carried my agony circling heavenward like smoke. The perfumes mixed to a rich pungency from distant lands, potent in their ability to transcend.

Attioc placed before me a bowl of smoking charcoal bits. He sprinkled the powders onto the glowing nuggets. The powders now became alive, infusing vapors as they melted, releasing the purest scents of calling. I held still, leaning over the coals, waving the smoke into my nose. I breathed in the incense, its sweetness filling my lungs. The smoke carried the gift of my sacrifices up to the clouds for the gods to enjoy.

Zuka came to me with the last bowl of olive oil, the symbol of peace and health. Wind whipped her hair around her as a veil. She handed the container to Attioc and moved to watch me. Old, gnarled knuckles gripped the olive oil, raising the jar over his head. His voice was loud and steady against the wind, calling upon the traits of sight and wisdom, all while the rites of words formed on my lips, calling forth my commitment to healing and light.

Attioc finished his prayer, placing the olive oil jar beside my bowl. The containers had traveled for many springs from various trade posts, crafted at the hands of the finest potters. The olive oil pottery bore the markings of a specific shell pattern. I blinked, thinking for a moment that I was dreaming. Each potter of trade status had distinct styles especially notable in the pattern. In my haste to see the markings closer, I knocked the jar, almost spilling the vessel, but caught it. Zuka watched as I ran my fingers over and over the shell pattern, trying to see the all-too-familiar indents. I looked at her full of questions. A nod and nothing more gave me the knowledge I was not alone. Mother's presence was in my hands. Tenderness entered my fingers. I cupped the pottery of my mother, allowing myself to pray by rubbing its smooth sides. She had come. A trade set in motion many springs ago brought fulfillment here when I needed her reassurance most. The wind lifted the thinning hair off the back of my neck. The grass around me ruffled and bowed. The holiness of my mother's love and her suffering entered my rite. Gently, I poured the liquid green flow of life's oil over the incense. The fragrance, rich and pure, enveloped me. The container felt light in my hands as I cradled her memory. The holy man's chanting started as mine turned more to sighs, and the sounds, the smells, and the storm circled around me, taking me to a height reached by eagles.

Standing over me, the holy man poured the ceremonial oil slowly on the center of my scalp. The heaviness of liquid spilled over my balding skin. The oil slid down my scalp onto my forehead, my cheeks, and my mouth. I raised my head to the skies, my eyes closed. The trickles down along my eyebrows followed the path down to my jaw. More liquid covered behind my ears. The oil trailed onto my back and traced my spine. Some oil landed on my hand. The color turned my skin a warm, leathery color. I breathed deep, so deep. I breathed to feel the hands of Mother. I breathed even deeper to find the vibration of life inside the everlasting words. I breathed in a fresh, new fragrance of who I am.

Drops of rain began falling on my upturned face. The storm had arrived, bringing droplets, mixing with the oil. Attioc took the coat from Zuka and placed the hides upon my shoulders. The rain's beading droplets, trapped under the heavy coat, warmed my skin with the chill of wetness. The goat skins, arranged in an alternating pattern after the tradition of the holy men, included a black stripe positioned over the heart. Every breath of a holy man was drawn from the remembrances of life's balance with death's finality. The black hide held the sacred exchange close as a reminder. Thunder rumbled, but rather than cracking the sky, the lightning chose to flicker, flashing light, reflecting on the bottom of clouds. We needed to go, but the final act had not been offered. Attioc laid his hands on my head.

"Gaspare, seer of the light, rise and take your place walking among the secrets of nature. Lean into the lessons of Cheala and Akeala, the goddesses of wind and earth; they have chosen you. Be for your people a source of healing and strength in wisdom."

Standing, I felt my spine stretch from my shoulders to the base. My head leveled. My mind focused. The rain came heavier now, drumming on the stone altar and on the ground. Tiny fingers of water ran across my face. The lights in the lard pots went out. Each person gathered a container to carry back to the village hall. I took Mother's jar. I stood holding her memory, looking at the people. I knew the course I must take to find inner healing: I would need to face Aroden and not give into the weakness of my hatred. Rain's cleansing rinse, a final act of grace, lingered in the oil and water, darkening my skin with a fresh shine. For the first time since leaving the mine, I knew the heart of freedom.

# CHAPTER 19

# MOUNTAIN PASSAGE

The first snow came early. Our time to go was now before another snow could follow. The moon's fullness would peak in two more nights. Zuka brought her package of meat and medicines. Natika stood by her side. Haliam gave the whistle he had carved to Natika, and we headed for the final trail home.

"Aren't you going to take her with you?"

"I'll come back," Haliam said.

Haliam hummed us out of the village towards the last leg of our journey. His cadence carried us through a flock of startled sparrows. We passed along the river, and Haliam continued to work his way to remembering parts of words that hid in the memories of his happiness.

The sun climbed and so did we. The mountains opened as we crested the passage's peak and saw weighted gray clouds cloaking sunlight over the distant mountains. Snow blew gently up in swirls. Wet kisses stung our cheeks, melting quickly upon their touch. We breathed in the sharp freshness of the crisp air. We made our way to the tree level, walking under the bowing branches covered in white. Cracks boomed from within the woods, revealing the life still moving around the dying leaves. The snow's reflected surface glowed from above and below. Winter, a time of sleep, death, and stillness, gave us hope of a waiting life's presence. The fresh chill attacked our breathing with a promise of change, and each step took us closer to fulfillment. Each step I came closer to answers. A sense of achievement bolstered our courage. We bore the cold in our fingers, knowing a fire would warm us soon enough.

A boreal owl perched on the gray bark overhead, his brown and white speckles almost masking his presence. Sharp, yellow eyes peered out of a round face, catching our movement. His head quickly pivoted, tilted looking to capture our sound. Silently, the owl launched himself from the branch, sailing safely to a newer place farther from our path.

His wings glided across the air. White spots on the feathers patterned with brown stripes helped him blend into the forest. The sound of snow dropping from the branches surrounded us, and then the space was quiet, yet very alive.

"Did you see him?" I asked, pointing where he had flown.

"Yes, he was effortless."

"If only we had wings. We would be at Ankwar before their dinner grew cold."

"We're moving at a good pace. The weather is holding. Soon, we should be there. Are you ready to see your people?"

I grunted. Haliam's phrase "your people" shifted my focus from the warm hearth to the public gatherings at the well. Faces long not seen came to mind. The wind carried voices of the dead past my ears. I could hear them and wasn't sure what I longed for the most.

"Yes, I believe I am."

"Zuka said depending on the weather, we had two, maybe three suns to travel before seeing Ankwar's valley," Haliam remembered.

"The part of me that is still not ready should be by then."

The light snow covering crunched underfoot along with crisped leaves and pinecones. We passed a tree showing signs of erosion. At the trunk's base, where the land had washed down, icicles began extending drip by drip, creating white roots to the dirt floor below.

"Nervous?"

The snow's softness seemed to cover all the space, allowing me to imagine new shapes underneath. A covered log could be a rock or even a forgotten and lost pack. No one knew what lay under the snow.

"A little," I replied. We walked on. I gathered a handful of snow to swallow, feeling the icy sharpness enter my throat. My breath steamed up in front of me like fog lifting off the pond. "I'm mostly tired of running."

Haliam grunted, knowing the same sense of exhaustion. He set down his birch bark container and began looking for pinecones and any other dry fuel. I pulled my own pack off my back and stretched, rolling my shoulders up and back, opening my chest to make room for my lungs to fill it. Soothing calm stretched across my widening chest. I held the air and kept the tightness inside, tickling at my nostrils to escape. The air felt good. Deep breaths cleared my focus. A calmness freed my answers.

"I think I want to hear Kaiya's laughter and see my brother Gabor's face when I tell him of the river crossings. I want to tell Esteban about the rutting rams we came upon."

"Yes, Brother. How about the exploding bow or the tracker we threw down from the cliff?"

"*You* threw down. I couldn't even stand on my ledge."

"We've seen so much. How many waterfalls did we pass?"

"I still see the tree growing out from the rock - impossible, but the tree grew anyway, wrapping its roots around the boulder like a gnarled old hand." Life around us had demonstrated a hard nature. The more we struggled and worked, the more valuable the fight became. Each obstacle helped us concentrate our purpose on why we were traveling. Looking up at the stars at night had created a longing to know them from my homeland, to be assured we would be all right. My life's plan hid under so many unanswered whys. Greater than any tribal calling as a holy man, greater than any need for vindication, somewhere deep within wavered the sense I needed to belong in someone's love.

"Is there a woman who waits for you, Brother?" Haliam asked.

I focused on blowing the embers from the birch container till a thin line of gray smoke trailed up into the air. I blew once more, gently this time, stopping to breathe in the taste of smoke.

I glanced at Haliam and shrugged. "If there is, she isn't mine to claim."

"There must be a woman. No one would go through what we have for a brother or a village."

"Oh, that's right. You are returning to how many villages for your women?"

"Woman. Natika. And yes, I will return for her."

"Why didn't you bring her?"

"This village you are taking us to, do we know anything about how life is there? Last time I was there, I was on Anak's rope as a boy. Last time you stood in the village, they tied you to that rope. I will go back for Natika when I know you are safe."

"Haliam, you didn't need to give her up for me."

"I didn't, Brother. I will return for her." He pulled out some of the smoked ibex Zuka had given us and cut a piece, tossing the chunk to me. The smokey flavor of the meat heightened the smell of the fire. "I couldn't let you go alone."

"Thank you, Haliam." I laid my grass mat on the ground. The snow crunched under my weight.

"You remember the owl we just saw?" Haliam asked.

"Yes, of course."

"Have you ever seen little birds mob a bird of prey, driving them from their territory, keeping their young safe?"

"Yes, I have, but sometimes the owl doesn't care. All their bombing and screeching at the owl doesn't loosen his hold on the branch he has gained."

"True, but the determination of the little birds together can drive an eagle in flight or harass a hawk to distraction, pushing the threat away from their home."

I sat looking at the fire. The snow cracked a branch nearby. Nature's ways were pure. She knew how to keep life living. She perfected balance. In nature, the small were not always the weak or the eaten. Haliam was right. Sometimes they banded together and became strong. We would know in two more suns if my owl would fly away. If only we could rally help from other small voices to drive away the danger.

\* \* \*

A journey of three suns became a trek of four moons. The storms had blocked our way. The missing sunlight did little to warm us. Views to the north explored mountain-overlapping mountain-like pups sleeping at their mother's teat, their backs rolling into the freest sky. From this vantage point, the top of the world couldn't be higher. The snow of our travels preceded us, coating the grounds crisp and clean, echoing the very crunch beneath our boots. The bottom of the lake mirrored the sky clear and strong, turning the world upside down in her reflection.

A large crack above us gave the only warning that a boulder had broken loose. The freeze and thaw had created an avalanche. The first boulder crashed into another large rock grabbing more rocks in motion down the mountain toward us. As the rocks slid and rolled, some of them split, sending debris scuttling along to gather more rough bits. Dust rose into the cold. The rocks were dangerous enough. Fragments stopped in or near our path. Smaller stones kept going like a mad bear stung by a colony of bees.

The little rabbit darting in my brain contemplated the force of a falling mountain versus a possible path through the hazardous wake. My decision to dodge and dash forward was taking hold. My eyes focused on the rattling onslaught betraying the insane contemplation. The noise increased as the rocks tumbled down.

Haliam grabbed my arm. "No, it isn't safe!" he yelled, pulling me backward as he spoke. "We need to pull back!"

A boulder of great size caught the air, gracefully extending time and space before crushing a little pine below us. Rock fragments chipped into my legs, bouncing off my hides and boots. A larger stone hurled through the air near my waist while Haliam continued the retreat, pulling me away.

Another stone launched and struck Haliam's thigh, sending fragments of dirt and dust into our eyes. Little pebbles slid under our boots. Stumbling, feet sliding, hands catching the ground, heads ducking, we scrambled out of harm's way. Tremors shivered up our legs. The mountain shook off her unwanted weight.

Chamois above us stood clustered, watching, deciding which way was the safest to run; their brown, wooly bodies jostling among each other, little hooves stamping, holding on, feeling the vibrations. Their little white faces studied the rocks.

Urgency dulled as the rocks lost interest and the avalanche stopped. The noise ceased in a final echo. Quiet returned, interrupted only by an occasional scuttling stone.

Haliam checked his thigh. Already the skin was coloring from the bruise forming. "Let's stop here to rest," he said.

"You should elevate that leg."

"It'll be all right. Just need to take a moment." Haliam leaned back against a rock wall and slid to the ground.

"That fall happened so quickly," I said, scanning the slope. "Just heard that boom and then rocks flew down like hail."

"Maybe the mountain wants to keep us from going farther."

I glanced at him. It wasn't good to tempt the fates.

"Think about it. Maybe the mountain knows the danger ahead is too much for us."

Taking deep breaths in the high altitude, I turned, surveying the lands, and nodded in agreement. We couldn't be far now, but neither of us knew for sure. A wrathful landscape couldn't change our course. Rest mattered.

Overhead, a shadow crossed the land, its formidable, blackened shape circling. I could see light reflecting from its whitened spots—a golden eagle had come to hunt. Silence carried the bird's form on the fingers of the wind as he circled, scanning the rocky terrain for a meal. From our position, we could see the glint in his eyes. His fierceness captured our attention; he looked as though he'd spotted something.

Further down below us, an unfortunate fox came up a path making her way to her den; her mottled fur concealing her among the rocks, but not upon the snow.

The eagle displayed its magnificent wingspan. Gathering height and angle, we watched him dive with speeds to mock a fish swimming with the current. Moments before impact, the eagle spread its wings the length of a man. His outstretched flight feathers curled up like hands releasing hold of the air, shoulders arched to support the weight of force from the eagle's pursuit. Head bent, talons extended, he punched the fox from her feet, and in a moment, there he stood upon his prey, gripping fiercely in his powerful talons, subduing the fox to ensure his flight would not be impeded by a struggle, shredding her fur to find the warm, stringy entrails. Nature's gruesome dance with life was finished.

He extended his enormous wings, showing the power beneath the blackened layers of feathers. He lifted himself with the folded body in his talons, bringing down the air with each stroke of his mighty wings. Gaining altitude, hoisting himself higher, the predator left to return to his crag on some side of the mountain. We couldn't see him anymore but heard the high-pitched screech announcing a successful return. Sometimes the small won, but not this time. Nature's balance was maintained. The air was quiet again.

"Hopefully this will be the last night we are out," I said. "My tinder for fire is low."

"We're above the tree line. It'll be hard to stay warm and heat our meat tonight."

"We have a little more sunlight left in this day. We can keep going."

"I need a little food and rest. We don't have to light a fire just yet." Haliam absently rubbed his leg and removed his pack. He rummaged through and pulled out some remaining jerky.

"If we need tinder, my pack is light. We can combine our load. I'll take your pack and burn mine for fuel." I pulled out the liver from our hunt the night before. It had stayed packed in the snow till we began hiking this morning. The liver would not be enough. We could only rest, not stay the night. I laid the meat wrapped in old mosses on top of my pack. The moss brushed off easily, a few tendrils sticking to the meat like tiny hairs. My dagger sliced through the organ meat easily. I took my piece and handed the rest to Haliam. Sitting on my mat enjoying the rich, bitter twang of liver on my tongue, I watched the valley and the way the setting sun played with shadows from the clouds on the land.

Haliam walked to the bog at the lower end of the gully. Kneeling to break the ice with a stone, he stopped suddenly freezing mid-strike. Never letting his eyes leave their mark, he motioned for me to join him. He pointed straight to where he was looking. The sun's golden retreat stretched shadows longer. At first, I couldn't see what he meant. My eyes focused, trying to see a shape softer than the stone. Only grays and browns blended with the cold front of snow on the rocks.

Then the slightest movement caught my eye. Out on the slope below us, a solitary wolf sat erect with the sun behind her, the thick fur of her winter pelt parted slightly in the breeze.

"Did you bring your bow?" Haliam whispered.

"No."

"We can't let her roam here, not if we're to rest and leave safely."

A light breeze blew around the corner of the rock wall. Cheala's breath lifted my hair a little. The wolf was unaware of us, watching the horizon, her straight back proud and graceful.

"I won't shoot her."

Haliam looked at me, astonished. "We won't be able to sleep with her or any pack she might be joining. These hills are dangerous enough."

I studied the curve of her back, her straight ears, eyes that were sharp and keen. She scratched the spot behind her left shoulder, extended her front paws, and lay down. Serenity blended her dignity with a near-human quality I remember.

"Gaspare, really, we cannot let her go."

"I won't shoot her, Haliam."

Sitting back on his heels, he looked from me to the wolf, shaking his head. "Why, Gaspare? How can we be sure to see tomorrow's sun if you do not?"

I looked for a last time at the wolf, looked at Haliam, and turned to go back to my mat. "We can move closer to the rock wall. We will be moving soon when the light of the moon rises."

Disgust mixed with worry on Haliam's face. "The moon's fullness will call the wolves." Haliam walked back to the bog. The sun made a final stretch below the clouds. Reds played within the orangeness. Haliam squatted at the bog, watching, nervously trying to find a better solution. The darkness would come. The moon's glow would illuminate the snow's bluish tint.

"Relax. You'll lose your body heat quicker if you stay tense."

"I would be more relaxed if you had shot her."

"It was too far to be sure," I said. I settled back more into the cold ridges of the mountain.

Darkness encroached, carrying the calls of the predators ringing off the stones and rocks. Soon we were nothing more than outlined shadows. We turned back-to-back, keeping our kidneys warm, and leaned against the rock. When the cold reclaimed our space, we would need to begin our trek using the moon. Before closing my eyes, I searched the night sky. There, near the horizon, the blue twinkle of Chealana shone. She would see me home.

# CHAPTER 20

# THE RETURN

Brown hens pecked the dirt around Mara's feet. The light of day hurt her eyes; her pupils hadn't returned to normal. She dropped the last of the seeds. The scattered, dusty chaff floated to the ground as the chickens scratched. A chilled breeze from snow on the mountains chased a dry leaf across the hardened dirt of the pen. She watched the leaf scuttle with little interest. The rough noise grazed the ground of her thoughts.

More wind lifted white clusters of smoke from the village houses. The smoke mushroomed, pushing up into the air. Cold space chased the denser smoke, pulling and spreading tendrils out into clouds. More wind felt the ends of her hair. She hadn't combed it since she last saw Tianna. Each strand hurt. The wind blew the dark hair across her eyes, willing her to notice, to do something, but Mara didn't. She stood with her back to the house, facing the mountains. She stared with glazed emptiness at the shadowy peaks. Heavy clouds hung low on the snowy cliffs, filled with more promises of snow. All the farm's noise behind her quieted, drowned out. Standing solitary, steam from her breath mimicked the village fires puffing out into the morning air. The mountain ridge stood cold and distant. The last skeletal colors of yellow from the changing leaves couldn't brighten the continual storm the rocky edge had created. That ridge had finally won. Mara stopped looking toward the mountains with hope. Now she only saw the impenetrable wall of her prison.

At home, the walls had become rigid as well. Cool uneasiness was settling in. The men had changed. Her brothers-in-law didn't stay long in the same room. Gabor seemed especially distant. Even Kaiya looked away hastily, dropping eye contact when they worked together. Her sister Tianna's visit had only tightened the strain. She had met to exchange some ground einkorn and milk. Aroden saw and thought the sisters had exchanged something more. His reaction had been as hard as his insistence that Mara knew something and was planning against him again. She told him nothing. It had only been flour and milk.

The blood that should be warming and pushing through her muscles seemed quiet. Taut skin around her temples and cheekbones didn't hold the ruddiness of her age, but rather a pallid tone darkened by a swollen shadow around her eye. This was not how she had imagined her life. The slight churning of nausea in her belly told her an all-too-familiar tale. Her sisters-in-law would have to take care of her daughters.

Pulling her shawl a bit tighter around her shoulders, Mara turned toward the river. The wind's stirring held little sway. Her last thought of care was to shut the gate behind her. Her finger caught on one of the sharp sticks of the closure. A little red dot pooled up on the tip before getting smeared unnoticed on her clothes, her arms limp at her sides. With each step, she kept convincing her will to lie down alongside her dreams.

A lighter breeze playfully pushed her, nudging her to the side, tossing up little pieces of dirt, trying to make her cry. The direction of the wind changed and headed back toward the village, back toward the family. The goddess Cheala seemed to push against her, but even a deity couldn't intervene. Instead, Mara tucked her head a bit more, continuing to walk. Glittering frost still crusted the grass, choking the moisture from within each blade. The frosty sparkles crunched under her. Heavy seed-bearing tufts hung low from the taller grass in other places. Only a stick of the once-green stem stood erect yet broken. The wind had long since scattered any seed, and the animals had ingested any tender leaves. The earth lay quiet under the cold numbness winter had brought.

Mara's feet continued toward the river. The water's frigid bite frosted the air. The moisture dampened deep beneath her shawl. No shudder came. Slumped shoulders held the covering against the cold. If Mara's suspicions of the nausea held true, the little one just starting to grow inside would never suffer.

The grass got thicker and higher the nearer she came to the river's edge. She would look for a place with large rocks to catch herself under. Little divots in the grass opened to trip her foot, tangling her progress. She stumbled once, cushioning her fall in the layered grasses, another little red smear from her finger wiping off on the frosty blades. The sound of the water working caught her attention. Closer now, the river was so loud, chaotic, rushing, bubbling past, bumping into rocks, shuffling under the stems along the shore's edge. Cold shards of her breath sliced the air around her face. A deep, wet sense of freshness pervaded the air, opening her lungs. Under the river's surface, the unseen tug of a current loosened a reed's stalk. The river's power permeated Mara's heart with awe of the indifference of life's rushing greatness. Static sounds played the river's song like the force of wind in the tree's tops. The noise teased her with questions. Where Cheala's wind couldn't achieve, Shal's water succeeded. Mara stared at the intensity before her, the wheels in her mind reversing slowly. The water rolled as if boiling, a force of power pushing boundaries, feeling the way to a purpose. She shook her head, trying to reclaim her reasons.

Clutching her shawl, she stepped through the crusty edges of ice with both feet before the water's enchantment could hold her. Instantly, shivers swirled around, bumping off her legs, quickly being carried away not noticing her at all. A rock slid under her foot, tilting her forward. The smell of water's fullness filled her senses as her arms waved in the air seeking balance, making her alert. The cold bit her legs. She pulled a foot back in a moment born from life's resistance to release hold. Reminding herself there was nothing left, she braced harder for the next step. The sharp coldness that met her legs only matched the dullness inside. Not to be outmatched, the wind pulled her hair, twisting it like a rope, the tendril of a breeze whispering in her ear. Mara stood looking between strands of hair at the cold rushing depths. She waded in a little deeper. The water unconcernedly eddied around her calves. The tingle had turned to a burn. The bottom of Mara's feet pricked from bone-needle cold. Each step broke her ankles. The heavy weight of not feeling waited in her toes to begin the climb up her limbs. The river, merciless in its beating, kept her legs upright, shivering. A chill began at her knees, spreading quickly to her shoulders and ears. Deep in her core, she ached from muscles trying to hold her extremities in unison. Breaking and bridging, the freeze pulled and pushed Mara's mind back into focus. The frigid water set her teeth chattering, talking out the sense of needing to live. The absurdity of the water's concentration on completing life's tasks struck a sobering contrast in Mara's mind.

Whispered prayers rose around her. Strands of her hair blew upward, and the edge of her shawl flipped outward, looking to create discomfort and response—life tugged tighter. She went a little farther. Another leaf floated by her submerged knees. A shiver ran down her spine like fingers. Nature's purpose stirred the stillness of her despair.

She was more alive than she'd believed. A breeze caught her breath, waking her to the final realization of her error. Her chest burned tight under the tension of living. She stepped back, splashing, flipping cold water up and around in her retreat.

Falling on her hands and knees, the nausea won as she gagged and gasped. Her lungs gasping, widening, filling fresh with life's precious elements. Spittle dripped from her chin into the rushing water. She wiped her lips and caught the iron taste of her blood on her finger. Closer to the surface now, Mara saw a clear picture of the rhythms around her. She gripped the riverbank's edge, and dirt pushed under her nails, rooting her. Determination resumed as she stood wiping a dirty streak across her mouth. The smear of grimy nutrients slid over her tongue with a gritty taste. Biting her lips, the signs of life returned under the deep blue hue of her skin. She knew hunger once more.

On the shore, she quickly shook the icy water from her feet, beating some warmth back into her body. She was more than this. He had almost won.

Coming within a breath's kiss of death brought tremors throughout her body. The sky shone bright, reflecting the snow from the mountains. Her eyes darting from clouds to tree to bending bough, she sought to connect the dots of being alive. She continued beating warmth into her arms and legs. Her will of life found a pulse of its own. Mara looked around, checking to see if any witness would need an explanation. A marmot, thick with winter's preparation, sat up on its hind legs, inspected the area, and, seeing no danger, disappeared into the tall grass.

Just above where the creature had been, another movement caught Mara's eye. In the distance, two shapes slowly shifted to define men. The world stopped spinning as her focus zoomed in on a remnant of hope. Hair still dangled in front of her eyes, obstructing the tiny images. Her hand kept fighting back the brown strands in the breeze. Coming closer, the figures caught her imagination. The sun's path angled just before midday. The whiteness clouded distinction. She held up a hand to shade her eyes.

The cold began to strike her toes, so she hopped from one foot to the other. Her eyes never left the figures growing in the field. Mara's thoughts stopped and collided as they reached to hold onto an abandoned possibility. Despite blood rushing and coursing through her, shivers shook her lips and chattered her teeth. The breeze's sharpness blurred her vision, drying the water from her eyes. She stumbled over some of the ruts along the way. The closer she came, the more the belief in his name returned.

"Gaspare." His name silent for so long broke the air and she called again even louder, "Gaspare!"

The men were still too far, but her heart's pounding affirmed each fiber of her being. He had returned. The others needed to come. With each step shattering her legs, she pounded the path, beating feeling back into her lower body. Tripping her way around the tangled grasses, she dashed past a cow and scattered the chickens toward the house. Her teeth chattered. She stumbled more. Hair teased in numerous directions crowned her head as she raced into the home of Tandor.

She looked for anyone to help. The shaking had seized her body, and she found it hard to stop. Gabor sat in tense silence, whittling an antler.

She thought twice and asked, "Where's Kaiya?" barely waiting for a reply.

Gabor didn't look up from his work. He nodded toward the smokehouse. She hesitated. The chattering of her teeth became loud. His indifference didn't require the excuse she was working on, so she ran to the smokehouse, almost knocking Kaiya over as she stood on a stool hanging strips of meat over the smoke to dry.

Mara's words tumbled out. "Kaiya, come quick. He's here. I know he's here. I saw him. I saw them coming in the distance. Oh, Kaiya, please come."

Kaiya stepped cautiously off her stool. "What is in you, Mara?" she asked, examining her wild eyes and mud-streaked face. Kaiya saw Mara shivering, shaking, and moved to get her towards the smoking embers.

"You've got to get Gabor and follow me."

Kaiya took in her wet legs and filthy fingers. "Where? What?"

"Kaiya, I don't know, but I just know we need to go."

Kaiya caught Mara's shoulders, squaring her to look into the wrestling of hope found in her eyes, "What are you talking about, Mara? Why do you want Gabor?" Mara's shoulders shook in Kaiya's grasp.

"Because I think he's come home."

Kaiya never let her eyes stray from Mara's face. She reached forward, gently moving aside Mara's hair. Mara returned her gaze steadily and sure. Seeing no sign of betrayal or doubt, Kaiya said nothing but walked straight into the house. Moments later, she returned with Gabor and a fur. Gabor's doubt in Mara's strength of mind showed under his furrowed brows. His skepticism blocked what she said.

"What is all of this, Kaiya? What are you two doing?" Gabor asked.

Kaiya put the fur around Mara. She turned and placed her hand on her husband's shoulder. She said, "Mara needs you."

"You must come with me. Please, Gabor," Mara pleaded. "Please, just come."

Gabor folded his arms across his chest. "Not unless you tell me what this is all about."

Mara didn't have time for these doubts. She turned to go and staggered a little.

"Gaspare is coming." Stopping the question Gabor was forming, Mara hurried on, "I saw him coming from the mountains. He's coming home."

Instinctively, Gabor's eyes critically scanned her wet appearance. Her lips had a bluish tint. Her teeth now chattered uncontrollably. Her face was smeared with dirt. He rubbed his hand over his chin, carefully considering his next questions. Mara reached for his arm. Her touch caused him to recoil. The movement's subtle nature couldn't be taken back. Mara dropped her hand, looked to Kaiya in desperation, and fled the smokehouse.

Her feet tripped a little, trying to focus the adrenaline. Before she could pick her path, Mara staggered again and fell against the smokehouse wall. The world around her head spun, and stomach bile regurgitated into her mouth. She couldn't see straight. Kaiya came and leaned her forward, placing a hand on the back of her head. She said to Gabor, "She hasn't eaten, and I don't believe she sleeps."

"Do you believe she's able to tell reality from her illusions?" Gabor asked.

Kaiya held her hand on Mara's back, holding her hair as her shoulders heaved.

"Yes, Gabor, yes. I believe Mara saw men. I believe she saw her answer, and I shall not take that away from her. Will you?"

Mara vomited between her legs, drawing Kaiya's attention back. She brushed more of Mara's hair back for her. Mara shook from the cold setting deep within. Gabor ran his hand over the back of his head.

Kaiya continued, "If strangers arrive, the village will not be hospitable. If Gaspare is one of them, he will need warning."

Gabor shifted. Kaiya's words contained a lot of ifs, but he had never known his wife to dwell in tales.

"Will you go to them?"

Gabor nodded and left Kaiya to tend to Mara. First, Gabor went back to the house for his dagger and walking stick. He ignored anyone so as not to stir any conversation. Heading toward the mountains, Gabor wondered which question's answer held priority. One question tagged another and another, till a swarm of locusts buzzed around his thoughts. Those mountains had brought little good to his family. Gabor wasn't sure if this phantom's return would be a harbinger of prosperity or more doom.

He veered away from the river to stand more in direct opposition to the mountain path. As Mara had said, two men approached. From his position, Gabor could see only one bow. They were not heavily armed. They didn't have large packs either, so they were not merchants or traders. The men saw Gabor. They stopped. The smaller one reached out with his left hand to grab the other's arm. Then he let go and began waving. Gabor could hear a faint "Hoi" cross the valley, so he started walking toward them. The smaller man slapped the other traveler on the back and pointed straight at Gabor. The bow in his right hand at his side, the little figure began jogging. Had it been ten or eleven summers since Gabor last saw that run? The smaller man sprinted, and Gabor returned his fervor.

The two brothers met, reforging the bonds that had been waiting among the shadows. Hearty slaps on each other's backs reinforced the fact this was no dream. The euphoria of being found temporarily forgave much. Gabor extended his arms full length with Gaspare on the other end; he inspected him for signs of familiarity. The lack of hair and the clothes only masked the eyes that Gabor knew well. The patterns of voice were those of his younger brother. If omens were to be trusted, then maybe this winter would bring a season of change to Ankwar's council and to Tandor's house.

# CHAPTER 21

# HOMEFRONT

Gabor said Grandfather's hut was the best place to hide both Haliam and me. In two suns, the council would meet, and I would attend. No one knew except Gabor and Kaiya. Gabor chose not to confirm Mara's belief that I had returned. He suspected what Aroden would do to her if he knew. Instead, she sat in the despair and nausea for the two days while Kaiya stole across the fields to bring us food.

"Is there anything else you'd like from the house?" Kaiya asked. "Grandfather lived sparsely out here."

"No, we'll be fine," Haliam answered.

As she turned to leave, I said, "Wait, Kaiya, could you bring me one of Mother's bowls?"

She looked at me for a moment and then smiled. "Sure, I know just the one."

I hadn't told anyone, not even Haliam. "I held one of her jars when I was in Undoura."

"You did? Are you sure?" Kaiya's surprise affirmed my need to tell someone of mother's presence.

"Yes, Mother always twisted her patterns to the left, arching the smaller shells."

"She did, yes. I always thought they looked like droplets on the waves."

"I always imagined the splash when I skipped a stone."

We looked at each other for a moment, enjoying the memory.

"Kaiya, how long ago did Grandfather die?"

"He's been gone now maybe six or seven springs. He got sick not long after you left."

The conversation ended as she stumbled into the awkwardness of why I didn't know. She looked hastily at me, then at the door. The angle of light coming through a crack in the ceiling danced with dust particles lifting and lowering in the beam. She turned to go but stopped at the door.

"Gaspare, I'm so glad you are home," she said quietly.

Neither of us stopped her again as she left for the farm. I could feel Haliam's stare on the side of my face.

"Is that why you skipped stones so often?" he asked.

I shrugged, "Maybe . . . I don't know. Maybe."

Haliam left to go outside.

"Brother, don't go far."

He looked at me confused, then looked at the color of his hand and said, "I wouldn't fit in, would I?"

His smile answered for me, and he entered the openness of the outside. The sun had left, pulling with her the darkness across to the tree line and mountains. A lamp couldn't be lit. If a glow were seen from the window, my advantage would be sacrificed. Just the darkness and I sat in the quiet of the night. The hut hadn't changed since I brought Chealana here as a newly born pup. I had forgotten to ask about her. How could she have survived Aroden's punishment? Cradling my head in my hands, I sought comfort, but my brain pulsed with harried thoughts.

Attioc had suggested a talisman for me to hold, something tangible to look at for my path as a holy man. Doubters would attack my calling, but no one greater than my own mind could assault me best. Attioc believed if I had something to hold, my mind might find the path toward understanding. Deeper questions haunted the corners of my mind, portents of my future failures never clear. I could feel a swirl of a storm in my memories. Nothing much remained in the hut except Grandfather's mat and a few blankets with frayed strands of woven fabric meant little gnawing sounds in the night. I hung our meat from the rafter and found some old hides. This would suffice for the next two nights.

A partially blackened sage wand hung in a corner. I risked lighting it, waving the smell of Grandfather back into the room. The smoky tendrils wafted through the air, chasing the evil spirits from our shared space. Gabor had said the hut became the source of clandestine meetings of late. A growing handful of trusted men came to talk and plan, but mostly talk. Since they had disturbed the dust of the room, the dank smell of emptiness barely lingered. Grandfather's earthy feel of calm came as I waved the bound sage.

I fell asleep early, not stirring when Haliam returned. Sleep cradled me until the moon reached the middle of her path. My mind skirted reality, lingering in the visceral shades of dreams. I couldn't pull myself out of the slumber. Instead, twisted memories unfolded before me. I remembered the feel of the rain on my skin from Undoura's ceremony. In my dream, the lightning flickering across the clouds turned much darker than in my memory. I no longer stood with the face of Attioc before me. The storm coming to me came from further in my past. I had only seen a storm like that twice in my life. The first time had been the day Father died.

Still ensnared in sleep, my dream turned to the blackness of rain, and a vision took shape. An impression formed from within the fog. I saw Father, his left leg deep in a hole washed out from the storm. In my dream, Father turned. He said something, reaching out his hand for help. Instead of help, an axe struck him. I couldn't see who held the weapon. I could only see Father. Father's blood mingled with the rain. I fought to hold on in the tidal wave of destruction this vision poured down on me. My legs kicked and thrashed in my sleep, while my hands worked to pull the mat back. Sweat formed under my arms, drenching my blanket. It beaded on my lip as I watched. My hair matted down my forehead, yet I slept. Nothing could wake me from this dream. My eyes raced back and forth searching for reason, anything that would end the rain and make Father whole again.

The hand that held the axe grabbed Father's arm and dragged his body toward the mud. The hand pushed a fallen tree to cover his head. If I could just see beyond the hand to the man's face. The rain hid the owner of this foulest deed. Father's end came from someone's soured core of a jealous heart. The rain pulled back just enough for me to see the hair and watch the defiant toss I knew well. Aroden's hand had killed Father. Understanding reeled through my sleep. The dark storm clouds broke torrents down upon us all, as I stood alone as a silent witness.

The vision snapped and I sat upright, sweat soaking my clothes and mat. Never had a vision been so visceral. Those visions in the mine had been more of symbolic renderings or shadows. This dream had felt real. Grandfather's hut had been more than a talisman. The room was silent except for the gnawing of a mouse. A dark shape on the floor near the door indicated Haliam had returned and was sleeping.

The sun wouldn't grace the sky for a while. If I stayed under this wet blanket, I would be too chilled to sleep again. I risked a venture outside.

Under the moon's glow, my restless feet found familiar ground on the path to Tandor's house. Standing outside the walls, my heart swelled with longing. How could he create so much chaos? No one would stand against Aroden. The man had willingly thrown his brother on a slave line and murdered his father. The side of the house's stone and mud felt cool to touch. I leaned into the strength of the wall yet felt nothing but isolation. The target of so many of my nights now left me cold. A groan escaped my lips. Who would stop him?

Attioc's words echoed in my mind. The old holy man spoke of duty, forgiveness, and justice. He said that the rightful expression of my anger would be fulfilled in justice, not revenge. This brother's filth, however, stained this threshold, binding my home in agony. Remembering the wet fingers of the rain, the spread of oil over my face, the freedom of my vows caused a twisting squeeze around my heart. I did not feel that peace. Now the moon's soft glow contrasted the crisp cold of winter's coming. Feelings of anger had diluted into confused longing. My encounter with the she-wolf on the mountain felt more like a promise. My dream, however, tore at me like a harbinger of a lie's brokenness.

A cough came through the blackness. I pulled back from the house, cloaking myself behind the nearest tree. Shuffling into the small space of moonlight, Aroden stumbled into view. His gait had a noticeable stiffness in his right leg: Chealana's mark. He stopped to relieve himself. His back was toward me. He seemed small and weak. My hand reached for my belt, looking for my dagger. There I stood, hidden behind darkness. I watched his every move. What was I waiting for? My feet stayed. My hand froze on the sheath. When he turned, I couldn't see his face; the darkness of the night blended with the darkness of his features. All I recognized was the churning in my stomach. He reached the door, paused, and went in.

I smacked the tree. The strength of anger's passion had amounted to nothing more than burning cheeks and acid in my mouth. In the moment of seeing him, my anger's fire had turned to ash. My shoulders began to shake and jerk under the frustration. I bowed my head to muffle involuntary sobs. Loss, a hide stretched too thin, strained to be heard like the beating of the tribal drums. My head throbbed.

Staggering back to the shadows, I retreated to Grandfather's hut. Cries from a forgotten place strained to reach the sky. Only silence reached my mouth. The pain's unresolved intensity dropped me to my knees. Grief found me there under the moon's light and wrapped her arms around my sagging shoulders. I thought my anger would have been enough to face him. Somehow, the strength I needed had to exist. I hadn't come this far not to find justice. However, to follow a bear into his den wouldn't be wise, especially with my lessened fury to embolden my resolve for vengeance. Yet did I only desire to see him suffer? Not knowing the answers, I would have to face my dreams one more night.

* * *

The night of the council meeting arrived. Pale yellow light lingered on the edge of the earth with the darkened clouds blanketing the fading sun. The scent of snow was crisp in the air. The night moved into the approaching stillness. I waited past the sun's streaks as she pulled the hem of purple clouds deep into the skyline with her. My time had come. Glowing from the moon's fullness, the path stretched ahead of me. Haliam stayed back at Grandfather's hut. We decided his presence could prove fatal and would distract too much from the purpose of my time with the council. We had agreed to meet at my father's house in the morning.

No matter the amount of time I had to prepare my thoughts, I still had no idea what or how I would act the first time I saw Aroden's face. In the darkness when I'd watched him, I hadn't seen his eyes. Would they carry any sense of regret or just the burning hatred from my return? The moon hung heavy, full of the burden of creamy light. The wolf's moon shone tonight—the same as the moon that had marked my Mennatti. The space filled with light closed around me, softening the darkness.

I walked past Tandor's house. A house that should be filled with laughter resembled memory's shell, closed tight. Pausing near the goats, I listened to the gentle shuffle of animals as they settled to sleep. The smell of the farm's blend of manure, feed, earthy water, and animal scent was comforting. My feet had traveled far from the time when I guided these beasts to the fields for pasture. If I were going to have any future in Ankwar, I needed to keep moving toward the council hall. The men were all in attendance at the meeting. The only ones left to guard the village were the younger boys.

In the village center, the menhir's dull gray sides picked up the moon's reflection. Shadows played in the light, and darkness intertwined around the stone's base. Entering the council hall could wait. Slowly, I approached the great stone. Palm out, fingers eager, I reached to stroke the surface. A cold, dimpled stone filled with the trace of ancestors met my touch. Much like the stone altar, the ripples and bumps presented imperfections I wanted to experience. My fingers rubbed the place I had touched so many springs ago when I came here still as a boy of Ankwar. The stone's hardness comforted me. I could feel the porous surface that had a thousand touches and thoughts left in a moment of need. Here is where Mara had almost burned at the hands of her husband. My heart began racing. A familiar sweat formed on my upper lip. I could not carry this anger into the meeting.

Little grains of sand in the gray stone, waiting to be released, rubbed against my hands. Leaning in, I breathed deeply the smell of the minerals from the mountains. The robust scent filled my nostrils with the earth's potency. Nerves in my fingertips tingled from a sense of belonging to the aged time of men.

The force of a whisper pushed my breath to the surface: "Blessed are you Hekor, blessed the god of our ancestors." Resting in my sigh, the fervent words continued, "Do not put me to shame." I placed my forehead on the stone. "Deliver me in your greatness." My petitions rose like the curling smoke of an extinguished candle. "You brought me back from Sheol's grasp. You preserved me from Death's touch. Have mercy on me and grant me this victory." My lips sent my breath out across the menhir's surface.

I lay the side of my head against the stone. The ancient traditions held in the cold surface warmed my cheeks. A slight breeze came from the dark and nothing more. No matter what I faced inside the council, the menhir assured me of my place among the men of this village. The time had come; I could delay no longer.

# CHAPTER 22

# COUNCIL

L ight from the council hall reached me before the noise of men. Grandfather's pelts smelled old. Tufts of fur stood out from balding patches on the hide. I tugged at the pelts on my shoulders and adjusted the headdress one last time before entering the gathering. I wore Grandfather's pelts and my dagger in the sheath that Natika had woven. I had fashioned a headdress from a goat skull found behind Grandfather's hut. The goat's symbol of vitality and durability suited me. I looked my part of a man of the tribe.

Inside the council room, luminaries in the shape of constellations filled the pock holes in the walls. The earthly stars were said to guide the council's decisions. Chealana's star twinkled as I walked past and into the room. Council members crowded around the front; some arms folded while others stood in clusters, shaking their heads. No one seemed to notice me in the dim light. The room was filled with the questions of men like fissures erupting from broken courage. The apu-ah hole that had taken Father's spirit back into the Earth's belly waited in the center of the room. I wished I could pull him back from the depths for strength.

Gabor stood in front of Mother's wall hanging depicting the history of our village. I saw Taran, who stood toward the back, near the candles. He watched more than spoke. My friend had grown. I wanted to edge nearer to speak with him, but he was not why I had come.

Finally, I saw him. Aroden leaned back, surveying the disruption he had obviously caused. His eyes sparkled with the personal satisfaction of playing everyone as a fool. He enjoyed tipping the cart, and then watching the scattering of everyone's focus like a bunch of rolling vegetables across the ground. His work amused him.

My focus locked on Aroden's eyes. The flush of anger stained my cheeks. I walked into the circle, my stride even. The men moved. They only recognized the tension; they didn't recognize me. Gabor looked over. He turned to get Esteban's attention. Esteban, who was heavy in conversation, didn't notice.

As I stopped before Aroden, the room silenced. Mine was a moment to stand and touch the sky. The smug coolness of Aroden's look shifted to a smirk, bemused with a tinge of curiosity.

"Aroden, son of Tandor," my voice firmer and deeper than when I had been a boy, "you must be removed from this village council for your corruption of our people's ways."

Aroden tipped his head, considering me. "Corruption? In what way have I committed corruption? And who are you, goat man, to stand in our private council?"

"You slew your father, Tandor, in cold blood, and you now defile his seat in this council."

Aroden's gaze hardened as he leaned forward, "Who are you to stand as accuser, in my village?"

His eyes sought to pierce the goat skull and furs he didn't recognize. Light from the oil lamps caught on the curved, yellow, ivory fangs on a strand around his neck. He had taken to hunting wolves, collecting the essence of their spirit to wear. Each tooth was the length of my smallest finger and able to rip the meat from sinew and bone. The teeth jangled together with his movements. He considered me like a predator, assessing the threat I posed. His slow and calculated response assumed I could only be a trickster or a traveling menace, who performed visions for food and shelter.

Gabor's hand moved toward his belt. I stood straight and ready.

"Have you no better accusation with proof to make? If not, you should be the one to leave this council."

"You slew Tandor and brought his blood upon his house. You sold your younger brother because he guessed at what you had done. Your guilt cries from the apu-ah." I gestured to the sacred hole.

Aroden shifted a little. His brow furrowed. His dark eyes held a dangerous look. The strand of teeth slipped behind his cloak with his movement. He shifted and rose to his full height. The shuffling began as a murmur around me.

"Who are you to bring these lies before me and our council? Declare yourself!"

The other men began expressing louder uneasiness, like cattle when a storm was coming.

Aroden loomed forward as a snake seeking a bird. "State your name or leave my sight. Your impudent lies seek to create chaos."

Gabor spoke from behind Aroden. "This is Gaspare, our brother. The brother you banished."

Hissing whispers of "bear hunter" swished through the crowd, filling the council room. The shushing intake of shock rolled like a wave before the torrent of speculations began. Hands flew to cover mouths. The men gawked. A spirit walked among them, bringing condemnation from the evil intent of their having done nothing.

Holding my ground, I repeated, "As a holy man called by this tribe, I declare you, son of Tandor, the one who should leave, for murdering our father and throwing me on the slave route."

With my announcement, I drew my dagger and moved to stand within range to inflict harm. "I know what you did. You killed Father. His leg could have been freed from the mud. He reached for your help. No tree fell upon him. Your axe brought his demise. You do not deserve to wear the badger pelts of our council's leadership. You do not deserve to walk the floors of this sacred house because you walk with the blood of our father and my youth."

The air tingled and sparked around us. A circle widened behind me, giving way for a fight. Aroden reeled back from the sting. He searched my face for any sign of a lie, or perhaps for familiarity. Gabor moved closer from behind while Esteban stood stunned as a young calf. I heard Sulvak declare a prayer of relief, and Chal moved toward me. Like Zuka, he wanted to see the scars I bore. Chal reached for my arm, the same Zuka had sought, the arm with the charcoal cuts. He pulled back my sleeve and checked, rechecking, verifying that indeed I had returned. Chal raised my arm up, declaring me Gaspare. Energy coursed through my veins and around the room. A vibrating hum turned to a deeper panicked realization filling the room.

Taran now stood beside me. I could feel the straightness of his spine. His shoulders were squared. Together, we faced Aroden.

Gabor walked over and grabbed Aroden's arm. Juri, the blacksmith, moved closer but didn't intercede. The balance of the room shifted.

Sulvak came in between the brothers. "The apu-ah hole is not big enough or deep enough for this council to continue the path toward bloodshed, nor should the floors of this sacred place be stained with hatred." Sulvak's voice carried strong.

"The sacred hole contains voices from beyond seeking justice," Chal said as he lowered my hand and joined Sulvak.

"I know the marks that were pressed into Gaspare's body. It was I who watched his journey back from the dead," said Taran.

Juri spoke, "He was cast out as a curse. Now he returns to fulfill that curse upon this village."

Murmuring rumbled through the room.

Turning to Juri, I answered his accusation. "If I had carried a curse, I have paid for wrongdoing with the suffering of the mines at the other end of Anak's line. I have absolved any pestilence that my life may have invoked by living the death of the damned, working underground to bring copper for your forges."

Sulvak added, "We will not make a hasty and rash decision. The claims brought before this leadership must be weighed to determine the path we will follow."

"We are all present now," Juri answered. "The decision can be made easily as it was made back when we threw this totem of doom from our village."

"No decision can be made with the heat of disturbance," countered Chal. "We have our traditions to hold us to a sense of order and we must follow them to preserve the integrity of our honor."

An ugly sneer lowered Aroden's eyebrows. "You speak of honor and traditions as a wounded animal that crawls into their burrow to die," he spat. "If we are to move forward as a people, we must shed this primitive thinking. We must learn to stand as men." Gabor's grip on his arm tightened as the grumblings intensified. Men muttered around the room like bees. The room hummed with convictions. Aroden continued, "Who is this self-proclaimed holy man to come and cause such turmoil?"

"He is a man who walks the way of honor, Aroden." The voice came from beside me. Taran declared his allegiance knowing full well the weakness of his village's will. "He is a man of conviction and truth, one who has returned from Sheol's darkness. Gaspare is a man who should lead this village away from the cliffs of discord we have perched upon. You, Aroden have wormed your way into the fears of our minds. You stir the turmoil you now accuse Gaspare of bringing."

"If we wait to decide," Esteban's voice rose above the noise, "Aroden will be free to continue working his divisive schemes. He should be banished tonight like he banished Gaspare. Did he give my brother a council meeting? Did he wait for us all to be gathered?" He walked to meet Aroden, no doubt remembering how his wife gave birth to their son in a field while Aroden destroyed the family. Reaching Aroden, Esteban leveled his glare and directly said, "Brother, you will leave before I kill you myself."

Gabor and Esteban together grabbed hold of Aroden. The path opened before them as the crowd closed behind them. They dragged their brother kicking and fighting through the village. Doors opened in the houses along the way; women peeked out, then quickly closed the doors. The brothers dragged Aroden to the path toward the mountains just past the village well and threw him into the edge of night. He sprawled on the ground, struggling to catch his wits, his badger pelts skewed in a ridiculous fashion, the strand of wolves' teeth twisted below his chin. His eyes were wide. Aroden looked at the crowd and licked the sweat from his upper lip.

Sulvak and Chal stood beside me. Sulvak quietly said, "The way of the holy man is to heal."

I watched the pathetic display. Aroden turned onto his stomach, his feet splaying, trying to make traction on the snow to stand, his control vanquished in his pitiful struggle.

"Is this rash casting out of the past the way to healing?" Sulvak asked me.

I saw my brother stand and then stumble from a lack of balance.

"If he goes from the village in this manner, there will be those who do not believe the words you speak. He can still cause harm from afar." Chal added quietly on my other side.

Aroden stood and faced his attackers, moving the sweaty hair from his eyes so he could see, alert for a path to restore him to his rightful place. The wolf moon showed the wideness of his terror.

"No one has proof of his murder outside of your vision. We need more to cast him out. We need a vote." Sulvak concluded his advice.

"We need the strength of the council," Chal added.

The two elders waited. The decision became mine. If the council were to be restored, we needed to purge the manipulation and workings in secret that Aroden had developed. We needed to come together as men and speak.

Gabor and Esteban stood with daggers firm and feet spread in a fighter's stance. Someone from the crowd bent to find a stone in the dark. Inside my tightening chest, I felt the empty truth of anger's wrath. I did not feel the freedom I had known to be possible. I did not feel redeemed, seeing Aroden suffer. I did not find satisfaction. Instead, a glimpse of remorse took hold. Aroden shook his head, raising his chin in defiance like the numerous times he had done with Father. While responsible for his choices, Aroden acted from a heart plagued with the fatigue of rejection's hurt. He walked every step in the pain of knowing Tandor hadn't found pride or pleasure in calling him son. Looking at my brother in the darkness, I found pity.

A chill from the coming snow brushed across my cheek. I shuddered. For all he was and did, Aroden didn't deserve to be cast out in the dark to freeze like an animal. I would not have his memory be a martyr between the village and healing. That was not my calling as a holy man. The first stone flew, barely missing Aroden's leg. Two more men stooped to find a stone. Frustrated from the silence they had maintained under Aroden, these men wanted vengeance for their impotent tongues.

"Wait, no!" I yelled. Picking up on my insistent tone, Taran and the two elder men rushed toward the crowd, echoing my plea. "Wait," I repeated. "Not this way. We must give Aroden a full council's decision."

Gabor turned. The shock was evident on his face. "Why should *he* have fairness?"

I walked to join my brothers, and the three of us stood facing the fourth. "If our village is to heal, we must find a path to true justice. We must return to the understanding that our strength doesn't come from fear, but from unity."

Aroden scoffed. "Is that what they taught you, Holy man?"

Esteban looked to harm Aroden, and I placed my hand on his arm. "Esteban, you know this is not how our village should make decisions." Esteban started to answer, but I hurried and added, "We must crave discipline and order, not wrath that sways us like the rattling seed pods. We must seek the strength our fathers worked to create."

Esteban's jaw tightened. "I will not have his corruption any longer."

"I will not have this puny curse lording over me," snarled Aroden, staggering a little, dodging another rock.

I looked Esteban in the face. "I will not have him be a martyr for those who still wish to believe his threats." My voice dropped low. "Please. Only I know what he did. Given time, his acts will bring the proper judgment. People will know him for his actions. If we send him out now, like this, doubt will work against us like the weeds work the fields."

"Then we need to tie him so he cannot escape or cause more disturbance tonight," Gabor conceded. "If I watch him, he won't make the morning light. Who can stand guard that we can trust?"

"I will guard him," came a voice from within the darkness. Out stepped Haliam from behind Aroden. His light skin startled those near him. Aroden looked at Haliam's face, stunned, amazed by the moon's light on Haliam's light features, unsure of what he did not know. Haliam came and stood before the council among the four brothers. "I will guard him, and, on my life, I will kill anyone who tries to help him escape." He leaned forward to whisper in Aroden's ear, "Breaking you over my knee would bring great pleasure."

Haliam's presence made the men uneasy. He was clearly an outsider. We had all had enough surprises thrust upon us for one night. The decision was made to return Aroden to the council hall and tie him there till the meeting could be held with dawn's coming.

I smiled at Haliam. "I thought you were staying back as we agreed."

"You agreed. I was curious and wanted to see this great figure you carried with us from the mines." Haliam's lips never smiled, but a certain light danced in his eyes. He would be true to his word and not let a soul enter or exit the council hall tonight.

# CHAPTER 23

# HOME

Gabor entered Tandor's house first with Esteban. Following behind my brothers, I could hear Gabor's booming announcement that Aroden would not be returning tonight.

"Gaspare has returned," Esteban said. "Bring the mead and let us eat and drink." Their voices carried warmth out into the night.

Gabor continued. "Tonight, we celebrate the return of our little brother."

I could hear the bustling inside. The sounds of laughter reached me where I waited. I paused to touch the threshold before stepping into my home. So many nights I had spent dreaming and longing for this feeling surrounded by the familiar walls. The hearth stayed as I remembered. Kaiya welcomed me back with Aleya, Esteban's wife. The women brought a plate of meat to eat with some honey mead and a few roots left from the harvest. Warmth fused with the movement of words and bustling to prepare a feast. Aleya ran quickly to find Mara.

Taran walked into the room. In my mind, he moved to the side, and behind him came Chealana. She walked slowly, a slight perceptible limp in her hind legs. Yet here and now in the room, only Taran stood watching me. My friend saw my eyes scan the area around his knees. He read the look on my face. I had held out hope in a silly, romanticized way that she would be waiting for me. Chealana was not there. Taran came over, held out his hand, and pointed to a faint line on his palm. We had cut that scar as blood brothers. He had made a promise sealed by our blood.

"Did Aroden kill her?"

"I kept her safe," he whispered.

"He has teeth, wolf teeth around his neck . . . Are you sure?"

Taran nodded and indicated we would talk later.

I choked back the many questions, dropping my eyes, and nodding my head. It had been too much for me to expect her wild nature to be tamed so easily. My last sight of Taran scooping her in his arms, lifeless, would be all I had. My childish mind needed to keep something safe. She had remained preserved in my memory as the young wolf cub I had found and called my own. Never had the thought occurred to me until tonight that Aroden might have destroyed her. The evening's success soured in my mouth. I had longed to pull Chealana close, working my fingers deep within her thick neck fur and resting my head on her back. Her keen wolf eyes would bring my sense of home. She would have smelled like a memory of the woods with sunlight beaming through the branches.

Sibaccian entered. He came late and held back closer to the door, his brown eyes like Father's watching the dynamics in the room. He preferred invisibility.

The room filled with life. From within the house came various sizes and ages of children, who should be sleeping, some hiding behind an elder cousin, some running with a sibling chasing, each bearing characteristics of our family. One taller girl came into the room. She brought with her a smile of sunshine as she picked up the smallest child. She certainly looked like a beautiful winter flower. Her face had a familiar oval shape yet paler, like a young fawn's speckled coat. She smiled at the little one in her arms and her eyes were warm; her cheeks held a vibrant glow.

She went and stood near Sibaccian. Her eyebrows framed large eyes so much like Mother's. She must be Zaria, all grown up. Mother's twins had grown up. Their fate had not been desolation. The house of Tandor had continued.

Mara came into the house and caught her breath, frozen in the doorway. She didn't move. Her chin quivered slightly. Tears she had believed empty filled up, tickling her cheeks, quietly running over her lips. She wiped her nose with the back of her hand. The movement caught my attention. I looked beyond Taran and saw her. There stood my Mara.

A flush rose around my neck, making the room feel warm. Mara did not move. Kaiya, removing plates from the table, glanced from me and then back to Mara before changing directions to move the children up the ladder to the eaves, making room for the adults. I took in Mara and the full room.

Aleya handed me a drink. The cup in my hand contained Mother's design. On a shelf stood Mother's pottery holding a variety of herbs and objects. Father's place at the table still had the oil stains from his hands darkening the wood. I had lived away equally as long as I had grown under this roof, but the smells of the room, the dirt-packed floor, and the faces I knew surfaced in my heart as a place I had called mine. I felt the bridge built between both sides of my past to bring comfort. So much sorrow could be forgotten when surrounded by those we love. Family, the source of conflict, became the fount of forgiveness. Familiarity brought remembrance of the value I held for this place. The thousands of footsteps and nights sleeping in the wild seemed to end here at my parents' hearth.

I had come home.

* * *

As the mead settled, so did the conversation. Esteban seemed the most doubtful of our council's ability to stand firm against Aroden. Gabor believed the silent members would find their voice. Sibaccian stayed quiet, occasionally asserting the defense of Aroden's actions. He seemed the most conflicted with the topic, and with the changes, and with my being home. We had moved from speculations of who on the council might doubt my claims to interpreting the depth of corruption Aroden had created. He needed to face his consequences, but would the council carry out the degree of banishment? Frequently, the strands of discussion trailed off into silence. Daily life in the village would be beyond tense if he stayed. I had worked too hard to return, so I didn't plan on leaving.

Tired from the seriousness, Taran stood to leave. I walked him outside.

Pausing before entering the night, Taran turned and said, "Chealana stayed with me till she came into heat and then she left. She headed toward the mountain."

I looked into his eyes and saw only the urgency of truth.

"She walked free among the mountain pines. I know that I saw her there a few times, Gaspare. I saw her in the mountains."

"Taran, I saw a strand of teeth around Aroden's neck." My question never fully formed.

"He has taken to hunting wolves, yes, but he did not shoot Chealana. I saw her a few full moons past. Or at least I believe I saw her. She never joined a pack."

"They probably wouldn't have taken her. Where were you?" I asked.

"Near the hunting rock on the other side of the mountain. She looked good, but alone." Taran put his hand on my shoulder. "She's safe up there with her mountain."

"Other wolves might have torn her apart years ago," I said. "How can you be sure you saw her?"

"She has a little bit of a limp. I followed her once to what I think was her den, but she lost me in the underbrush."

I smiled. "I'd like to think I saw her up in the mountain pass when I was crossing with Haliam."

"Maybe you did, Brother. Maybe you did." As Taran called me brother, I felt a familiarity warm inside my heart. Only Haliam had called me brother. Haliam and Taran: they were the ones I trusted most in life.

"Taran, thank you for standing with me tonight."

He stopped and looked at me. "I've waited a long time to stand with you, Brother." He left into the night.

The day had been long and filled with waiting. The night worked her quieting rites, stealing thoughts into the shadows. The brothers' conversation had been divided by my thoughts of Mara. She stood near the men, but her actions did not make it clear if she stayed near for me. When Esteban and Gabor roused passionate frustration in circles above the table, I stole glances at her, watching her interact with the other women.

Now that the talk of what to do about Aroden and village troubles dissipated, I looked at Mara and went to the door. She understood and excused herself from the women's company, heading out to the chickens.

In the same piercing moonlight as the night before, the farm looked lonely. Snow sharpened the moon's light. I crossed to the tree I had watched Aroden from and now looked to see Mara in the blackened shadows. A call from the darkness had told me where she waited. Sitting in the same room had been torturous. Doubt had mingled with hope. An awkwardness tugged at the corner of my mind: *What if she didn't* . . . But the closer I came, the more determined I was to tell her.

Mara stepped into the moonlight. Her body relaxed, drinking in the delicious breath of the crisp air all around. A small laugh began to form on her lips, creating a blush of life that came rushing to her cheeks. Her eyes held light and color. The sight of her warmed the air around me. She finished the distance between us. I held my Mara, her warmth filling my arms.

The shuffles and cooing of the chickens behind us created the knowledge that we had won. Enduring whatever either the mountains or the village had thrown at us had strengthened our belief in each other. The guilt I had borne slipped away when I lifted her chin, soaking in the excitement of her. Brushing the strands of her hair away from her eyes, I searched for forgiveness. I found a smile.

"You were my evening star guiding me home," I whispered. I brushed her cheeks, never losing sight of those eyes: the beautiful golden flecks that had lit the darkness in the mines. Her response to my words blossomed like morning flowers fresh with dew. I wiped an errant tear, and she held my hand in place on her cheek. She moved her lips to gently kiss my fingers.

Lifting her to swing around in a circle, my heart felt fullness. Still holding her, I slowly eased my arms back just enough to see her entire face with my own eyes.

"I wished upon that star many times, waiting for you to come home," she answered.

Being so near to her confession, the iced reality I had lived under for so long began melting. I shook my head, shaking off the ghost of an empty life. I looked at the length of her nose that led to the fullness of her lips. I leaned into Mara's love to claim the protection of the present and future. The desire to claim the life I should have had gave me courage.

Gently cupping her face in my hands, I searched for my answers. I found trust. Those eyes that had guided me so many nights, the eyes that had been the last to leave my dreams and the first to return looked at me with a longing for vulnerability. She whispered my name, calling me back. My thumb traced the curve of her lips. The iced coating inside me slipped away. I felt the breath of a hundred springs crack the remaining cover of hard coldness. The rebirth of the man believed dead broke through. Awakened at last from my icy sleep, I dared to claim happiness.

Not caring about tomorrow or the council's decision, I pulled her face close. Everything momentarily forgotten, our lips neared each other, creating a deep rumbling born from the depths of waiting. The sound of blood pounding in my ears silenced any further hesitation. Mara's face flushed. Instead of seizing her tightly, I gently placed a kiss on her cheek. It would have to be enough for now. I could not ask more.

As I pulled back to gaze upon her face, Mara grabbed my head in both hands and pulled our lips together, fusing our fate and future.

# CHAPTER 24

# TRUTH'S REALITY

The council denied me attendance while they decided Aroden's judgment. Some council members argued I had not officially been elected to the council, as my Mennatti was incomplete. Others believed I had been gone too long from village life to have a clear perspective on the needs and state of life in Ankwar. The arguments held perceived truths, but not the truth. Fear's coils girded about the council with a steady suffocation. Chal assured me he would represent the insights of the holy man's role in the decision. For me, I needed to wait. Mara waited with me.

We walked together to the livestock and made sure they had food. A fresh snow had come to the valley, and the skies looked to hold more. The families that would move the cattle down lower in the valleys were preparing to leave by the next full moon. I hitched an ox to pull the cart, and we went out into the field. We loaded cut fodder from the stacks into the cart and pulled the food down to the enclosure.

Before the last haul of food, I lay back down on the hay. Mara lay beside me. I pulled some hay out of her hair. Our fingers intertwined. We stayed for a moment, me looking up at the sky's shifting clouds and Mara resting her head beside me. She was another man's wife. The passion we had shared was stolen just like kisses in the night. The pains of longing drew us to the forbidden fields. Forgetting the council met, forgetting she belonged to Aroden, forgetting the family needed to be strong again, we fell further into Salir's song of denied love.

Snow scented the air. The breeze pulled the heavier clouds over the field. We needed to get back; more work waited. The luxury of time that I wasted made for a guilty pleasure. Even as a young boy I had worked. That is what being a member of Ankwar meant. We worked. If we wanted to eat, we worked. Food meant survival through the winters. Lying here with Mara went against my family's loyalty. Even the most estranged family required a sense of unity. I shifted her weight from my arm to get up, her gentle protests voicing what we both felt. Together we walked back to the animals, pulling the last load behind us. We were comfortable in our quietness together.

None of the men had returned from the council meeting when I went to get some water. Zaria worked in the space outside the house, banking the fire in preparation for the day's meal. Once the mud oven absorbed the warmth, she would push the ashes to one side and put her loaves on the other side. Zaria's clothes looked like Kaiya's style of weaving.

Smiling, I approached the girl. Zaria glanced at me, and her face quickly sobered. She quickened her working pace. Wiping her hands, Zaria looked down. Long lashes shaded her eyes. No mistake could be made—she looked like our mother. She was the only daughter of the house of Tandor. Zaria embodied Mother's slender form and hair, the way she held her head, her mannerisms . . . I could see our mother's fingerprints all over her. A sorrow twisted inside me as I watched her. She never knew her.

Zaria's hands deftly moved the coals inside the oven. Her silence did not dissuade me.

"Let me take that for you," I said as I reached for the bowl with meat. She glanced at me, held back a little, and decided to risk the help. I held the bowl up, looking for Mother's traditional markings. Instead, I found an unfamiliar pattern etched on this bowl.

"I've been working on a new design," she offered. She moved the pieces of dough to the front of the oven.

I replied, "You made this?" Some meat juice poured out when I tipped the bowl too far forward, looking first to Zaria then the bowl and then gazing at the girl.

Smiling shyly, Zaria answered, "Yes, I've been making bowls for two springs."

"You're quite good."

"Do you like the design?" Zaria asked. Too young to hide her pleasure at being complimented, Zaria bloomed like the winter flower she had been named for. Her face opened toward me, dropping some of her guard. Her voice was light, filled with innocence.

"Yes, I see the smooth lines on the sides of the bowl." Holding the bowl higher, and this time more carefully to examine the sides, I said, "You have a very similar style to Mother's."

Zaria quickly glanced at me. I hadn't meant to say that out loud. Once our sibling connection had been acknowledged, I nervously continued looking quickly down to a rock or leaf for help with my words. I began again quietly, "Our mother held the title of being the best potter in Ankwar. Did you know that?" A hint of pride lingered on the question.

Her eyes widened. "No, I didn't realize."

"I lived for two springs in the village of Undoura. I found one of her jars there. They used our mother's jar to hold the sacred olive oil."

Zaria's eyes grew even wider, and her mouth formed a circle that now looked more like Kaiya's gestures. I smiled at her, putting her bowl back in her hands.

Zaria tilted her chin down, smiling. Her face held intelligence and curiosity. "I hope to begin selling my bowls at the trading markets in the spring."

"You must do so. That would be good for you, for our family, to have pottery once again distinguished on the trade routes."

Zaria's smile tugged at the corners of her mouth and eyes, and I saw her relax a little more as she added the meat to the oven.

"You must have eleven springs now, right?"

"I have thirteen . . . well, almost. When the moon reaches full again, Sibaccian and I will have thirteen springs together."

At the mention of my younger brother, I decided not to linger any longer. Something about Sibaccian didn't feel right. I couldn't identify why. He seemed nothing like Zaria, and yet they had shared the same womb. The smell and sizzle of meat inside the oven tempted me to stay, but I needed to keep busy. My mind didn't need the quiet or too many questions.

Haliam found us. At his approach, Zaria backed closer to the oven. Haliam slowed down, extending in his hand to Zaria a freshly woven rope. His peace offering brought a glance from her, but she didn't reach for it.

"You should take it," I said. "Haliam's ropes are second only to Kaiya's."

The hesitation lingered a moment more and then came a smile just for Haliam. The purity in her gaze made Haliam smile.

"A sweeter flower cannot be found till spring breathes her warming breath across the apple trees," Haliam said, handing her the rope with a low bow. As Zaria blushed, Haliam asked, "That is what your name means, Zaria? Winter's flower?"

Zaria looked down, gave a little nod acknowledging Haliam's words of friendship, then accepted his gift, pulling the rope close to her.

Aleya came to the door and called for her. Zaria left for the house.

"Brother, you do not need to stay out at Grandfather's hut. There is room for you in my father's house."

Haliam's turn for quiet. "Your village needs me as an unbiased outsider. The time may still come when they will call upon the strength of those not infected by your brother's ilk."

"I hope you speak the wisdom of our tribe's counsel. Thank you, Haliam. I couldn't have come home alone."

Taran arrived. The meeting was over. The look on his face told the tale of the village's answer. A decision had been made.

# CHAPTER 25

# THE DECISION

Taran's steps came with the swiftness of his news. "There you are!" he called in greeting.

"What news do you bring us, Brother?" I called back. I poured him some water.

He reached for the cup, drank all the water, and looked me in the eye. "They've decided he must go."

No chanted trance or rhythmic drums had ever brought me a deeper sense of relief. Tension from my shoulders released as I lifted my face toward the heavens. I closed my eyes in disbelief. A small flake landed on my lips. I whispered a prayer of gratitude. Could redemption be mine?

"Was the vote unanimous?" Haliam asked.

"No, never that easy. Gabor and Esteban should be back soon. Esteban was talking to Juri when I left."

"Where are they keeping Aroden now?" I asked.

"They tied him to the menhir stone while the council met. I believe he is still there."

"I will go and make sure," Haliam said as he turned and headed toward the village center.

Gabor came into range and saw me talking with Taran. "Fair enough news, little brother," Gabor started. "I assume Taran told you the council's decision."

"Yes, I find it hard to believe."

"We all do," Gabor said. "What we do know is the village is not ready for a chiefdom like the one Aroden posed."

Taran shook his head. "I'm not interested in provoking fights with nearby villages or engaging wandering foragers to help raid fields and flocks."

The snow became tiny pellets of tight crystals falling. A few bounced off Gabor's hat. Three or four gathered on Taran's shoulders.

Esteban came near. His face didn't look as triumphant as expected. We greeted him. He motioned for the house, and we went in, anxious for his report.

"I spoke for a long while with Juri," Esteban said.

"I never understood his alliance with Aroden," Gabor said.

Neither did I. Juri's betrayal of his marriage agreement with Father for Mara and me to wed never felt right.

"Juri was bought by Aroden's threats against him," Esteban answered.

We all looked at him shocked and interjected questions simultaneously until he raised his hand.

"Aroden approached him, suggesting attacks and raids on the village might happen if Juri didn't align with him." Esteban's shoulders sagged under the weight of words. "Our brother used Juri's status as the smith of the village and his relationship with Father to push his way into the voice of the council."

We quieted our questions, wondering who else Aroden had coerced. Esteban finished with, "He sealed the negotiation with his marriage to Mara."

Gabor and Taran turned at the noise they heard, realizing this animal sound came from me. Something snapped. Deep inside, a crevice tore my mind from reason. I backed away from the men and pushed myself back toward the door, away from the hearth, yelling from somewhere lost in me. Fierce tears burned the edges of my eyes, drowning the sounds of life. Squeezing my eyes shut tight, I fought back. My fists clenched as tight as my teeth before I threw back my head and opened my mouth to be heard by the stars.

My body sought ways to expel the tantrum waging. My feet looked to kick. My fingers sought anything to throw or to break. My eyes saw Zaria's bowl. I desired destruction matching the feeling of broken pieces inside me. I needed to break something to match the shattering inside. A surge seized my brain, and I began to wildly look out the door toward the village. Taran ran to me, followed by Gabor. They feared the ideas they saw in my eyes. Taran grabbed my arm. I shook him off. Gabor reached me and held me back. I twisted and shrugged.

I pivoted on him with rage, "Don't tell me not this way! Don't tell me to let it go. I should have confronted him at my Mennatti. I should have smacked the arrogance from his face then when he told me he would have Mara." My words finished with another yell of frustration. I tried to tear away from them, but they continued to hold me.

Gabor's words came quietly, but they made their mark. "You are right. You are right. I shouldn't have stopped you." He released his hold on my arm. The anger pulsing in my ears pounded away at my thoughts. Something in his tone slowed my body enough to listen and to hear. What one brother destroyed didn't have to end in a ruined family. Gabor offered no excuses. He didn't hold me back anymore. My breathing steadied as I turned toward him.

He looked ashamed. "I was afraid that so soon after Father's death," he said, "if you had made a scene at your Mennatti, your actions would be seen as rash, impulsive, and weak. They would hurt your chances of being accepted by the council. I stopped you . . . I . . . didn't know."

Taran looked at me and added, "Gaspare, we cannot make any excuses. Anyone of us could have stepped in and none of us prevented what Aroden did."

"You were a boy, Taran. I was a boy." My voice shook, but my words were not strained.

"You both were boys. You are right. It was my responsibility to put Aroden in place. I am the eldest. The work should have been mine," said Esteban.

I looked up to see Esteban beside me, his hand on my shoulder. "I didn't think he would take his cruelty so far. I underestimated him. You . . . you were . . . I . . . I am sorry, Gaspare."

The shame and feelings of being hated lowered my temper. "I never knew why . . . I could never understand why . . ."

The band of brothers stood in a circle, silent in thoughts of what should have been. Finally, Taran spoke. "Do you think you should be there when the council exiles Aroden from the village?"

"I hadn't considered otherwise," I said.

Before my blood pressure could rise again, Taran added, "Your voice has credence now. If you were to go and show anger and spite, the village might turn on you as an instigator of a family feud."

Taran added, "I won't go if you would like for me to stay with you here, Gaspare."

His offer felt like a dove's wings of peace. I wouldn't be alone anymore.

"I will go and stand for Father's house," Esteban said. "Gabor and Sibaccian will be there, and Haliam too, as a neutral party. Let me go and have Mara pack Aroden's things for him."

I looked at him. "Mara?"

Esteban nodded. "She's his wife. She goes as well."

My heart ceased its beating. "He can't have her. Not again," I said, desperation rising in my voice. "I won't let him take her from me again."

Esteban shrugged his shoulders. "She is part of his house. If he goes, he takes with him his house."

Taran interrupted. "They couldn't mean Mara and the two girls should go out into the snow. Esteban, hasn't Aroden caused enough suffering?"

"The council was clear. They want him gone with no ties or reasons to come back to Ankwar." Esteban eyed my stance. "This is his right." Esteban turned to head back to the Council.

"Right? Where was my right when he stole her from me through lies and threats? Where was my right as Anak dragged me over the shadows of the mountains? He has no claim to a right. He spent his share and then some of mine as well."

"Esteban," Gabor called. My eldest brother turned, and they shared a knowing look. No words passed, and Esteban left for the village.

"I'll take her and leave. We'll go right now. I will keep the children safe." I began to pace to find my direction.

"Don't be a fool," Gabor said. "No one is going anywhere except Aroden. Grandfather's hut worked once to keep you safe. There's no reason the hut can't keep Mara and the girls out of sight now. But we must move fast."

"If the village thinks she should go, there will be no possible way to keep her here."

"Let's deal with that after Aroden leaves. First, we need to hide her." Gabor moved toward the door as Mara and Zaria came in from the ovens.

A sacrifice needed to be made.

# CHAPTER 26

# DEPARTING

Zaria quickly went to find Mara's two girls while Mara gathered more blankets and food to carry out to Grandfather's hut.

"I just don't think this is going to work," Mara mumbled as she looked around Tandor's house one more time. My doubts remained silent. I'd seen the determination and fear of this village. My faith in their newfound courage didn't have the roots of an oak tree. Gabor left to join Esteban and Sibaccian in the village. He would stall any advances that he could. Taran carried the embers from the hearth. Mara wouldn't be able to have a large fire, but she wouldn't need to freeze either.

Carrying what our arms could hold, we headed to the hut. The girls' questions drifted across the field and down the path like birds flitting for seeds from dried grasses. A chill breeze blew on our backs, pushing us toward safety with the breath of a prayer. Not till my hand touched the doorway of Grandfather's hut did I look back. The fields lay quiet. The snow, however, did not. The field showed numerous prints, including small child-size prints. No one saw. But Zaria knew our hiding place. My compliments for her earlier hadn't earned me such loyalty as to come between twins and secrets.

"Haliam will stay out here with you till we have a better plan."

"Will he be enough?" Mara asked.

"I trust him with my life. He's more than enough," I answered.

"He has taken ownership of the village conscience. He doesn't fear them. In fact, quite the contrary. The village isn't sure what to think of him," said Taran.

"We must hurry back," I said and took one last look inside the hut. The girls were huddled together in a corner near the blankets, not sure what to do. Mara looked at me and nodded.

Taran and I left quickly across the field. The little snow pellets were bigger now. They began to lie down on top of the branches. A fresh blanket would be upon us soon if the snow remained steady. Looking closer, our tracks didn't leave a deep print, yet there was no denying the activity of numerous feet, both little and large, from the morning's movements. I tried to shuffle through the prints the closer we came to the house. More snow would be a blessing and a curse. If the village delayed in sending Aroden away, then Mara's hiding would be compromised. She couldn't stay out in the hut with the girls.

Back at the house, we saw Zaria talking with Sibaccian. He had returned early from the village. He looked up when we approached. His eyes darted from Taran to me and to the direction we had come in, and back to me. Seeing him standing there with the stark contrast of the whitening snow against the darkened sky seemed familiar. His thirteen springs had not been filled with a sense of childhood. No father, no mother, a family remnant fractured from sibling discord suckled him in a wearied trust. My youngest brother reminded me of something I had forgotten.

Kaiya came out holding two full bladders of milk. Aleya followed with a sack of einkorn flour and dried meats. One of the younger children carried the ember container, followed by another with a pack. Sibaccian went into Aroden's hut and came back with his bow and arrows, a knife, and Father's axe. Zaria gathered a fur hat and grass mat. They all held items for a journey.

Taran asked, "Where are they keeping him?"

Sibaccian answered, "Sulvak believed we should keep him in the village and not at home. Too much strife had already been stirred."

"Are they determined to send him out?" I asked.

Sibaccian looked at me, pulling back. "Isn't that what you sought?"

"I'm looking for justice and the safety of this village," I answered. None of this was about revenge. Aroden was a danger to the village. Our tribe needed to be cured of his vices. Sibaccian looked down. The large bow overwhelming his small frame made him seem more of a child. The look across his face said otherwise.

He spoke quietly as he looked up at me. "Why is it he must leave? Now after all the loss? Wasn't Mother and Father enough for you?" His words were ice water to my face with his cold delivery.

"What has he told you about me?"

"Because of you, Mother died."

"He's a liar."

"He's not the one hiding someone else's family. Wouldn't that make you a liar, too?"

Kaiya reached to stop him.

Taran placed a hand on my forearm, turning me away from Sibaccian to look at him. "Will you go to the village with us?"

That question had been churning inside me since the early morning. Did I need to see for myself the injury now inflicted upon my brother? Would that make me free from the pain?

"No, I don't think I need to go."

"Are you afraid?"

I looked over my shoulder, seeing the challenge in Sibaccian's eyes, his chin tossed up defiantly. "No." Blood was pulsing through my arms to my clenched fists. This younger brother of mine had set his course on feuding with me.

"Then you're a coward," Sibaccian said.

Kaiya put a hand on Sibaccian's shoulder while everyone rushed to correct Sibaccian's statement.

I walked closer to the challenge I heard in Sibaccian's voice. My eyes narrowed, indicating the barb of his arrow had struck a nerve. "What good would it do me to see my brother cast out? How does not watching make me less of a man? The things I have seen would crush you under the weight of evil and hatred. I have no desire to continue that path any longer."

Taran told Sibaccian to head to the village with his load. He took the food from Aleya and Kaiya, placed it in the pack, then tossed the pack upon his back and turned to the village.

Kaiya looked apologetically toward me. My chest heaved from the restraint of not breaking Sibaccian into the fragmented child he was. "He didn't mean it," she said.

"Yes, he did."

"He's just a boy. It hasn't been easy for him, Gaspare. He's always been a bit of an outcast in the village. Can you imagine growing up under the shadow of your parent's death and the village, this village, thinking you a harbinger of sorrow?"

Nothing further was said, but my mind ignored the silence. I changed my course. Turning my back on the house, I headed into the center of the council's chaos. I would not stand the challenge of a coward, even if it was from a mere boy.

# CHAPTER 27

# INTENDED CLAIM

O ur village didn't have a lot of experience casting one of our own out into the fields. In fact, before me, I can't remember another who had met such a fate. Zuka, but she'd escaped in the night. We did have our ways of handling tribal disputes and punishing those who trespassed on the village's wellbeing but casting them out was not typically one of them. We were a small group formed from the convergence of three eastern families. We needed every hand to make our village function. Our punishments could be harsh, but generally, once every ten springs was enough to keep the outliers in line. We worked around the age-old squabbles and clashes that came from various interests. We tolerated the insanity of Henig, who had died a pauper with a curse on his lips. We celebrated the new spring with a festival of promise, complete with cups of mead and salted meats. We sacrificed our autumn harvest on the great stone table to stave off the evil of winter's hunger. But we simply did not cast one of ours out as the atonement for our blind ignorance. That just wasn't done.

I neared the crowd formed around the council doorway. Haliam saw me and approached. He pulled me behind the menhir and into the shadow of a tree nearby.

"Gaspare, quickly, tell me where is Mara? The men will be coming for her soon."

"She's safe."

"You don't understand. They intend to send her with Aroden as his rightful claim. She's not safe to stay in the village. Once they made up their mind, they became bent on a full purge. They will cast out not just the serpent, but all that he has built in his lair. That includes Mara."

"She's at the hut. You think they will look there?"

"I would."

My breath steamed the air like water on the hot embers. Snow still fell upon the layers already coating the earth.

"Haliam, what can I do?"

"You must stay here. I will take Mara to Undoura. She can stay with Zuka. She will help her."

"But the girls will never make it in this snow."

"The village can overlook a couple of girls. They will not be the target of their angst. We can carry them over the mountains once spring has returned. But not Mara. She must leave now."

The crowd shifted in the cold keeping their feet warm. They grew tired of waiting for an outcome. I looked at my friend, Haliam. I saw Taran on the other side of the crowd. They were my two brothers, closer than those of my own blood. Beside Taran, I saw the scowl carved into the features of Sibaccian and I knew.

"Haliam, please take her. Take her now. I will stay here. I will find a way to distract them from her whereabouts. You must go."

"I'll head toward the river."

"No, you must climb up now into the tree line. Take the harder path, away from the village and past the animal enclosures. Follow the sun's trail. Mara will know the way."

"Will Mara make the hill?"

"She will. She must."

"Then we shall head for the upper tree line."

"I will follow you later."

"You must not come till you bring the girls. You must let me take her away from sight and memory. Do not be the wounded fox that brings the hawk to the den."

A tightness seized my gut as I watched my friend turn and make his way swiftly toward Grandfather's hut and Mara. I had just found her and now I would lose her again. The sight of her hair sprawled across the hay with streaks of white melding with the pieces of golden hay would be my lasting memory. How did the gods find a way to give me so many heavy goodbyes?

Time did not allow me to ruminate my misfortune of the stars. The crowd parted, and I could see the leaders including Esteban coming from the council hall. I turned one last time to see Haliam and caught only a glimpse of his shoulders darting behind one of the village houses. He would see his mission through. I had to stand, making sure nothing more could follow to hurt her.

# CHAPTER 28

## CAST UPON THE SNOWS

Esteban cut through the crowd. Fury's burn and the look of newly sharpened flint in his eyes made people step aside. Following behind him came Gabor, Juri, Sulvak, and the elders of the tribe. Behind them came the bent form of my second oldest brother, held tight between two men. The parade marched past the menhir, past the well, past the last house in the village, and to the edge of the lake of green waters facing the stark skyline held back by the dominance of darkened mountain peaks on every side. A timely wind swirled the top layer of snow, adding depth to the ominous task ahead of Aroden. Taran and Sibaccian approached with the goods they had retrieved from Tandor's home and Aroden's house.

An elder came and helped Aroden place the pack upon his back. He turned to present him with the first bladder of milk when Aroden saw me. His nostrils flared and his eyes burned with the contemplative murder of a hawk focusing on a pigeon. Snarling like an animal, he lashed to be free. He harnessed hatred and threw off the arms and the pack from his back.

"You!" he called out, saliva spraying from his lips. "You have come here to mock me."

"I have come to ensure that you leave and nothing more." My voice held a calmness not from me.

Rage filled his legs, his arms, his mind, and seemed to seize hold of his heart, squeezing out every ounce of spite. Lunging for me, Aroden caught me hard with his arm. I staggered back but took the bait of hatred and lunged at him. We embraced, bound by the end of death alone. He would see me die before he left.

The crowd stepped back, making room for the thrashing of two brothers. Aroden's wild rawness gave him strength I had to adjust to. In one of our twists, our feet slid on the wet ground, toppling us. We rolled. He ended on top, his hands around my neck, strangling the air from my pipes, crushing the veins' ability to carry blood to my brain. I gasped, choking deeply. Pulling against his hands didn't work, so I focused my elbows and arms to pivot my weight. Regaining my ground, I found a foothold to throw my weight upon him.

I broke his grip when we flipped over; I was now holding him to the ground. One of the canine teeth from his necklace pressed into my wrist. My lungs sought to be filled. While heaving each breath as deep as I could gulp, my mind scattered to Mara, and I knew what I needed to do. I threw myself into the many seasons of pain he had caused me. Sitting across his chest, I allowed rage to direct my fury. Blood shot across my face from a hit to his nose. My hands pummeled him for Chealana, for my childhood, for my Mara, for the curse I wore. He had savaged more than just my freedom.

Aroden found his way out from under my weight, boring down on the side of my head. He neared the fallen pack. He found the dagger Taran had tied to the side and held it out. He would see me bleed.

Gabor took his dagger and tossed it to me. Aroden and I circled each other, eyes locked. Before either of us could strike, I felt myself pulled back by strong hands. Aroden was hauled back as well. Esteban held him. Taran and Juri held me.

Sulvak stepped into the center, his old age not intimidated by the hormones of the men bound around him. "Enough!" he shouted. "Enough of this nonsense."

Aroden wiped the blood from his nose with the back of his hand. I had broken it, giving him something to think about tonight in the darkness.

"We must not delay any longer," Sulvak continued. "The snow will show no mercy to anyone. The time has come."

Some of the men looked up into the gray sky. No presence of the sun could tell us how much longer the light would be with us. Snow mixed with mud, blood, and grass stirred into slush at our feet. We would soon be cold and in need of shelter.

"Gabor, trade your boots with Aroden." Sulvak gave Gabor no room to question. "We cannot send him out with damaged gear." Gabor obeyed.

The men restored Aroden's pack and supplies to his back. They returned to form a barricade across the way to the village, standing shoulder to shoulder. Remembering Haliam's mission, I quickly scanned the valley. Had I given them enough time?

"Aroden, son of Tandor, we release you from Ankwar." The words Sulvak pronounced echoed like a drum, sentencing my brother's exile. "You are to leave and never return except upon punishment of death."

"I will not leave without what belongs to me!" Aroden shouted. "Where is she?"

Aroden looked at me, scanned the crowd, and then returned his look to me. "She is mine. I will not leave until I have what is mine to take." He held my gaze.

Sibaccian spoke up, "She's in Grandfather's hut." His eyes glanced at me, showing where his allegiance lay.

Sulvak sighed. "That hut is too far away."

Aroden seemed to sense his leverage. "I will not leave without what's mine."

Sulvak directed two men to go and get Mara. Sibaccian volunteered to be one. Taran tried to stop him, but he shook his hand off. Sibaccian's eagerness to retrieve Mara made one thing clear: Mara would have to remain a secret, never to return to Ankwar. She would only be safe if I stayed away from her.

Aroden watched me under hooded eyes. The fight seemed to have tamed his bitterness for the moment.

The way to Grandfather's hut took a lot of time. His cabin was located on the other side of the village, beyond the first field. We neared midday. The snow had stopped. A single ray of sun pushed through the gloom momentarily before closing behind the gray barrier. The men returned carrying two little girls. The children's mouths were open in sobs. Confusion marred their childlike beauty and innocence. Their discomfort came from the heart. Mara did not join them.

Coming up behind the men, Kaiya hurried to reach the girls.

"She's gone," Sibaccian said.

"Gone from where?" I questioned him.

"She's gone from Grandfather's hut where you hid her." Sibaccian sensed his defeat. He had tried to prove his manhood too soon.

Aroden raised an accusing finger directly at me. "Where is she? What have you done with her?"

I did not give him a response. Rather, I turned my gaze back to Sibaccian to push the prick of failure deeper. "Why are you so certain she was there? Did you see her go?" I asked Sibaccian.

"No, but I know she was hiding there. Zaria told me so."

"Maybe you misunderstood Zaria," Gabor said.

"We found these two there with blankets and other supplies," Sibaccian hurried, grabbing the wrist of the youngest, his redemption nearby.

"Did you find her or not? We must make haste. Much time has been wasted now." Sulvak's determination steered the focus away from Mara and onto the path that stretched ahead into the mountains.

Aroden made to lunge at me again. Esteban blocked him. The barricade of men moved to ensconce him.

Sulvak sighed from the depths of his soul. Time did not remain for another brawl. "These two children cannot make their way into the mountains. Is there any to take them and raise them? I'll not have innocent blood upon our heads again." Sulvak turned a weary face toward the gathering.

"I shall take them," stated Kaiya. She gathered the girls to her side, wiping their faces.

"Our family shall help as well," added Taran. "They are the children of my wife's sister. They are welcome in our house."

Sulvak nodded. "So, it is decided. Before the sun travels any farther, we must part our ways here and now," he said as he turned to address the men. "I ask for ten men to ensure that Aroden leaves."

Men began to raise their hands and step forward. The strength of healing could be felt at our fingertips.

I moved to join them, but Sulvak stopped me. "Not you, Gaspare. There is enough bad blood between the two of you."

"I will go to represent the house," said Esteban, stepping forward. "My brothers will remain here, trusting that I will see the job through."

"Very well," Sulvak continued. "Your band of men will travel with him to the mountains. You will stay till dawn to ensure the distance is cleared." The wives of the men hurried to gather supplies for them. Sulvak turned to Esteban and added, "Take no part in harming him. Leave his path to the gods and his destiny."

Esteban nodded. The group headed out toward the granite wall of cold, toward the boundaries of the mountain's crest. The remaining members of the village stood watching the procession. One by one they returned to their lives and warm fires. I remained, Gabor and Taran at my side till they, too, turned to go.

In the distance, the group became a small cluster. Ant-like, they made their way. I could only pray Haliam and Mara had gained enough ground to hide their path. With Sibaccian's hurt pride and hatred of me, I would have to bide my time and keep her location a secret only

Haliam and I shared. Maybe there would be a day when we could live together in Ankwar. Like Aroden, Mara and I would have to find our way, as would the village of Ankwar.

# CHAPTER 29

# A TIME TO SOW

The spring after Aroden's leaving brought fresh green grasses thrusting up into the cooling breezes, warmed by the sun's beams. They stretched tender sprouts further each morning. New buds burst open for bees to pollinate, filling the air with perfumes and heavy branches. Calves and lambs fell out from swollen wombs upon the earth for the herds to grow. A fullness of fresh life surrounded Ankwar.

Two springs later brought Sibaccian's Mennatti and his place under the mantle of a black kite among the council of men. His kill had been soaring above and had landed in a tree with massive black wings splayed above talons gripping a torn squirrel.

Another five springs, and by summer a drought ravished the valley of Ankwar, cracking the ground open. The earth's soil that once lay fertile to our hands now produced only weak sprouts that dried before becoming tender. Our dandelion dreams of a good harvest dispersed, scattering on the dry breeze. Each new sunrise came clear and scorching, launching the radiant orb to travel through blue skies while the running rivers lowered. The parched furrows left from our awls cried out for water to nourish their impregnated seeds. The land hardened rock-like, snaring the strands of grasses barely able to stand. Families came together over lost crops and cattle. The winter following the drought, we lost several members: Sulvak, his age weakening him, and Aleya, who always struggled to be strong; both fell to the Harvester's cut. Esteban carried Aleya to the mound. The dirt was piled over the chamber once again with the hope that clover and flowers would return.

Another spring brought the traders, and another spring brought rains of new life. Twenty springs passed in all from the last time I saw Aroden. His daughters grew, taking their place as wives in the village.

They passed me like little ghosts of their mother. Twenty springs came and left since I saw Mara.

In the early seasons, when I tried to steal away to Undoura. Sibaccian had determined to shadow me. I took him into the mountains on various paths, but never to my love. She stayed safely hidden.

Once Sibaccian married, his time became filled with more work on the farms. Tandor's family had many daughters but needed more sons. Even with his distraction, I didn't risk exposing Mara's hiding place. Time left her safely in my memory alone.

My gift of languages helped Ankwar with the traders, who brought new goods and words from afar. Through their paths, I learned of Haliam. We found a way to send brief messages. He had taken Natika to be his wife and had a family of four fine sons. His skills as a weaver of rope made him desired by the workers of Undoura. Without mentioning her name, Haliam would tell me my dove had grown more beautiful. She longed to fly to me but would wait till I believed the way clear of hawks. And so we stayed, parted yet safe. Mara was safe and that made the difference in each day.

I worked in the fields planting the new crops, organized the families to rotate the herds on southern pastures, and sent valuable items to villages I knew on the trade routes, growing our standing as a valuable tribe. I grew in standing among the council's trust. Esteban grew into the role left by Sulvak. Chal's weakened state and age diminished his ability to endure the longer meetings. I stepped into his place as a holy man through my knowledge of medicinal herbs and remedies. Gabor continued his position of leadership alongside Esteban and me on the council. His perspective brought clarity to the focus of the village's plans to thrive. Juri found work for Sibaccian as a knapper. His precision with the flint made him necessary for cutting implements. The points of his arrows penetrated through hide, muscle, and arteries to sever the heart of an ibex at thirty paces or more, so clean were his edges and lines pressed into flaked stone. And so grew the men of Tandor's house. We took our places in the village leadership of Ankwar. All except one.

Eventually, word reached me on the trade routes of raiders and dangerous men. Attacks increased against small settlements, villages that showed outward weaknesses, farmers grazing flocks and herds far from a call for help, alone and vulnerable. A recent tale from a trader told of a digression into immoral behavior. We spoke in muted tones a language unfamiliar to my people. Before the men left, I found Esteban and shared with him the word from the trail.

"Brother, he speaks of a band of men, savage in their intent."

"How many? Did he say?"

"No, the reports vary."

"Is he sure there is just one group?"

"It appears to be, but no one knows for certain."

"How far away are the attacks?"

"They are north of here more towards the edge of the mountains. I am a little familiar with the area." Mara stayed more east, for which I was thankful.

Esteban almost questioned me but realized my past had trails he didn't understand. He turned toward the north, seeming to me that he willed a vision of these marauders. We both wondered the same. Neither spoke. Rather, we chose to speculate and wonder.

"Ask him to learn the number of men and frequency of the raids," Esteban said.

"I will need to pay him to earn his eyes on our behalf," I answered.

Esteban sent me to Juri, and I returned quickly to meet with the trader as they were loading their bladder bags from the well in preparation to leave.

"Wait," I called. "Have you but a moment more?"

The trader began to show hesitation. His path was long, and the way no longer felt safe. He had wanted to make it to his next village by the morning.

"Will you keep an eye out for us? Let us know what you learn of these men? How many raiders might there be? How often the attacks have occurred? What seems to be their target?"

The trader rubbed the hairs on his chin and moved his hand to rub the back of his head. He extended a hand and waited. I would need to make his information a worthy trade.

I pulled from my pouch a dagger of excellent quality. Sibaccian had outdone himself knapping the length of flint for this blade. The handle identified the carrier as a man of status with a loop to display upon his belt. The trader's eyes widened, and his eyebrows raised over pursed lips. He took a breath with a slow exhale and reached his hand hesitantly to hold the dagger. Trying not to appear eager, he overexaggerated his wait to reply.

Turning the blade back and forth, he ended by shrugging his shoulders and said, "*Ennai, ennai.* I tell. Next time I here, *ennai* . . . I tell."

"*Dennaki*," I replied. "*Dennaki*. Thank you."

The trader gave a crooked smile. "*Dennoki*," he corrected.

I nodded. "*Dennoki*, thank you, *dennoki*."

The trade had been deemed worthy. His valuable information raised his status as he hung the dagger from his belt. Neither of us could see the amount of crimson stain he would lie in from a bad deal. Neither did we know that he would eagerly trade his information to the wrong people. What we did know is information was a tradable asset; an asset I tried to control with each negotiation.

He gave his dagger one last admiring pat on his belt and left on his trade route. I relayed this success back to Esteban and Juri. We would need more daggers to gain the reach necessary to understand what trouble lay out there on the horizon.

# CHAPTER 30

# SOUTHERN SIGHTS

As the flint traders brought more word from their separate paths to the north, the east, and the west, the picture became clearer: these attackers hunted at leisure, targeting the weak, shooting children, women, old men in the knees or lower, crippling them from any hope of escape. These raiders seemed to live from the power of fear.

The villages affected were peaceful people. They didn't have organized defenses. Nor did we. Our expression "if they come" turned into "when they come" and yet we didn't have a plan for preservation. As word of the threats increased among the traders, I began to see a need for stronger alliances between villages. Our valley ran rich and full from east to west with an emerald-green lake marking our way to the summits. We could be accessed easily from either direction the sun walked. I approached my brothers for a travel plan. They agreed. I would travel to a smaller village to the south of Ankwar. They could need our help and would be a close resource to return the favor.

First, I would need to return to the mine and to Malek. The traders had made clear the path Haliam and I should have taken from the copper mine had we only known. I understood the visceral strength of the mines. If I headed east for help, a flint knife or some arrowheads would not suffice. If I sought help from the north, a gift of status would be needed. Gabor pledged to journey with me to get the copper. Sibaccian insisted on joining us as well. Haliam would have been my preference over both Gabor and Sibaccian, but he still lived far away. Traveling alone back to Malek was not wise, so I agreed to go with my two brothers, and we made plans to leave.

I rubbed the top of my head. My hair was gone after all these springs. Would Malek remember me? If he did, he certainly wouldn't simply allow me to walk in and out of the mine. I reached for my bearskin cap. This would help hide my features. The trail would be cold, but not as cold as the reception we would have if Malek recognized me.

Gabor returned from the meeting with the village women. We would need to have as many hands as possible smoothing and polishing beads that we could trade if the deal I wished to negotiate would work.

* * *

Three brothers, wearing the tunics of Tandor's house, left with pledges and hopes for strength. The red threads of Father's sign lay upon the chest of my shirt. I reached into my coat and rubbed the itch.

The southern foothills began our journey across the varied shades of new green grass; only the birds chatted around us. At night, Sibaccian sorted various flints and knapped arrowheads, borers, and other tools to barter and trade. We had just gotten a new amount of flint on the last trade that came through Ankwar. He finished shuffling through the clinking pieces of stone, finding the one for which he saw a purpose. His focus matched the rhythmic snap from the precise pressure he applied to create a smooth, beveled edge that would sink the arrow into her target. The resulting arrowhead held a good value for trading. Gabor smoothed the branches he worked into shafts. I held the yew wood, turning the core into the strength of a weapon of distance once the arrow was released. We sat around the fire with the sounds of snaps and scrapes together with the crackle of the fire popping. The night sounds surrounded our group as we sat in silence.

As the sun rose on the last day, we made our way to the mining compound. Familiar smells of fire and burnt malachite reached us in the breeze as we passed a field of goats. Care would need to be given to not cause alarm. A hare darting off at our approach startled me. The sudden flapping of two large crows from a tree above quickly drew my attention. Gabor and Sibaccian looked at me, but I offered no explanation. I did not wish to become a slave trapped under the earth again.

Our path widened as we approached the boundary of the chieftain's copper fields. Each step forced the next step. Had it not been for the sake of my village, I'd never have seen the wreckage of the mine again. Nothing, however, looked familiar.

My steps slowed instinctively. The points of arrows and a loud deep voice stopped us. The grass, knee-high around the path, seemed to stand still as well. Holding my hands in the air, I motioned to my brothers to copy me. The voice spoke again. I recognized the accent from the traders and called back, "May I lower my hand to show you my pass?"

The arrows' tips did not lower their aim, but the voice considered my request. A grunted permission allowed me to slowly reach for my claim to the mine's wealth. The pouch I had received with my vows from Undoura hung around my neck. The voice received my pouch, examined the leather and contents, and motioned with his arm as the arrows obeyed and lowered.

"What do you want?" asked the guard.

"We need to make a special gift. The copper from your mines is the best for this gift."

The guard looked at me, considered my dress of skins and the pack I wore, glanced over Gabor, and then regarded Sibaccian's young face of stone. The guard's eyes, hooded under dense brows, questioned every part of us. He rubbed his crooked nose and pursed his lips from under a thick mustache. Finally, the guard nodded his head, motioning for us to follow.

When we arrived at the house of the chief, the guard motioned for us to wait outside. Looking around, I could see the familiar smelter's station. We were near a newer mine than the one I had helped dig and the one I supervised being dug. The fires were smoking, and the men who worked the minerals into valuable commodities ate rich cuts of meats and drank their fill as all men of the craft were inclined to do. Working the fires required knowledge. Knowledge earned power. Only those of weaker resolve worked the ground to bring out the malachite. The bodies only obeyed through a lack of understanding.

The guard returned and motioned me inside. Behind me, he placed an arm to stop Sibaccian and Gabor. We were to be separated. Gabor had common sense. Sibaccian had his arrowheads to help him trade for negotiated safety. I nodded at Sibaccian, letting him know to obey, and went in.

The room had two oil lamps burning on the table and beds with furs surrounding the walls. A darkly tanned man stood at the entrance. He bore the carved face I remembered. It was Bretasko. My stomach seized, freezing me to the spot with the memory I last had of him and Anak on the trail. Beyond him, filling the seat, Malek sat watching.

"What do you want from us?"

Finding breath, I steadied my words, "I seek the quality of your mine's finest copper."

"You did not come all this way just for copper you could get on the trade route. Why are you here?"

"I have come to learn if the attacks that have been made in the north have reached down here."

Malek leaned back, his hand darker than mine reaching into a bowl for more olives to eat. He considered my information and replied, "I have heard news of them. They have not come this far south." To emphasize his words, Malek pushed the tip of his dagger into a juicy fruit sitting next to the bowl of olives. He brought the fig before him and slowly began to peel the skin, watching me with questions.

"We have heard they are raiding to the north of Ankwar where we are from. The traders are afraid and don't always return."

"So, you came all this way for questions of my safety?" Malek watched me closely. A sneer lingered around his words.

"I desire fine copper to mold an axe."

"Do you wish to give these raiders, as you call them, something worth stealing?" His eyes looked amused but guarded.

"I seek allegiance with other tribes. The axe is a symbol of our pledge. You have the best copper. I cannot risk the traders to bring the best."

Malek leaned back and rubbed his chin, considering my request. He didn't seem to recognize me, which steadied my gaze. I wanted the copper reserved for the finer trades I knew Malek to have.

"An axe poured from our copper would be a fine pledge indeed. What are you able to pay for such metal?"

Opening my pouch, I removed a thread of five cream-colored marble beads polished smooth. Each disk had a small hole in the center. The beads sat clustered on the thread like the puffed grain of a ripe einkorn. One bead had taken our best crafter two days to finish. Turning each in my fingers to feel the strength of my people's hearts, I laid them on the table before him. I knew the worth of the prize I offered for the treasure I aimed to gain.

"Each of these beads represents one basket of beads from the finest white rock that I will have delivered to you. One basket will arrive every second full moon. They will make a fine addition to your celebrations."

The man nodded. He picked up the thread, feeling the smooth care of identically formed beads. The promised prize would take this man's entire village two moons to complete.

"When will you deliver these promised baskets? Do you intend to trust them to the trade lines?"

"I can have the first basket ready to move before the next full moon."

Malek ran his fingers through thick, dark curls. He leaned forward and reached for the beads. Feeling the smooth surface rolled between his thumb and forefinger, he meditated on his offer.

"This is good," he stated. "Let us share some mead, from the finest honey the color of our copper."

As I reached for the cup placed on the table, the dark hand quickly grabbed my wrist. The point of his dagger pushed into my blue vein. I looked at the sharp blade of flint and then at the man I knew well, controlling my signs of fear. A vision of fire came to me.

"If you betray our deal and no payment arrives, or if they come, shall we say, of lesser quality or amount promised, I pledge to you my three strongest and surest men led by Bretasko here will hunt you down like a pack of wolves, tearing the breath from your lungs. And then I will exact payment from your village. Do I make my pledge clear?"

His hand holding my wrist brought a vision of a fiery shadow. His anger didn't burn as strongly as the Malek from the old days in the mine had, but there was no mistake: the heart of this man was the same. Bretasko's presence behind me loomed the truth of Malek's words. I knew what it meant to be hunted by these men.

"I come here, holy man of Ankwar, son of Tandor, and leader of men among my people. I have seen the fire that burns within you. I recognize the shade that crosses your past. I have sworn an oath to deliver. May I cut myself down before your pack of wolves if I betray the words I speak."

The knife lowered aim from my arm and eventually rested on the table beside him. His sun-darkened hand sat silent on the handle. He sat back, a deep look of thought in his manner. I pulled my hand back firmly and placed both hands on the table, palms flat on the surface, and leaned forward, ready.

Malek studied me. "There is something about you."

I never took my bear skin cap off. I hoped his memory would slip past any details of me. He poured a full cup and pushed it toward me.

"It will come to me," he said, "but now we drink," and he lifted his cup to me, the mead sweet and cool on my throat that had gone dry.

From my meeting, I found Gabor with a stash of food he had traded. We visited the stone pits to gather sufficient malachite to carry back with us to Juri's forge. Tables were lined with women and older men grinding the malachite in mortars. Sibaccian wanted to stay long enough to crush the malachite into dust for easier carrying. I wanted nothing else but to put as much distance between me and Malek and Bretasko as I could.

I put my hand on Sibaccian's, stopping the pestle from grinding. Sibaccian scowled and sprung back like a snake. The stone mortar jostled from his jerk, scattering fragments of green shards across the floor. The people to the sides of Sibaccian shifted uneasily. Their pestles barely ceased grinding.

"What did you do that for?"

"We need to go. There's no time to crush the malachite here."

Sibaccian pulled the mortar closer to him and began grinding again. "I am not hauling all of this heavy rock back across those mountains."

I reached to stop him again and he jerked back gruffly, raising his voice. "Let go of me." He moved further away down the table.

I froze, realizing how close my brother had come to using my name, a name I never gave to Malek during our negotiations. Gabor came over to see what the commotion was. The tables were full, and ears were listening.

"We need to grind enough stone for our traveling purpose," Sibaccian insisted as he pushed harder on the pestle. Gabor looked at me as I walked away in frustration.

He followed me to the quieter section of the tables. The gentle swishing sound of the spinning pestles against the near dust whispered behind us.

I grabbed Gabor's arm. "We've got to go!"

Gabor felt the extra squeeze in my hand because he slowly moved his arm out of my grip. He studied my stance, my eyes that were unable to rest. He read the blood between us. Nodding, he turned to Sibaccian, whispered something in his ear, and motioned for us to go. With shoulders hunched, Sibaccian sent me a glare and shook the green dust into his pouch, tying the end shut.

Upon returning home, an axe blade would be poured. I would see to the process myself. For now, heading across the hills back toward our mountain and putting as much distance from Malek seemed critical. I could feel the change happening in my demeanor.

From behind us, I heard, "Hoi!"

There came Malek. His steps were long and with purpose. His thick brows were crossed. He pointed directly at me. "Hoi," he repeated. "I remember you."

A rabbit never felt more fear from the talon at the scruff of his neck. Gabor, seeing my panic, stood a bit in front of me. As Malek approached, Gabor smiled and raised his hand toward Malek in greeting. Malek scoffed. "Not you. The one behind you."

I reached to hold the edge of a nearby table. My breathing caught. My knees weakened. Malek pushed past Gabor and reached for my shoulder, saying, "You used to come on the trade lines from the old country in the east, didn't you? We don't see many people looking like you around here."

Malek seemed satisfied he had found his answer. My reply mixed between a laugh and a cough. I squinted my eyes more so he wouldn't recognize his error. "Oh, you mean my father," I lied.

Malek stared, his eyes sharp as a hawk's. The time lingered, drawing on my last reserves of strength. Then he shook his head and turned back, muttering, "No, that cannot be it," and walked away.

Before my knees buckled, I grabbed my backpack and left—with or without Sibaccian, it didn't matter. I passed the forges before stopping. The warmth in the air seemed suffocating. Using bellows from long reed pipes, four villagers blew continually as they worked the heat into the center of the clay pit. The heat pushed against their faces. Orange to white the flame pulsed, surrounding the crucibles until a final change appeared and the copper came forth to be cooled in the water. The heat burned inside me. Ankwar's cost of being redeemed seemed too much to bear.

# CHAPTER 31

# A HOUSE DIVIDED

B ack in Ankwar, the men gathered at the council house after the day's work had ended. I stood before them, the axe head in my hand shining in the light. The smooth surface of solid copper made it an object of great value. Esteban smoothed an aged yew handle to attach to the blade. A length of leather cording was found for the final assembly of the axe.

"This is nothing more than a vain display," a council member shouted from the side of the hall. "How much has this idea of uniting villages cost us in the form of that one head?"

"The price is not yours to worry about. The house of Tandor has taken on this action," I said.

"Gaspare has made a trade with men from the western mines," Sibaccian spoke up. "The house of Tandor cannot make all the baskets of promised beads in time."

Murmurings and side conversations filled the space of the room. Thick arms crossed in resistance of this idea.

"A trade like that would take the village a full season to create, or drain our storage meant for our fall ceremonies," said one of the councilmen.

"How full will our fall harvest be if raiders come and burn our crops or kill our herds?" another councilman asked.

More murmuring and eyebrows darting, looking for alliance in reasons.

"Is that trade wise?" called out one. "Are they not worse than any band of robbers?"

"Won't such a trade lure their attention here to expect more?" came another.

"Do you wish to lure the raiders or mercenaries here with such a blade?" another asked. The murmurings ruptured into rumblings born from envy-inspired fear. I gave a sharp glance at Sibaccian. He stood with his arms crossed and head raised, looking directly at me.

I raised my hands to silence the crowd. "I seek strength and unity among other villages."

"We have established trade with a number of the villages already."

I looked to Gabor and Esteban for support. They were discussing something between themselves. "Yes, we have," I said. "This axe will be a sign of power, brotherhood, of protection with larger villages farther out."

"If protection is what we need, then leave the axe here in Ankwar and we will protect ourselves," shouted a voice from the other side of the hall. Murmuring and nods at the idea of Ankwar's virile men passed from one to another council member, each viewing himself as the great defender worthy of the prestige.

"We cannot afford enough axes for our entire village," Gabor said, standing. "What have we here, thirty-five, thirty-eight men? But if we join with another village, then our men become sixty or seventy, and that's protection." A scowl had formed across his eyebrows. The weakness of the men didn't sit well within his idea of who we are.

"We have enough axes and daggers in this village that every man and woman could be armed," Esteban added. "We need to ensure the raiders are intimidated to come this way when they see houses standing together against them."

I stood and walked to the center. "We have bought valuable information from the traders. We know trouble is out there in the north and now toward the east. Mere daggers will not buy what I seek. If we know and do nothing about the danger, then we shall suffer greatly from our weakness."

Juri stood. "What Gaspare says proves clear. We cannot live in fear of attacks, nor can we go out and face the thieves head-on. They are a small band. They could be anywhere. We need a plan."

"Do we have such a plan?" called another.

"I shall make my way east as far as Benaki, to see if Krenden still leads his people," I said. "They are strong and good friends. He is situated in a good position on the mountain passes between the valleys to the east."

"East? You're heading straight into the trouble. Why not just leave our chickens sitting out for the fox and owls to carry off?" exclaimed the first councilman. The other councilmen briefly laughed.

"How do we know you won't bring the trouble here, attracting attention to us when we might go on quietly and unseen?" asked another councilman.

"I don't know that, but if we don't go, I guarantee we will not be hidden. We lie on a trade route. Our presence is known," I said. "How much flint did each of you trade already just in the past moon? Tell me, where did the rock come from that you use as borers and arrowheads? Some of the stone Sibaccian knaps come from a two-day journey in either direction. I tell you our presence is known, and we need to prepare, not sit and wait."

Grumbles rippled through the council hall. Seats shuffled. Heads nodded. Backs bent in thinking and questioning. Some suggested a trap. Some expressed fear of becoming a target. I feared doing nothing. Ankwar sat on the verge of becoming her lesser self once again.

"I leave with the sun's light," I said. "The council's blessing is sought, but not required. Something must be done. I will not sit idly by."

"If you do not go with our blessing, you do not go to represent us," cried one from the back. More muttering followed the outcry.

Taran stood. "Then let us vote," he said. "Gaspare will know the voice of Ankwar if we vote."

A nod of agreement joined the murmuring.

"Brother," Sibaccian said. "Together we will represent the hopes and desires of Ankwar village."

"We will continue our travels together," Gabor added.

Esteban put the council to a call for votes. The majority agreed we should go, but only a small majority.

I didn't want to venture that far with Sibaccian. I didn't want to take him anywhere at all. I needed Haliam. How could I convince my younger brother he would be more useful going a different way? Twenty springs had passed and not once had I ventured to Undoura to see Mara. This shade of danger increased my desire to go to her, but could I risk exposing her even now? The sight of my younger brother's eyes that narrowed when he looked at me told me all I needed to know.

"Sibaccian, take the first load of the promised baskets west to the mine. Payment must be made as promised."

"Why aren't you taking the pledge?"

"There is no time. My way heads north and east to a village only I have been. The way is a treacherous path, and I must hurry."

"Then one of the men, who normally move the cattle west for the family, can take the bargained price. I should attend to the trails with you and Gabor."

"I need to go quickly and unseen. Three are easier to track."

"The council agreed to send us."

"The council barely agreed."

"I shall make the arrangements with one of the men, who deliver the cattle. He can extend his journey with the beads. I will be ready to leave with you in the morning."

"If they leave by tomorrow, they should arrive with the payment in six, maybe seven suns."

"Yes, I will tell them to leave before the new moon."

"Make sure you do." I turned to go and remembered the shadow of the hand, Malek's hand, pressing the knife into my wrist. For a mere moment, stealing in like vapor through my mind came the silent voice I didn't heed. Could I trust my brother? Lingering less than a heartbeat, slower than an eye blinking, a questioning thought interrupted with a gut feeling attached before the choice became chosen, destiny decided, and consequences waited for us to arrive.

# CHAPTER 32

# EASTERN WINDS

Before the rays of the sun could push past night's coverings, I was up preparing for the journey. Gabor, Esteban, and Kaiya worked to see if we had the necessary supplies. Sibaccian had returned late in the darkness wrapped in tension. When he entered, I shoved an extra tunic into my pack more forcefully than intended. The tools we needed didn't meet inspection. All the edges from the family stash of flints, flakers, and more had dull, blunt, or worn-out usefulness. All tools needed a fresh sharpening.

"Is nothing sharp for us in our own home? The village walks around with ready borers and flakers, yet in our own home we are but poor mice waiting for a crumb from the village knapper." I tossed the borer and my dagger to the table and turned to face Sibaccian, watching for his excuse.

He grunted before replying, "I can sharpen the tools on the way."

"We're not stopping for great lengths of time. This isn't a berry-picking excursion."

"It won't take long."

Esteban picked up my dagger lying on the table. "Gaspare, this dagger of yours needs a new flint soon."

Feeling the edge from the tool he had handed me, I grunted, casting a disgusted glance of disappointment toward my younger brother.

"My dagger has lasted me this long; the blade will have to manage this trip."

"We haven't gotten any decent flint from the traders lately," Sibaccian said.

He spoke true. The flint needed replacing. My blade slid into the sheath and hung from my belt. Natika's weave and the sheath's prominence hid the weak status of the blade within, but Esteban was right. I had gotten the flint over several springs spent. Going east to Krenden, strong tools were just as necessary as strong legs and backs.

My pants made from last winter's sheep tanning covered my thighs and lower legs. The sheep skins would keep my legs warm for the long journey. Kaiya's oldest daughter had stitched the hides into the fitted pattern. Putting on my boots reminded me of the time under the tree with Haliam and Natika. As I stuffed the grass cage around my foot with dried tree bark and other grasses, I found myself excited to see my friend despite the conditions. Too much time had passed.

Esteban brought the holy man coat, but not the one Attioc had covered me with in Undoura. He gave me a new one Kaiya and the women had made. The black hide over the heart reminded me of the lessons of life's constant existence with death's presence. Kaiya had added black and white hides from last winter's goats and sheep, each stripe strategically stitched to show the strength and wealth of Tandor's house. Five different animals from our herd, domesticated from a variety of lines, had been selected and arranged. The weight of the elders, the responsibility of our house and village, was placed on my shoulders. My words carried the wishes and pledges of more than just mine. The effect of the hides made me feel larger. Gabor's and Sibaccian's coats contained similar construction of goat hides, each color placed to indicate the region and achievement of the wearer and the village. The more hides represented the more wealth assumed. The house of Tandor enjoyed supplying the village with livestock.

Gabor brought out the bear cap he had saved. "This may not be the staff I made you, but this is your bear. Not sure why I didn't give it to you sooner, but here he is."

I touched the fur, rough between my fingers. No words came to signify the sadness this bear represented. I have hunted many bears since. I have earned the fierce title of bear hunter whispered as I passed people, but with each carcass, I found I couldn't erase the shadows from this first beast. Pulling the fur down around my ears, I lifted my chin to tie the hat firmly. The room quickly became too warm.

We put our quivers and packs on, along with our grass mats. Kaiya returned from the smokehouse with a bundle of fatty bacon and another of fresh goat meat for us to eat. We would need lots of fat and protein to sleep on the mountain. Zaria, who had come from her home, gave me einkorn and some flatbread. I could still feel the warmth on the browned crust; she must have pulled them from the heated stone moments before coming. She placed them in the backpacks with the other supplies. Pausing for only a moment, Zaria knew she needed to return to her husband and sleeping children soon, but she wanted to see us on our way. A look of surprise crossed Zaria's beautiful face, her eyes still full and round with innocence.

"Do you have your pouch?" she asked me.

"I never take it off," I replied, patting my chest. The leather lay against my skin. I smiled at her; she was so different from her brother's hardened distrust. My pouch contained my gasper stone, beads made from marble, and the stones of the mountains, a single red stone with green flecks, along with other herbs and dried mushrooms known by the holy men for healing. I wore the pouch around my neck to remember.

Esteban approached with the copper axe. In his hand, he held our village's future.

"Gaspare, take this," he said. I motioned for Gabor to take the axe, but he shook his head. The copper reflected the light from the lamp. The yew wood had been carefully selected by Esteban himself and smoothed, rasped, and fitted to tightly hold the blade with leather cording the length of seven arms. The axe showed the luxury of care from a craftsman. Finer axes of this quality didn't exist in our village. I gently hung the axe from my belt next to the sheathed dagger.

I reached for my longbow. The yew wood had been freshly cut at the first signs of spring. The cow horns were secured tightly to the tips. My smoothing had begun to shape the wood the way I asked the grain of the wood to go. Like Sibaccian, I would need to finish working this into a final bow along the way. Holding the length before me, I admired the smooth sheen, and the balance made by the symmetrical curve. I tested the bends in the handle, feeling the tension within the core of the wooden shaft. Strength was there. This would be a fine bow. Just needed more evenings around the fire to continue shaping and smoothing. At my age, I needed more of a walking staff to cover the terrain we headed toward. The joints of my legs, the tightening in my chest: all reminders that my mornings were shortening.

Kaiya brought me a string made from lime that she had twisted into a cord.

"Your ropes always were the best," I said.

Pleased by the compliment, she handed me the cording. "Use this for your bow string or if you get in a bind."

"I will. Thank you, Kaiya." My hand lingered on hers for a moment. She had been my confidant and friend, more of a sister than I ever knew. I placed the cording in the bottom of the quiver.

The quiver held eleven unfinished arrow shafts. A condition I didn't feel at ease with. The lack of arrowheads made one more point of irritation with Sibaccian. I shot him another glare.

"I'll fix your arrows along the way," he said. I was out of flint, out of time, and out of patience. We needed to make haste. Esteban saw me count each fletching. He went to his quiver and pulled a longer arrow and two medium-length arrows from inside. As he walked toward me, his thumb felt the tip of an arrow. He placed the fourteenth arrow in the quiver and turned me around to face him. Holding both his hands on my shoulders, he braced me and looked me in the eye. A wizened depth of pride and worry blended his eyes and countenance.

"I've never asked more of a brother than I ask of you," he said. "Be safe, stay on the path, but if you should run into old trouble, remember you do not win to hunt with revenge. Revenge is an arrow that shoots both ways."

I met his gaze and nodded. We stepped out into the new light. Outside the hut, we could see the white caps on the mountains in the distance. In the valley, the layers of snow had begun melting already, the freshest green of grass pushing through the sod, but the weather further up on the slope could change in a moment. Cattle grazed in the lowest field, already finding nourishment in the juicy stems. The echo of a goose honking for a mate as he flew over the green waters of the lake carried through the waking air. White fog stretched above the surface as the hillside began to awaken to the morning.

"I will send word if we are successful. Do not look for me till harvest. The path we take is long."

"Send Sibaccian back if you need our help. I will come for you." Esteban's grip on my shoulder tightened, reinforcing his intent to uphold this covenant.

"Our village deserves more than to live in fear," Sibaccian said. "This discord must be squelched."

"Deserve?" Gabor turned to him, studying the man he didn't recognize. "What precisely does Ankwar or any of us deserve? I go seeking strength and assistance so we will not be vulnerable."

My younger brother turned away from me. "I fear we go seeking Gaspare's old vengeance with Aroden. That can only lead to destruction," he said. "But we must go."

Gabor and Esteban both carried a scowl upon their brows. Zaria ran up to stop us. In her hands, she carried two birch containers. She had prepared the embers from our hearth in young maple leaves. I shared a final smile with my winter flower. Compelled, I reached to brush the hair from her eyes—so much like Mother's. She stood there with her silhouette framed by the shadows from the lamps that faded into the darkness from the open door. The earliest shades of dawn pinked the skies above her hair.

The sun stretched over the mountains, lifting the night's blanket with the tip of her golden orb. The clouds rolled over, revealing delicate underbellies, and began to wake. The time had come. I looked once more around the village. Turning, I left the house of Tandor with two of my brothers for the last time. The screech of a hawk searching for another cried out from the treetops. The branches of the larch trees held clusters of tiny green needles. Their fragrance would fill the woods soon. We walked out into beauty and hope. Before my feet crossed the edge of our village, however, my last breath had already been measured.

Our little band of brothers headed up into the mountains, while the length of seven suns westward in the copper mine, hands slammed the slab of the table, grabbed a nearby dagger, and plunged the point of the blade into the wood. He had remembered where he knew my face. Malek had remembered. Bretasko, unleashed from the blackness of Malek's scorn, set out from the copper mine with his men: a wolf pack of hardened guards sent to hunt down missing payment for copper and the life of a runaway slave. No one had arrived nor would arrive with the promised payment of beads because no one had been asked to take them.

Each step I took led the treachery away from Ankwar. Sibaccian followed behind me, never indicating his broken word. His plan to keep a promise was not with me. His promise that held greater weight was forged by a secretive handful of the elders, who stewed and worried about the danger associated with me.

# CHAPTER 33

# LOST BROTHERS

The morning chill as we entered the higher ground of the mountain caused my joints to stiffen. My age showed at the slower pace I needed to go up from the valley. Sibaccian grew impatient, but we still made our way. Gabor spotted a hare in range. Retrieving his kill, Gabor asked Sibaccian, "Why don't you go find some new wood before we get too high up the slope beyond the supply of limbs?"

The tall trunks of the trees on the lower part of the slope created great shade but made cutting branches difficult. Sibaccian went off into the pines.

The shadows lingered around the trees. Tall, straight, gray lines created an eerie feeling. Could a man sneak up on us undetected or were the tree trunks too narrow to hide someone? I sat perched on my heels, feeling the deep stretch in my thighs. The hare roasted on a stick. I wiped the blood on a small portion of my coat before remembering this coat came with special honor. Reaching for the discarded rabbit hide, I finished wiping the blade in the gray fur.

Sibaccian came into the fire circle. He held a dozen branches that he had found farther down the slope. He dropped his pile near the light and reached for some water.

Gabor tossed his tools toward his youngest brother. "Before you begin on that food," he said, "you need to make good on your promise to sharpen our tools. Mine are rather useless in doing the work needed." Sibaccian grunted, put down his bag, picked up a tool, and inspected the edge.

I turned the rabbit, continuing to brown the meat. A howl sounded in the distance. Another answered near the first. I counted six different wolves as they sounded their location. They were on the hunt. There was no denying our need for protection. We finished eating and headed out of the tree line into the open space up the incline. We were visible here. There were a few larger boulders along the way, but looking back and looking up showed a grand space. The moss thinned and the rocks stacked in layers as we came closer to the summit. The path would be much the same once we crossed to the other side. Gabor hoped we would reach the other valley by nightfall. I thought we would do well to make it to the next line of moss on the other side. The stones pounded our legs and back, making progress slow. Fresh springs spouted from the mountain all the way up. Even under the snow cover, we were able to find persistent water nearby. The snow on the rocks made the way slippery. Looking up, I eyed a wisp of cloud, knowing the danger such a dark little fragment could mean.

On the other side of the slope, we neared a good stopping place. The slope's steep ascent outmatched our advanced age we carried. We had stopped four times that morning and I could feel the frustration in our progress. I turned to look to the right, remembering the diversion Haliam and I had taken many seasons ago. We had the mountain falling down upon us and had cut through to a gully due to the rockslide. The memory of the colliding rocks contrasted with the quiet this evening offered. Haliam had seen the wolf at the gully. Laying out my grass mat, I looked at every dark shade of stone, checking for movement. Even though I knew too much time had passed, I still found myself searching the rocks for her silver back.

A labored silence existed between us. I decided to let the silence work its peace and looked to the sky. The clouds rolled quickly over the clear spaces of blue. No harm would come from these clouds, but the ones on the horizon might hold a threat. Tomorrow we would need to make it past the hunting rock and to the valley down where the river cuts through the hills. The path should be easier being back in the tree line and down on more grassy turf. The distance to Undoura, however, made twice the path we had already crossed today. Sleep might help, but no guarantee came that we would doze.

I rolled over on my mat when I heard Gabor ask about the payment.

"Whatever happened to the delivery of the beads?"

When no one answered him, I rolled back over to find Sibaccian. "Did you send the payment to the mine?"

Sibaccian's face did not show but lies began to sprout around him like the first blades of einkorn wheat in the early spring. Gabor looked up from shaping the arrow in his hand. He watched Sibaccian over the flames of our fire. Gabor's eyes narrowed as he gauged the intentions of his little brother.

"Of course, I sent the payment. What do you think I would do?"

"When did you send them? I saw the collection of beads still waiting the day before we left." Gabor leaned in over the fire and pointed his arrow shaft toward Sibaccian to get his attention.

"I told the son of the farmer tending the cattle to have his father deliver the beads. He will do it."

"You fool!" I spit. "Malek is not a trader. He's the chief of a mine. Bretasko and his men are hunters, and right now they are out there with one purpose: to exact payment for this axe." The firelight glinted off the blade as I held the axe up. "Bretasko will not wait for some shepherd's boy to remember. He will come to exact payment from Ankwar."

"The village will be fine—"

"The village is in great danger and so are we. Why did I listen to you? Why? Why did I trust you to do one thing right?"

Sibaccian shrugged his shoulders, making light of my worry. "We can go back now to Ankwar and just make the payment."

"Bretasko has changed the price of the copper," I said, remembering Malek's knife on my hand. "He doesn't want a bunch of beads. What is he going to do with baskets of beads? Have his guards carry them like beasts of burden? This axe will cost Ankwar dearly. If we return in the morning, we are still behind as the payment needed to be to the mines before now."

Anger gripped me and panic shot through my mind. Bretasko would show no mercy. *I'm closer to Undoura now than Ankwar*, I thought. *I could go on ahead and get Haliam and other men to join me. Together we could all return and help protect our village.* Taking Sibaccian there would not fare well for Mara. If Sibaccian betrayed us willingly then he wouldn't hesitate to do so again under pressure. He could not be trusted.

Pointing at Sibaccian, I shouted, "You should go straight back to Ankwar at this very moment. I'll go ahead to Undoura." I stood up and began packing my backpack. Gabor reached over to steady my hand.

"If this Bretasko is as angry as you say he is," Sibaccian said, "then you send me to my death, Brother."

"If you don't go, there's no telling what death has already been delivered to Ankwar. Maybe you think everyone is safe, but what about Zaria? If Bretasko's men learn that she is related to those who do not pay for the copper, he'll extract the weight from her, or Kaiya, or any of the children. Would you like to see one of the children, maybe your own, be slaves down in the mines, crawling in the dark, hauling rock? Or worse: never being taken at all?"

The memory of my time at the mines collided with the realization of the evil I had unknowingly brought upon my family. The tightening in my chest burned fiercely and my breath caught from the sudden pain.

Gabor stepped in. "No more arguing. I'll not hear anymore. "You," he said, turning on Sibaccian, "you errored by not sending the payment, and that is final. With any luck, you can make all the difference for our people." Sibaccian sat in stunned silence. "Gaspare, leaving in the dark, stumbling over those rocks will help no one, especially if you break your leg or worse. I will take Sibaccian back in the morning and you can continue to Undoura and get Haliam. We will make it in time."

"I won't sleep, Gabor. Not now. I need to go tonight."

"Not if going means getting lost or killing yourself in the dark. Sleep or no sleep, we need to stay here till the sun's light."

Proving Gabor's point, I slipped from standing too fast on a snow-covered rock. A curse upon the mountain, upon the rock, upon the darkness all came out of my mouth before I remembered how far voices carried on the mountain. I rolled back onto my mat, resigning myself to remain until light. Under the cloak of darkness, only those with nocturnal eyesight could move. Gabor was right. The path ahead curved along cliffs and had springs bounding through cracks in the path, either able to trip me and cause me to tumble off the side. Me blundering around behind boulders would help no one. Lying and doing nothing wasn't helping me. The shades of night passed me, never being fully awake or completely asleep. I waited for the morning light. My mind twisted visions and manipulated dreams of failure.

We planned to part ways in the morning with Gabor and Sibaccian returning up the slope and I continuing down toward the hunting rock. Our plan didn't account for Sibaccian seeing his older brother and calling to him.

# CHAPTER 34

# BOUND IN LIFE

roden had heard his name and turned to look. He had seen the quick turn we made, ducking and pulling Sibaccian with us behind some boulders. A look of amusement had crossed his face. Glancing back, I saw him reach over and hit the shoulder of one of the men he stood near. The man got the attention of two other men near him. Confirming my fears, I watched him, with full confidence, make his way to where we hid. He didn't hurry. He knew he didn't have to. The group of men approached us, a pack of wolves closing in.

The twilight brought wind and new snow. The wind threw swirls of snow into our faces. Any curses were saved as breath needed to be focused and not wasted at this altitude. With throats dried from the cold, we knew we needed to use the time and space to regain a plan. We considered the opening in the path. This clearing would have to suffice. There we would make our stand.

Aroden and his men came. He stopped near enough to see me, but far enough away. The men crowded behind him. A sneer formed on his lips.

"We want no trouble with you, Brother," Gabor called.

Scoffing at the familial term he replied, "Brother? What is it that you want here?" he asked. Looking at my coat, he laughed mockingly asking, "D-d-d-did they send you up here to trade your hides? Is that why you're wearing so many?"

Aroden's goading wouldn't work. I couldn't let him get to my pride. Sibaccian began to answer, so I interrupted, "We travel these trails like everyone these days. The routes have opened again from winter."

Sibaccian added, "We are heading to Undoura. Where do you go?"

Aroden slowly studied our clothes. The sneer deepened and reached his eyes. He turned his focus to my belt. "Let me see that."

I watched him carefully. Holding the axe, I turned the tool, showing the smooth surface. The craftsmanship of the pour told of the hand

Juri played in making this fine axe. The wooden handle fits snugly, holding onto the blade. I returned the axe to my side, but not my belt.

Aroden's eyes were hard, like a hawk watching a pigeon. "Have you seen an axe like this?" he asked one of the men traveling with him.

The man grunted and replied, "No, not in a while."

"Why won't you share this family treasure with your oldest brother?"

"You are not the oldest. Esteban is." I tried to steady my composure, but the bear cap hugged my forehead, and I could feel beads of sweat beginning to form. A thought crossed Aroden's mind. I could see the shift in his intentions. He raised both hands to show no harm intended and pulled back from us.

The group of men began backing up at Aroden's motion. They made way for us to continue. Deep in my gut, a tightening fear took hold. He had baited his hook and would wait for us to leave before he enacted his vengeance from behind. If we turned our back on our brother's treachery, one or all of us would be dead before dawn's light finished rising. There would be no way now for Sibaccian to return to Ankwar with Gabor. They would clearly be outnumbered and targeted. If we continued to Undoura, Aroden would find Mara.

I could hear the men's accent. They carried the thick sounds of a northern tribe. Aroden still had Ankwar's intonation, but he clearly communicated his wishes with them. His path of exile had been very different from my own. He had been a man cast out. I had been slightly more than a boy and tied to the line of a trader. Whatever Aroden's story, he had found his way to enjoy an amount of status. What had he promised or done for these northerners to accept his lead?

"What do you intend to do?" Gabor asked Aroden.

"Nothing," he said and ushered the way with his hand. "Nothing, Gabor. I just wanted to talk to my brothers."

I placed my hand on Sibaccian's arm to stay my thoughts and devise a plan. Turning our backs amounted to certain death. All the obvious options ended in death.

"I'm going with you," Sibaccian said. "Either with you, or I will go with Aroden."

"Of course! You're a fool, but a live fool, and you are another pair of hands against those men."

The sting from my remark settled on Sibaccian's face. He scowled and from under his breath he muttered, "The council was right about you." I never considered the darkness that had formed over his heart.

Two of Aroden's accomplices moved toward us, separating me from Sibaccian. Aroden kept his full attention on me while the other two separated Sibaccian from Gabor.

"That axe you carry must have cost quite the family fortune," Aroden said. "It's only fair that I have a part of this trade."

The two men grabbed Sibaccian's arms, pinning them back. Another man circled Gabor as Aroden approached me.

I wanted to hear the drums calling down the rain that day I took my vows in Undoura. I wanted to feel the smooth dripping of the oil poured over my forehead, running down behind my ears. I wanted to be freely who I was called to be, but I just couldn't get beyond being Aroden's brother.

"Did you hear what I asked you?" he said, pushing me backward.

"You didn't ask me anything. You just take as always."

His eyes narrowed on my face, and he pushed me again. "Who do you think you are?"

The question that had plagued my mind pushed me to answer. "I am Gaspare. I am Holy Man of Ankwar and son of Tandor. Get out of my way."

With that said, I pushed him back harder than he had anticipated. I put down my pack and took off my bearskin hat. I would not be off balance and sweaty against him. Being uphill, I created a significant threat.

Sizing me up, he began the circling of a buzzard searching for remnants of prey. I pushed my shoulders back and took my longbow staff in both hands. Together we danced: who would be the first to move, who would break the other?

"I've had enough of you," he sneered and lunged at my head. He still carried Father's axe. I blocked it with my bow, the impact reverberating through my arms. As his arm came down with the axe, I pivoted the momentum of the bow and smacked his jawline with the other end of my staff. The blow struck harder than expected.

"Seems I underestimated you, little brother." Aroden circled some more before returning with another lunge. This time he delivered two swings, and I blocked both, but on the second one my hand slipped down the bow. I could not follow through with a return hit.

The last man moved to help Aroden, but he held up a hand to stop him. Gabor filled the space with a blow to one of the heads of the man nearest him. Stunned, the man crumpled under the impact. Gabor finished the attack evening our odds. Aroden ignored their struggle. There would be no one to take this long-awaited victory from him.

Instead, without turning his eyes away, he said, "Kill that one. Wound the other but leave this runt for me." He saw us as berries hanging on a vine waiting to be plucked. He laughed and wiped some blood trickling from his lip where my bow had caught him. "Your gizzards will be great feeding for the buzzards with the sun's light."

He came at me with two more hits. This time my feet held my balance, and I pushed him back, hitting him above his ear with my bow. "Less talk, old man."

He shook his head, stepping back a little when I lunged at him, thrusting the horn tip of my bow into his gut. The air gasped out of his mouth. Instead of following through with another blow, I pulled back. I thought he now understood he wouldn't have an easy fight. He doubled over with both hands on his knees. The man holding Sibaccian moved toward Aroden, but Gabor threw himself into a harder attack and they couldn't spare any ground. Sibaccian worked to save his own hide as the slope of the mountains turned slippery from the mush and strain of the men's feet.

Aroden scoffed. "You're weak. Always were. You should have finished me because you won't get another chance." His breath huffed back into rhythm, and I watched him stand back to full height with a supporting hand on his back. My score didn't include death. That was my error. Aroden carried no goodwill inside. His advantage came in ruthless hate.

A cry came from one of his men as Gabor gained his advantage, pushing the blade of his dagger in deeper. We now stood three to three. Aroden wiped a trickle of blood from his nose. He needed to catch his wind as I proved more than he had planned for. Time was running out. Instead of his axe, he threw barbs. Taunts had seemed to stir my blood in the past. He began with his usual subjects: my manhood, Chealana, Mara. Nothing penetrated. I watched him and focused.

Shifting his weight, he timed his newest attack, "You accused me of killing Father with no proof. Didn't you know it was you who killed Mother? The entire village had to be out watching you fail at your Mennatti while she died alone birthing that brat." He watched the effect of his words as he repeated, "You have no proof. I have the witness of Ankwar. You killed Mother!"

And with that he launched himself at me, full force.

# CHAPTER 35

# BROTHER'S BURDEN

White lights of pain flashed within, blinding me. An instinctive block saved my head from being split open by my brother's rage. My right hand absorbed the anger from his axe, bones cracking upon impact. I staggered, dropping to one knee. All sense of familial rejection powered his hit, a dull hatred directed at me. Stepping back, he wagered whether he could easily kill me, or if I still posed a threat. He sneered, lowering his axe to his side. The cost to disarm me exacted a high toll. He stood watching, chest heaving. Sweat froze the fur on his coat. My fury seemed impotent in his eyes. I was nothing more than Gaspare, his little brother, one to be used and discarded.

But not tonight. True enough, I would die on this mountain, and one day soon, but not here, not this way. Deep breathing tightened in my chest, becoming short, unsteady intakes. I felt pressure around my straining heart. My eyes burned. I couldn't let them blur the sight of him. A decision had to be made. The horizon sagged low. Victory flared in Aroden's eyes. He tipped back his head, shaking the sweat from his vision; defiance squared his jaw. From under his furs, he pulled his string of wolves' teeth, ensuring I saw the ivory gleam. A raven landed on a branch. Head bent, it inspected the scene, cawing, alerting others to fly over and wait. I couldn't end this way. I needed to stand.

Aroden had aged since our last fight. He now had close to fifty springs to my forty-six. His hit had spent his remaining venom. Our exertion nearly spent, we took our places, desperate for air and time. He stepped back, chest heaving, to rebalance and savor his final decision of mercy or justice. My right hand dropped limply to my side. My left hand cradled my deeply bruised ribs. I rolled my head back, looking up at the sky. My heart, an internal fire, squeezed into a spasm. Blood dripped through my fingers. Aroden's blood was sprinkled onto my face and coat as well.

The snow crunched as he shifted his weight. His lips formed words my mind couldn't comprehend. Throbbing in my head pressed anything else out besides the pain. Even numb, I could predict his words. Even now I knew he told me he could take anything; anything I valued was his. He had told me before. I needed to focus. I closed my eyes, praying in the darkness. Sulfur brewed inside; I tasted blood; pressure gathered. Two more ravens crowded the branch. Three heads bent in inspection. Their sequenced cawing mocked us. Over the trees, the winds called, whipping the darkness to banish the light.

Something deeply wicked had been aroused within me. Revenge coiled a bitter head. Her venom coursed through my mind. My eyes opened. I stared alert, ready.

As heavy black clouds warned of danger on the horizon, I watched a flash of certain victory flare in his eyes and nostrils. The wind gathered strength, blowing branches down nearby, pulling his hair into his wounds. Matted and sticky with blood, he pushed his hair back away from his eyes so he could look at me.

I couldn't let him win.

"You just don't see, do you, Gaspare?"

I answered with a quick look of my eyes but continued focusing on my breathing. Somehow, I needed to stand. His words were garbled in my pounding head. I closed my eyes for a moment, keenly listening for any movement he might take, looking for the spark inside to ignite my will to get up. Over the mountaintop, a wisp of dark gray cloud hung. The potential of a snowstorm threatened to cover our tracks and more.

"You had a son. You destroyed him," I spit into the air. "His name was Balick." My words were unclear, I repeated the mantra forming inside. "You killed your son."

Aroden's suspicions that I mocked him now sharpened the hate in his eyes. "He was not my son. He was part of your cursed self."

"I buried him in the pit of the mines you banished us to." The strength from the cave came to my heart. Leveling my glare to watch him, I asked, "How's your hip, Brother?" With those words, I began to stand.

His nostrils flared as he tossed his head back in defiance. He needed to finish this fight. With me dead, his plans to bring a reckoning to Ankwar could begin. Arrogance filled Aroden. To me, he was nothing more than ashes. Ashes as cold and barren as that mountain night of my Mennatti. Ashes from the back side of the hearth as Mother, a widow, in her swollen condition, filled the birch bark containers prepared for me. Ashes from the smelter's fires. All Aroden's confidence and ill-gained power meant nothing to me anymore. Fire begets ash. Nothing remained of our brotherhood except blood.

As he reached for Father's axe, power surged through my legs, willing myself to propel all my remaining energy through the pain, through the space that separated us, through the memories of all he had cost me.

I opened my mouth. Thirty springs since he had sold me into slavery—winters working the copper mines, seasons of darkness creating the crucible to melt my blood cold. Warped in frustration's passion, the sound ricocheting off my lips broke free. From Chealana's star, from thousands of suns and moons, through suffering and hope, down through the footsteps of the ancestors seeking these lands, a vast, animal cry ripped through me, pushing me forward and stealing back my strength like the mountain's mighty avalanche. I saw the heat rising from his hair. I saw the axe shift as his grip released and tightened. Most importantly, I saw the look of disbelief—or was it fear? —as I stood one last time.

A primitive rumble came from the mountain. The other mountains answered back from hoary, snow-covered heads. The storm would cover us soon.

Aroden laughed. "What's this dog believing he can bite me?"

The strengthening winds scattered the snow as piercing ice bounced off the ground. A deep primal growl tore through my throat, expelling all the air from my stomach, and preparing me for the final impact.

I slammed into my brother, thrusting the smooth edge of my axe into the spot just under his ribs, deep into his liver, as we both rolled to the ground. With one final hoist, I pushed my blade to the depth of death and peered into the face beneath me.

What should have been a moment of satisfaction became a flat, dulling sensation as I watched Aroden's face register his fatal wound. He had underestimated me. That had been his mistake. I hadn't intended to bind myself through his death. That mistake had been mine.

Our lungs screamed for air at the high altitude. The tightening in my chest returned. Beside me, my brothers built on my momentum, targeting Aroden's men. Gabor dealt a blow to the one man's head, leaving him unbalanced. The second man turned and dealt a heavy blow to Gabor, allowing Sibaccian to break free and run to the edge of the path.

Standing there, Sibaccian watched as the attacker dealt Gabor's exposed head repeated blows. Fear must have seized Sibaccian. His instinct froze. With another hammering hit, Gabor groaned, falling unconscious in the snow. Sibaccian backed to the rocks, fingering for a stone to fit into a sling. Spitting blood on the snow, Sibaccian slung his slingshot, hitting Gabor's attacker in the temple, felling him with the hit. The man did not move.

I rolled off my brother, blade wet with his blood. Black ravens cawed from the boughs above, sentient spectators of the spectacle. Startled, dark-fingered feathers flew up as prayers to heaven, scattering death's confusion aloft. The eagles should have carried my prayers, but my unworthy stain reduced me to only the black heart of scavengers. The ugly carrion cry would bring no divine answers. No machinations of man could outmaneuver the wreckage of derailed desires that lay now in a pool of brotherly despair; we were no exceptions.

Aroden gasped for air like a trout on a rock. He looked unbelieving at the blood squirting through his tunic from his inner elbow where I'd sliced the vein on my way to deeper meat.

Gabor lay in the snow behind them. A red pool stained the whiteness around him. Sibaccian backed up toward the path to Ankwar. My bloodied face, my shattered hand weakly extended, was more than he could bear. I tried to call him but collapsed, leaving the words lingering with my own blood on my lips. Awed disgust clouded Sibaccian's face. Backing further to the trail, Sibaccian fled without looking back once. He left Gabor, Aroden, and me behind, leaving us on the ground with the skies heaving white flakes under the weight of their disappointed grace.

Winter had not yet relinquished her hold on these heights. Her length of freeze penetrated longer and deeper than I could remember. Winter covered the mountains in slopes of ice, extending down more each season. A glacier had been forming farther up, bridging the mountains. My view blurred as my brain eased the pain into unconsciousness. The battle had been too much. Ankwar needed to be warned that Aroden had been gathering what appeared to be a raiding party aimed at her borders. If not too late, Sibaccian could divert Bretasko's vengeance from our family. I needed to trust Sibaccian would save Ankwar.

My eyes weighed heavily. I heard Gabor groan and found him lying by a large rock. The man had beaten him severely. His ragged breathing formed little puffs of clouds from his lips. His hold on life gripped the edge of consciousness. My right hand throbbed as the nerves awoke under the savage wound.

I moved closer to hear any words. The amount of red-soaked snow around his head meant he didn't have long.

"Gabor, stay with me, Brother. We will get you to Haliam. The medicines of Undoura will heal you," I lied.

Gabor sighed. Blood pooled at his lip. A weak cough splattered down his chin. His tongue, dried from exposure to the cold, muffled his words. "I should . . ."

"Save your energy, Brother. We need to get you to Undoura. I will get you help."

Gabor gasped and focused his effort on being understood: ". . . should have come . . ."

Propping his head on my leg so he wouldn't gag, I answered, "You did come, Gabor."

". . . when you were taken . . . I should . . . come . . . Forgive me."

"Gabor, there is nothing to forgive. No, there is nothing you need to apologize for. Don't do that to yourself. Rest. I will get you help."

He feebly shook his head, a rattling in his throat, his eyes rolled back, and he tried again, "Forgive . . . me."

The cloud began to form over his eyes as tears formed in mine. His grasp on this world slipped.

"Gabor, no, please no. Don't leave me."

Barely perceptible, he shook his head.

"I can't do this alone. I can't."

With a slight squeeze of my hand, Gabor gasped, looking up to the sky.

"Brother, I forgive you, just please don't leave me." The forced words tumbled from my lips, and his head rested back. His body relaxed as if with a long sigh. Redeemed, he embraced the wind that would carry his soul to the house of our fathers. All had been spent. His hand went limp in mine. Bitter tears stung my eyes and froze in the cold. Aroden's last breaths sifted into the sighs of the wind behind me. The struggle to stay awake melted into numbness and finally the sleep I had sought.

\* \* \*

Hunger rallied my senses. The rough cawing of a crow nearby called me back. He came down from the tree as a scout for the murder of crows gathering. The larger ravens had already hopped on the nearest fallen man of Aroden. Heavy, fat snowflakes splattered on my cheek and forehead. The sky's darkening colors came into focus. An ominous storm hovered over a distant peak, opening her vest to reveal the heart of nature's fury. Thunder rumbled, and the winds pushed down the clouds carrying snow. I couldn't move, but I needed to. Weak from blood loss, I lay there dizzy from the spinning sky and trees. Next to me lay Gabor, and near us, Aroden, their blue lips parted—one in peace, the other in a curse. Snow covered their cold nose and forehead. This chaotic end had not been a dream. The fight had not ended in a win. The loss had been too great.

My first movement trying to lift myself reminded me I had almost been the one lying there dead. Mud from the fight squished under my hand, coating the deep axe wound from Aroden's blow. Swollen and raw, my hand welcomed the cooling seal of the mud. The water god, Shal, had found favor with me to allow such a fortunate puddle.

Turning to look in the other direction, I spied, with the last of the day's light, a blue cluster of campanulas rising above the white and clinging to bits of dirt within a crevice near me. This plant's tenacity growing from a stony surface reflected the strength the plant offered those who knew. The blossoms promised vitamins my body desperately needed. Great effort rolled me to my side, elevating bruised ribs. Sharp pains coursed through my chest. I grabbed a handful, crushing the delicate petals with my inability. Farther down the slope near the hunting rock, the hornbeam tree should have buds. For now, I would use the mushroom to treat and cover the wound until morning. Pulling the mushroom from my pack, I worked with my teeth to stretch and pull the fleshy fungi into place on my wound.

My mind clung to scraps like the roots of the little flower. The skies threatened to unleash floods upon my sin. I packed my backpack. Movements, any movements I made, pulled my muscles into a burning tension. Sitting on a boulder, I pulled off some smoked jerky that Kaiya had given me, chewed through the throbbing pain, and resolved to enlist Haliam's help once again in saving my village from Sibaccian's failure. Why did I trust him? I should have known. Sibaccian, that coward, had left as soon as he saw a chance. Hopefully he could get to Ankwar before Bretasko's men.

I reached into my pack and found kidney meat from a small chamois we had hunted. Gabor had wrapped the meat in fresh bracken from the valley for us to carry. The spring fronds would slow the spoiling of the meat. Blotches of fat snow fell on my shoulders. I needed to get out of this cold. I pulled some einkorn bread that Zaria had packed. Thoughts of her smile, as a summer's morning, warmed me. How like Mother she was. She would be watching for Sibaccian's return. I wiped my hands on my coat, mingling the brothers' blood from my wound with the meat. Hoisting my pack up on my back, I made my way back to the trail to finish my trek down to the hunting rock and on to Undoura. The strong, pointed lines of the hunting rock would provide shelter while I rested. Cheala's wind brought cold down from the mountain covered in fresh snow. She covered Aroden and Gabor's bodies as I left.

Watching the skies reveal their judgment upon me, I moved through the growing darkness, winding my way down. I could not be bound to Aroden in fate. Restitution must be made. My village didn't deserve to suffer from the vain and destructive paths of two brothers. My plans to unite the villages disappeared like vapors. Closer than any brother, Haliam and I had escaped numerous treacheries together, from the copper mines of Malek to the frozen hand of this very mountain pass. He would be the one I could trust. Haliam would find a way. Haliam would help me give strength back to Ankwar. I just needed to survive this coming day and the trek to him.

# CHAPTER 36

## UNDOURA'S LIGHT

I descended the hills to Undoura. The surging river had guided my way, each step agonizing, stretching muscles that needed more food, pounding on joints that cried under spasming muscles. Fatigue's tension kept one foot moving forward, then one more. The moon's shape rounded out the bottom of the new hunter's bow while the stars shone brightly after the haze of snow and rain. Smoke from the long home fires thinly curled into heights above the houses till, like a river, the smoke joined together, spreading, widening, and smoothing a course over the sky into the horizon. Over twenty springs have passed since I last saw this valley. Driven by hunger and fatigue, I focused my strength not on the sights and smells, but on laying down my burden.

I stumbled three times. The roots of the surrounding mountains exposed uneven terrain. The hides on my boots were heavy and wet, my toes freezing nubs. Thick, frozen breath carried the last of my body's warmth out into the air. My eyes blurred. The trees swayed and turned upside down. The ground came up suddenly. I rolled over, feeling nausea creep up my throat.

Through the blurry view, I saw a pair of feet in front of me. Hands grabbed me from under my arms, lifting me to lean into someone. My head dropped, bobbing down onto my chest. Someone else's will moved my feet. My knees buckled, refusing my weight. The firm trunk of a pine supported me; hands had propped me up under the fragrant greens. Shadows whispered assurance as the shapes faded away. My chin sank into the soaked furs of my coat. The dehydrated splitting in my skull crowned my head. Nothing focused.

And with that, I fell asleep.

\*\*\*

The warm smell of cedar's essence filled the room. The voices overhead only spoke briefly. Nothing recognizable. Nothing discernable.

My head felt hot. The light faded, and the warm smells of smoke and food filled my senses. I began to sleep again. More furs were piled on top of me as hands felt my face and checked my eyes. An arm elevated my shoulders so my lips could find the warm fluids offered. With food beginning to stir me awake, the wound in my hand came alive. Moans and wincing brought more feet, more rushing, shushing, movements surrounding me. Warmth I couldn't remember soaked into my bones. The warmth weighed my eyelids closed. I let go to sleep.

The splitting headache pounded me awake. More water immediately found my lips. Hands held the cup for me as I sipped. The gentle coolness of the water over my tongue and down my throat flooded my need for more. I tried to grab the cup with both hands, never wanting to let go. My stomach dumped the contents as I gagged. My head fell back on the bed. Movements around me, cleaning what I had expelled. Left only with the strength to move my head back and forth, I waged war on the voices inside my fever. A quiet voice from beside me repeated the words, "Kula, kula, shhhhh." Words from my childhood, words I had used to calm a dying beast, now came to me. A gentle hand stroked my hair all the while calling, "Kula, kula, easy now." I turned to hide in the breast of my savior and gave way to sleep once more.

Thirst and hunger woke me the next time. Still by my side and ready with a cup of water, the hand brought relief to my lips. The hand offered me einkorn bread. Only small pieces, so I wouldn't choke, followed by more water. The urgency of survival had left along with nausea, and I could take in the soothing routine of drinking and eating. Comfort granted me focus through the pain. With the last drops of the cup, I looked up to thank the one helping me and saw the eyes of a dream watching me. Salir's woman from the lake had come to me. Her song had guided me through the darkness. She had come to me at last. Here before me, I beheld a spirit with the eyes of my Mara. Her hair had gray streaks like the wings of a mourning dove, silvery in the light. In the crinkles near her eyes, a single tear lingered before touching her cheek. Her hand reached up and touched my forehead. My lake woman's hands had bestowed gentle healing upon me. I tipped my head to see better. She smiled. The softness born of life's hardness smoothed her face.

Wincing through the pain, I reached up to touch her. I brushed the tear from her cheek with my thumb, the soft wetness of a healing balm. She held my hand, kissing my fingers. Those eyes with flecks of gold, deep fires of heaven, warmed me, never once leaving my gaze.

"It's you," I whispered weakly.

Mara gave me more water.

"I thought I only dreamed of you, but now I touch your face and know you are here."

Mara shushed me and gave me more bread.

Feelings shivered like the last leaves of autumn, clinging to the branch, the wind tugging the stem to let go and live in a fiery freefall. Looking at Mara, feeling her tenderness, created a sense of possibilities.

"Mara, I . . ." My head hadn't quite focused. How do words find a surface when they have been scattered and torn for so long? The wind pulled the leaf a little more. The hardest part was letting go. "I . . . I want to . . ." Thoughts collided, and the room tilted. Just embrace the raging river pushing me to the waterfall. "Mara, I . . ." The room began to spin again. Losing sight, I felt sleep coming to take me again. "I love . . ." Instead of saying what I longed to say, I blurted out what needed to be said. "I must see Haliam." Lines blurred between reality and a dream. A sagging sense of sinking into mud filled the gap where courage had just flickered. A familiar weight of lacking sat on the ledge next to my love. I let the fever take me back.

\* \* \*

My eyes blinked awake at a nearby candle. Across the room, a woman stood with her back to me. Her long, dark hair, neatly tied behind her, reached to her waist. Her hips curved from childbearing. She worked quickly and smoothly. Had I told her of my love? I couldn't remember. I slowly sat up, knocking over the water waiting for me. Mara turned at the noise and came to my side.

"You are awake. That's a good sign."

"How long have I been asleep?"

"Since you came down off the mountain . . . for most of today."

Hearing the lost time, I quickly moved to stand. "I need to see Haliam." My legs wouldn't work, and I stayed in bed.

"You are in no condition to go anywhere." The seriousness in her voice seemed laced with disappointment.

"Then get him for me, please. I must convince him to return to Ankwar with me."

"Haliam cannot come to you now."

"But I need him! I need men to come back with me to Ankwar." I tried sitting up.

Mara shook her head.

"Why not? Has he gone out into the fields?"

"Haliam is not well. A deep fever has tied him to bed."

"Haliam? He's not well?" I shifted, trying to move. Pain and Mara's hand eased me back down.

Mara only nodded, her eyes saddened. Nothing seemed to work. Nothing was coming together how I had envisioned it.

"You fixed my fever. Can't you fix his? What happened?"

"He had a bad fall, breaking some ribs. He wouldn't rest and kept working. His lungs filled with a deep cough while fever took his energy."

She stopped. I shook my head. Concern for my friend collided with my need. The effort had drained the little reserve I had.

"This is Undoura. Holy men and women are trained here. Is there no one?"

"We've done the poultices. We've treated him with all we know."

"Have you given him lungwort tea?"

"Yes, and some dried peppermint from last summer's harvest."

"Did you try the tall yellow flower? Do you know which one I mean?"

"Yes, there were some newly grown, and we prepared the leaves. Gaspare, we have tried the rosehips from the fall and all different herbs to bring his cough down."

I reached my hand to hers, wanting to believe all she said was only a story. She would laugh and tell me she didn't mean any of it. Haliam would walk into the room. But she didn't. He didn't.

"Has his chest begun to wheeze?" I asked.

She nodded. "Yes, the wheezing came with the fever. The heat has covered his body in sweat for four suns."

"The fever is good. His body is fighting back."

"He is old, Gaspare. We are old. He got sick this past winter. He didn't come into the spring strong."

"Can you take me to him?"

"After you rest some more. For now, just rest."

I reached to get up. My body didn't cooperate. Failure surrounded every thought I had counted on to save me. My mind couldn't rest. My eyes grew heavy, my heart heavier. Noises in the room blended with dreams that kept me trapped on the edge of consciousness. I must have slept, but not the sleep of restfulness.

The light had shifted in the doorway. Mara returned with a young man. He looked like he had maybe twenty springs to his bones. She nodded toward the left side of the bed. He helped me stand; my broken ribs forced a wince. Mara noticed. She supported my right side more. Between them, leaning my weight into the man, I hobbled over to another hut.

The hut of Zuka was small but warm. The room held the pungent scent of tired herbs. The lard in the lamps added a headiness to the smells circling around a mat with Natika's incantations of hope. Outside, a child played on a flute. The notes came as a summoning of the ancient healers. Over near the fire, the mat had been placed on piles of straw with Haliam lying under blankets and furs. A line of sweat beaded on his forehead. Age stamped its crescent on his face with deep bags under his eyes and sallow skin.

My old friend looked up to me, his eyes glazed with fever. A faint smile crossed his lips before more coughing shook his shoulders. A frail hand reached from the bedding. Mara nodded at the young man. Everyone left. Haliam and I remained alone.

A sizzle from the fire accompanied the wheeze from his lungs. The effort to greet me created another coughing that shook him, making him look like a swallow's thin bone. Water seemed best, but after two sips he turned his lips away, dribbling some droplets down his neck. Something like a smile feebly worked the corners of his mouth. He had slipped into the shadows. The fork-like scar on his cheek had become lost in the wrinkles of the man I had known. My friend had been caught by age.

I looked down. I noticed a brown soak in the middle of my clothes. I brushed the crusted blood on my tunic. That must have come when I held Gabor, or was it Aroden? I couldn't tell anymore.

"Brother," he whispered. "How good to see—" He was interrupted by a slight cough and wheeze.

"Haliam, Brother." I grabbed his hand, covering the frailty in the once-strong hands.

His brow furrowed. "If you are here, what of Ankwar?"

"Ankwar has her troubles as always. That has never changed."

"But you changed. What did you do to yourself?" He saw the large blotches of dried blood on my tunic.

"I met Aroden. I killed him, Haliam. I killed my brother . . . I am afraid I have brought down Hekor's wrath upon Ankwar and my family there."

Haliam slowly shook his head. "The Gaspare I know didn't seek that fight." His shoulders shook with the next cough, but he continued. "Did you?"

"No," came my whisper.

"Ankwar always sought to blame. They haven't changed."

I turned away to stoke the fire.

Haliam sipped more bitters before continuing, "Even with my fever I can see you've let them change you."

"Gabor is dead. He came with me. I led him to his death. I shouldn't have killed Aroden, Haliam. We were brothers. I am a holy man. I heal, not kill." Looking down at the dried blood on my tunic, I sought the red threads in the pattern; my stomach twisted at the memory of my anger.

"You weren't your brother's problem. You never were. You only got in the way."

"I shouldn't have killed Aroden."

"Maybe, but someone would have. It was only a matter of time."

"As a holy man, it was not my place. As a brother, I . . . He just . . ."

Haliam coughed a ragged, chest-heaving cough. I could hear the wheeze from his lungs. "Don't hide behind being a holy man."

I turned my head; not sure I wanted to hear him. The flush at my lack of control reddened my cheeks. My hand began tugging at the blood crusted on my tunic. I shifted.

"You, Gaspare, are afraid."

"Maybe I am afraid. We're all afraid of something." My right hand lay impotent in my lap. My good hand continued twisting the fabric of my tunic. I had failed. I had brought shame to my father's house.

"Yes, but you embrace your suffering and wear it like the colors of your house." He took another sip of the bitters. He waited for the calming to assist his words. "You, Gaspare, are more than the bad that has happened to you." Haliam laid a damp palm on my arm, weakly holding me to his words.

Frustrated and angry, I pulled away.

"You've been beaten into believing suffering is meaning."

Anger flamed up within me. With my only good hand, I tore the tunic stained with my brother's blood off my body. Standing there, bare chested, I held the tunic, shaking it to emphasize each word.

"These colors?" I asked. "These colors? This house is dead wood." I threw the blood-soaked cloth into the fire. "What good are these colors?" As the flame sought to turn the threads to ash, I turned to look for anything other than my old friend, but a cough called me back to his side. Another cough shook his body, tightening his grip on my arm just a little. I could feel the weakness in him. I knew the weakness in me.

"We shouldn't talk. You should rest."

"I will rest when I am dead. Listen to the words of one who is dying. Do me that last favor."

I closed my eyes, wishing for the strength to leave, but nodded instead.

"Gaspare, life is suffering. Everyone suffers. But that is not all life is. Suffering calls us to a greater sense of happiness."

I scoffed. "What happiness?"

My friend would not be deterred. An excitement glimmered in his eyes as he said, "When we let go, there is something akin to happiness."

The light from the fire glowed from many surfaces around us as the threads of the tunic blackened in the embers, and shadows swayed in the corners of the room. I turned to look at my friend. He took short breaths and never stopped watching my face.

"I wish this happiness for you, Gaspare."

"Are you afraid to die?" I asked him.

"Sure, but not as afraid as you are to live."

I shook my head. "Mother's sacrifice for me . . ."

"Your mother loved you. If there is anything I have learned from watching Natika with our children, she would gladly sacrifice herself to protect any of them." A frail tightening of his hand on mine emphasized his passion. "Your mother was no different. She loved you." A cough shook Haliam, lifting his shoulders from the mat. The following wheeze filled the space between us.

I looked at the ground. "I close my eyes and only see darkness. I cannot see their faces anymore: not Mother's face, or Grandfather's, or Father's. And my dreams are dark. I do not see the fire within others anymore. My gifts have crawled back through the apu-ah hole. I have no purpose. Nothing."

"I am touching your arm now. Do you not feel that?"

"I only see darkness."

"That's not what I asked. I said do you not feel that?"

I looked down at his hand on my arm, his touch light with little strength, but I felt the warmth. I felt the gentle pressure of his hand and I understood reassurance. He knew me. I nodded and placed my other hand on top of his.

"You have a woman you love, and you have family that believes in you. Sacrifice only partially defines you, Gaspare. You've been walking backward for so long; you can't feel the sun." Haliam coughed again and motioned for some water.

"I am trying, Haliam. Ankwar is failing, and I am trying to unite the tribes to help her."

"Maybe saving Ankwar isn't the story you are meant to tell."

My shoulders slumped down. My chest burned inside.

"Go to the atonement stone. Find the stone that gave you direction. You need to select your stones more carefully. Feel the edges to get the greatest skip across the water."

I managed a little laugh.

"Find the stone that slips into your hand comfortably. The impact of that stone's flight will leave a changing impact on the surface."

I shook my head, smiling. "You use my words against me, old friend."

"Call her back, Gaspare. Take time with Mara and listen to the stillness within."

Another cough shook his back, and he seized his ribcage. He needed to rest.

Mara and the young man came and helped me out into the sunlight. They took me back to the smaller hut that stood near Zuka's place. Looking at the young man created a horrible thought: was he Haliam's son?

Seeing me watch him leave the hut, Mara said, "His name is Gaspar. I named him after his father's brother."

I looked at her, eyes wide in disbelief. His father? Aroden couldn't be. She'd left Ankwar and hadn't seen Aroden since.

"I was pregnant with him when you returned to the village. I had him here after Haliam helped me through the mountains. That man guided a vomiting woman filled with morning sickness and weakness from hunger. Your friend was better than his father ever would have been to Gaspar. He gave us a place to stay. Gaspar received his blessing to marry a young girl in the village."

"You had a son?"

"Yes, and he has been very caring of me. He doesn't have the temper of his father. He has the gift of herbs like his grandmother."

Mara's eyes lit up when she spoke of her son. She shared how he had learned the ways of the village. The more she talked, the more my eyes couldn't stop taking in her beautiful glow. Here I could gaze fully on my love, not in dreams, not by memory, but by seeing her eyes widen as she expressed wonder, or the way her hands became freer as she told stories about her days in Undoura.

Her brow furrowed, and a serious shadow came over her face as she began sharing how she had always watched for signs of his father to surface in her son. Her words became more rapid to reassure herself as she shared, "There were little ways, uncanny in how they had come through, but Gaspar's personality did not resemble his father in the least." I couldn't stop watching her mouth, the blush of her cheeks, the heady sense of her being real, and standing so close.

"Gaspare, Gaspare?"

She called me from my dream.

"Are you listening to me?" Mara asked.

The words of Haliam repeated like a magpie in my ears. The woman I loved . . . I loved . . . Before I could change my mind, I reached across the distance and pulled her into my arms. I have no idea what she was saying, but my lips had no trouble finding hers. I drank in the fullness of her there in my arms. I held her till there was but one space: Mara and me. Just to breathe the air with her in my world seemed holy. When I lessened the kiss, she picked up the intensity. We were locked in love forced to wait. I held her head to my shoulder. My chest swelled to the size of the heavens, her soft breath on my neck. Words fell away except for one: peace. I felt at peace.

I moved a wayward strand of hair from her forehead.

"All this time . . . all this time, all I wanted was to do this." As I said the words, her hand slipped into my own, smooth yet strong like the numerous stones I had skipped at the lake. A gentle squeeze before my calluses found the softness of her skin. Her own hands, rough from work, carried resilience and need: the need to be wanted. Restless, our fingers played together, entwining, fidgeting, holding onto the hope that our hands could touch the sky together. I would have given anything to have been able to have brushed her hand in passing or to have her touch my shoulder as she came from behind. The past's tenderness never known worked our fingers to dance on the tips of tingling nerves, swirling to feel the lengths of each hand ignited in the union. Comfort came alive with the strength of two bound in the cradle of what had never been.

How I had longed to look at her secretly while the families talked around us, clueless to the passion churning inside me. I had longed to see her with wisps framing her face, waiting for me to brush them away. How I had wanted to pull her to my knee and look up to the stars, showing her Chealana that had brought me home to her, to feel her lean into my chest and smell the sweetness of her hair as I told how her memory had burned blue like Chealana's star. The tenderness taken by time's sentry had only been mine to hold in regrets.

"Mara, forgive me. I stayed away . . . I stayed to keep you safe. I shouldn't . . ."

The words volunteered themselves. The guilt admonished from unspoken wishes pushed the confession from a heart in turmoil.

Mara only put one finger to my lips. She looked at me like an old lover and smiled. "You're here now."

Our foreheads touched, and I buried my fingers deep into the thickness of her hair. She looked at my right hand, careful not to bump my arm.

"I will send Gaspar for the herbs and mushrooms to set the healing in your hand," she said. As beautiful as the palest pink sunrise, the lost time fell in step with the present, and we began fresh together as a family. Remembering myself hearing her son's name as my own, I asked, "Do you think he would like this?" I fumbled one-handed in my pouch, dumping the contents of white beads and herbs into my lap until out fell my gasper stone. The sun caught the surface and danced light across as I tilted the stone.

"I think he would feel honored to have this stone."

"Would you give it to him?" I extended my hand in eagerness to make amends.

Mara closed my fingers over the stone, guiding my hand back to me. "No, you should give it to him."

"He doesn't know me. Why would he want a stone from a stranger?"

"He wouldn't. But if you gave him your stone, you could tell him the story of strength and courage the stone holds."

"That's not the story of this stone."

"Haliam has been a great father to Gaspar. We have never wanted anything except you. I would have chosen you to be the father of Gaspar. Your story is one of daring and determination and valor, everything a son admires in a father. You sacrificed everything to keep us safe, and that is the gift only a father could give."

"I was afraid Aroden or Sibaccian would find you and hurt you, so I stayed away."

"You stayed away because you loved me. That is what has gotten me through each day. Your gift graced another generation with hope." She smiled at me and changed the subject. "I have some food for you to build up your strength. After you have eaten, I will have Gaspar come and help you outside where you can both air yourselves."

"I will travel to the atonement stone, then maybe Gaspar will help me."

"Take him with you."

"Mara, I must tell you. Aroden is dead. I killed him up on the mountain."

"Aroden has been dead to me for many springs. Now eat and I will get Gaspar."

In my lap next to the beads sat the little red stone with green veins that I had pulled from the lake when Haliam and I escaped. The stone marked the beginning of my journey home. Placing it in Mara's hand marked the completion of my journey. Folding her fingers around the red stone, a sense of belonging matched with my feeling of being home.

# CHAPTER 37

## A SHADOW'S SOUL

Haliam passed as did the sun that day. I had sat with my friend as he drifted in and out of the threads of mortality. The thin skin covering his hand had already looked ready to release a hold on life. At last, he surrendered.

As he entered the next light on this side of the mountains, Sibaccian had already returned to Ankwar. He had returned with no brother, nor axe. Sibaccian's failure found him telling Esteban and Kaiya of Gabor and Aroden's death. His failure found him berated by the council members he had seen in secrecy before our journey. When Bretasko's men arrived with the next sun, Sibaccian was beaten severely. His only choice in saving his own wife and children came as helping the hunters find me.

The council members felt the urgency of Bretasko's presence. His stern, hawk-like features scanned the scene for weakness, anything that would betray fear. They believed if the village sacrificed me on the mountain pass, then the debt would be paid. But this was not the pledge Malek had made. This would not be the satisfied end the council sought.

The council members met in secret one last time with Sibaccian. Weakened by the beating, Sibaccian listened in the darkness. He heard the plans of the councilmen, who stood in the shadows.

He scoffed, "I've already rendered his weapons useless. He's basically unarmed. His body shows his age. Let the mountain finish him. You want me to betray my brother?"

"Have you not done so already? You want to be free to live? Then that is your price."

"There must be another way. Enough men from the house of Tandor have perished. You cannot ask this of me."

"There has been enough strife through famine and failed crops that the house of Tandor has brought upon this tribe. Tandor has been dead now these past thirty springs, and we are none the better for the counsel of his sons."

"You cannot mean to blame all of Ankwar's troubles on my family?"

"No, but we can blame the arrival of this Bretasko on Gaspare and you. We said we didn't want to make payment as a village. This latest evil that befalls us is from your household, as are a variety of other ills." The shadows lengthened.

Sibaccian tried again. "He only included the village because he wished to unite us all. The payment could easily have been made by our family. You stopped the transaction."

A gruff laugh came from the darkening space between Sibaccian and the elders. "His ideas are dangerous to our way of life. He grew apart from our ways while he was gone. He sees too much."

Sibaccian backed away. He rubbed his eyes, trying to find a way through these lies. This snare had been set, and he had blindly walked into this web of wills.

"You will take this guard Bretasko away from Ankwar and lead him to where your brother may be found."

"If I refuse?"

"We will turn you over to this guard's judgment. You can work the mines in payment for the axe you lost."

"You leave me no choice."

"There's always a choice. Yours is the fate of twins. It should have been so many springs ago when you were born under the black mark of death. Maybe it is you we should be sacrificing up on the mountain instead, since you arrived in the manner of the cursed."

Sibaccian backed further away. He had bartered with who to believe and had lost. Not only had he sold away the lives of his brothers, but the value of his own life held no consequence.

"Gaspare only cared for Ankwar. He believed he had a role in helping her grow."

"If he believes so, then he will gladly sacrifice himself for our safety and keep these wolves away from our people."

The bait had been taken, and Sibaccian had fallen prey. The guards would only wait until dawn's light. Until then they marked the village, noticing where the wealth lay.

Sibaccian entered the house of Tandor for the last time. He found Esteban. He gave him a warning to get the children and Kaiya far away from the village. In his heart, Sibaccian knew the truth of what was to come. As the remaining children of the house of Tandor prepared only the things they could carry, Sibaccian left to go to his hut. Only questions remained in the room.

# CHAPTER 38

# A LOVE LOST

A coldness had settled over me with the passing of my friend. Life in Undoura made sense. With Mara, I felt the greatest sense of completion. But Ankwar would be in trouble from Bretasko's men. I needed to go back, return the axe, and finish what I began.

"Take me and Gaspar with you."

"Only danger exists in Ankwar."

"Why? You said yourself Aroden is dead. I am free."

"You may be free, but I am not. It's too dangerous. There is snow up on the mountains. The face of her summit carries an unusual amount of ice for this time of spring. Any melting lower down makes the way treacherous."

"Yet you will go and risk losing us again?"

"If you have any desire to see your daughters again, or your sister, or mother, then I need to go and finish what I started in Ankwar."

Mara looked at me. "I do wish to see them, yes, but . . . Gaspare, don't go. Stay here in Undoura, please."

I reached for her. Looking into her face, I brushed back the hair from her eyes. Everything I had wanted I now held. But darkness covered my vision at night, and that same darkness blocked my view of our future together.

"I must go, Mara. As long as I hold this axe, I hold the debt of Ankwar. We must be free to live together here or there. I cannot stay knowing the wrath I have brought to Ankwar, to Esteban, Kaiya, and Taran's families."

"Sibaccian should be the one to clear the trouble with this copper mine. He is the one who failed to send payment."

"Yes, but I am the one who promised the village they wouldn't have to pay, and now Bretasko is coming to extract his fee from Ankwar. My idea brought him."

Mara searched my eyes for any turning from this decision.

"If my word cannot hold water, then I will drown in a river of guilt. I do not want to live the life of the hunted." I began packing my bag.

Mara joined me, staying my hand as I reached for the ember containers. "Gaspare, you cannot stand in the line of these arrows aimed at our village." Her hand tightened on mine, willing me to stop. I couldn't look at her. I just couldn't. "Then you ask me to make the widow's wail. I cannot see anything good coming from you leaving now." Mara relinquished her argument and prepared food for me. "If you do not return, I will know things did not go well in Ankwar and I will live as a widow."

Before the sun cut the darkness of the night's sky, I began my journey on the trail up the mountain. I turned and looked at Mara. She stood straight, the light of the hut cutting her silhouette into memory. She watched. She did not wave. I knew her eyes would carry me over the first ridge till I was out of sight. At the top of the rise, I turned. She hadn't moved. I sent a wave to her, my arm absorbed in the missing light. She knew. The small figure lifted an arm and then was gone behind the hill.

# CHAPTER 39

# FINDING A WAY

Morning rose and blended into a surer sense of the day. I had passed the hunting rock, the jutting point hidden by the new leaves. The river below poured over itself, passing rocks and swirling into corners. The point where the river bumped into the arm of an adjoining river marked my way up the final slope. My backpack needed shifting with each step as I sought to clear the summit before dusk.

Stopping only briefly to rest near the gushing springs, I eyed the field of rocks that lay before me. Nothing of softness between me and the summit except patches of moss and the smallest flowers. Their little blossoms bobbed in the breeze, offering me tokens of their strength and goodwill. The rocks layered on top of each other and shone brightly in the later light of day. Streaks of golden lines or silver branches decorated the surface like precious stones. The fierce incline of the slope offered resilience as I trudged on. These same rocks had cascaded down trying to bury Haliam and me, but today they lay quietly in the path. The pounding my legs took meant I would need to rest before facing more rocks.

The light began fading as I reached the narrow channel of rocks going down the other side. This mountain that I knew showed her treachery and would bury me if I let her. The moon had retreated into a sliver, forcing me to stop for the night. This last night on the mountain brought a sense of anticipation. The new day would see me back in Ankwar where I could right my mistakes. I laid my mat down on one large rock facing the sky and her thousand stars. The Raven would be visible again. I looked for Chealana's star. There she was. Her bluish light glowing, showing the way home, and yet my direction had changed. Seeing Mara had turned my heart from the hearth of my family. Ankwar no longer needed to be home. I would finish these dealings with the village and return to her. Lower down the slope, Aroden and

Gabor had lain. Their eyes didn't see these stars. I pulled into my coat, feeling an emptiness inside. How much control did I need to lose before I would let go? The wind lifted the edges of my mat. In sadness, I closed my eyes and slept.

Lower down in the valley, as the mourning dove's wings whistled on the air and the sun stretched a flame across the edge of the new sky, lower down at least two hillsides below the lake of green waters, Bretasko's men crossed the edge of Ankwar with Sibaccian leading them up into the mountains. The councilman had returned to his home happy to have solved the village's problems by offering Bretasko meat to eat along with Sibaccian as a guide. His deal sent Sibaccian to the mines to work three springs after he found Gaspare, but that would do Sibaccian good. Earning his payment of the copper satisfied the councilman's sense of justice. A grievous mistake must be demonstrated to the village for all to learn. He believed fully in the strength of his righteousness. Ankwar's problems left before they even heard the roosters crow at the arrival of the sun.

Sibaccian and the four men marched into the mountains. Up above a higher peak, a thick grayness of the clouds filled with snow that lay heavy above them. No one wanted to be buried in their sleep. They stopped for water at a spring, their backs against the rise of the mountain. The greenish water lay smooth as ducks called each other, and the chalky whiteness softened the water's cold depths. Ankwar's lake made herself a place of respite in the balance of a rugged life.

# CHAPTER 40

# THE CLIMB

I had reached the tree line when I saw the band of five men. Their backs turned away made it hard to tell who they were. I saw Sibaccian's coat and began to call to him but stopped when the man beside him turned and I saw the face carved by a heart of rock. Bretasko stood facing his men. His eyes pierced the distance. He addressed the other three men. A cold hand squeezed the heart in my chest. If I was going to survive this day, I needed to think and use the land to my advantage. The long length of these black pine trees could mask my movement, but no man could hide forever behind the trunks.

I slowly backed away among the trees toward the boulders as the men gathered themselves to resume their hunt. The softness of the moss cushioned my steps. I made my way to the farthest end of the pine forest. The men moved closer. Fear seized my mind. I wanted to run, knowing I would never clear the last tree.

Behind a tall tree, I risked looking up at the mountain. I could begin to hear feet kicking a stone, snapping a twig, pushing the way closer. The path up the slope would expose me easily as a target to shoot from behind. The wide space to the summit offered little cover. I needed another way. To my left, the gray clouds hung, but the path would be more rigorous. This way would take me to the highest peak and, if I remembered correctly, I could cut across once over the summit through to Haliam's little gully. That was my only hope to lose them. If I stayed in the trees much longer, they would find me. If I climbed up into the sky, they would follow. I needed to remain close in cover to the rocks and move through the hardness to a flight of stairs that could save me through the impossibility of the climb.

My body was already fatigued and didn't relish the prospect of taking the higher slope. The clouds warned of the fickle nature I knew all too well of this mountain, but another snap of a branch reminded me I had to try. Just a glimpse of twisted horns high above me darting among the rocks revealed a ram. I took him as a good omen and made for the path.

# CHAPTER 41

# A MOUNTAIN'S SHROUD

The sun pulled my shadow long and lean in front of the steps I took away from Ankwar. The warm spring air had been exchanged for the freshly fallen snow at this altitude. The wind fingered along the path, revealing the stubbornness of a few spring flowers holding on the slope. The warmth from the sun's rays was soaked up by twelve blackened bodies perched ominously on the rocks above. Their vantage point allowed them to scan the rise of the mountain in numerous directions. Some of the vultures stood with lifted wings, cleaning their feathers in the warm air currents. All of them, trance-like, faced the golden orb. The wind fingered down my coat collar, sending a chill down my neck. I missed my tunic. The black silhouettes blotted the morning with their presence.

Farther up the path, I relied on my walking stick to balance and help me up the steep incline. I had never finished carving it into a bow. My heart burned. My legs throbbed from rocks and more rocks. My pack swayed. My hat dropped over my eyes. The peak had brought a tremendous view of the green lake below and the folds of mountains draining into her waters. No one could be seen behind me. Nothing was there in the land of rocks. My plan seemed to have worked. If Sibaccian led them up the typical trail, the one I had descended this morning, then I could get behind them on the trail and track them instead of being the hunted one. I could risk a little time to stop and eat.

Leaving the trail, I worked my way to Haliam's gully. Soon I would be back on the trail to the hunting rock, but water and food could be risked here. Instinctively, I looked to where the wolf had been the last time I was here with Haliam, scanning the rocks for her gray coat though I knew seeing her again would be impossible. I knelt to take a drink as Haliam had and remembered all those now lost. This was as good a spot as any. I removed my pack and put aside my embers. I had some time, yes, but not enough to start a fire.

Digging through my pack, I found a package of meat. I undid my axe and my belt and leaned them against a boulder. My shoulders ached and appreciated the stretch that I was able to afford without my pack. Pushing my hands into my lower back, I stretched, leaning backward and feeling the pull of all those rocks my body had crossed. From up here, the world seemed possible and impossible. My wound ached along with my head. Snow began falling on me, so I put my mat over my shoulders and sat down to eat the fresh liver Mara had wrapped along with the final strips of dried ibex Kaiya had sent. Kaiya had sent enough for three men. Did she know about Gabor?

Resting here felt lonely. The air held a chill. The snow came a bit thicker, making a layer, covering a cluster of small, white flowers growing near the water. They promised spring and new life would return to this mountain, but the chill from up the slope indicated otherwise. I missed home. I didn't want to run anymore. I wanted to go home, home to Mara.

Spring meant festivals. I was born during the spring festival. During those celebrations, the people of the village had come together, celebrating with feasts of the leftover winter storage. People shared their goods, reaching toward each other with smiles and friendship. Spring meant the crops were sown in hope. Spring meant lambing season and the renewal of life. There endured a sense, neither good nor bad, that home had always meant I was not alone. Yet here on this mountain pass somewhere between Mara and Ankwar, I felt an emptiness that no taste of food could chase away.

I sat eating; my thumb absently ran over the edge of my dagger. The tip had broken off. That must have happened with Aroden. The thought of my brother's face dried the taste of meat in my mouth to powdery chalk. I got up to get another drink from the water. Everything hurt as I moved. As old as I was with my forty-six springs, I found the boy still inside scared and shivering.

I repacked my backpack. Looking up, I saw the shape of someone approaching. I recognized the coat as one from my house. *Sibiccian made it*, I thought. He walked alone. *Had he escaped? Did he know to find me here? Together we could survive Bretasko. I had been too hard on him.*

I raised my arm. He hesitated, then waved back. The span of my shoulders opened, allowing space for the arrow to come from behind and slice through my coat, my shoulder, and my vein. I had only heard the slight whistle as the shaft swam through the air. My breath heaved sporadically with sharp intakes. Blood pulsed into my chest cavity, dropping me like a large ibex to my knees.

I leaned forward, trying to push myself up from the ground. I needed to stand, but instead, I rocked back on my heels, letting the wind dry the tears wanting to come. Bretasko's man stepped out from behind the boulder farther up the gully that had hidden him, followed by Bretasko himself and one of the other men. I could hear his boots crunching in the snow. As I looked up, I felt the wet drops of snow hitting my cheeks. My eyes began blurring, yet I still searched for him. Sibaccian stood there, watching me fall. Behind him came the last of Bretasko's men, and my sight lost hold and focus. The sound of snow crunching increased. The hunter came. His words: a curse or blessing I did not know. A brother's betrayal cut deeper than the arrow had. It had been a good shot. One I would have been proud to have made.

Gasping at the mountain air, I grabbed at my chest. The valley sprawled before me. Cheala worked to bring a cover, carrying more snow on her winds. Across the way, a lone wolf sat, her gray fur smooth down her straight back. She turned, smelling the wind, and looked at me. On soft paws, she crossed the distance and came to stand with me. Chealana had come for me. I felt myself reach out for her. My vision began to cloud. The hunter yanked the shaft of the arrow from my back. The head broke off, lodging the flint deep within. My mouth opened, helpless to form sound. The oxygen was burning through my lungs. I tried to see Sibaccian, but only saw the gray eyes of Chealana. She waited for me. We would walk again into the forest and play in the sunlight dancing across the shadows there. Words choked on the gargling sound in my head.

The hunter threw down the broken arrow shaft. He pointed at me and looked at Sibaccian, who reluctantly nodded. The reality of watching his third brother die carved the depths of his mistakes upon his memory. He did not know the wrath Bretasko's men would pour out on Ankwar. He did not see his own feet swinging in the air as they hung him in the smokehouse. He did not hear the cries of those running past the toppled menhir stone as the buildings burned. He could not even notice the copper axe lying against the boulder where I'd left it. He couldn't see.

Tears came to wet my drying eyes. The wind brushed my cheeks, whispering in my ear. The hunter tore off my bear cap, exposing my bald head to the chill. The cap Gabor had made me. He had been proud of me and my bear. The valley began to sway. Sibaccian cut off the pouch I wore around my neck. I searched for Mara in the approaching darkness. There I found the last petals of hope opening to guide me. If I had to die, at least I would die knowing they would not have what they sought, and Mara was truly safe. With me died her whereabouts.

A numbness that had begun in my chest now spread up my arm, beginning to fill my thoughts with a drifting fog. Bretasko's hunter pulled back his axe. The impact from the blunt end on the back of my head swung my body into a twisted fall. The cold wind blew more snow, and my left arm flipped underneath me to brace my body. Perverse cruelty left my one good hand raised like a prayer or someone seeking alms: a gesture of charity and faith. The only tokens came from the snow landing in my palm.

Sibaccian had proven himself true to the elder's promise. He had led them to their prey. He assumed the elder would be satisfied. He assumed Esteban and those who remained of his family would find safety. He assumed three springs would go quickly, working the mines. Deceit mandated payment, but no offering on the atonement stone would blot out this evil. He did not understand the severe purge needed to right the depths of lies and treachery. He did not see my last vision of destruction.

With that hammering blow to the back of my head, my debt to the copper mine was paid. Blood within and blood without poured over me like the oils from my ceremony anointing me for a path of healing. With a sigh, my soul was caught on the wind. Chealana licked my wounded hand. I felt the rich thickness of her coat I had longed for and buried my face in her warmth. She was my girl. We were free to walk as we once had walked.

Cheala, the goddess of the wind, looked upon the suffering. She blew the cloud filled with snow, preparing the way for the glacier's approach. The men chose not to tarry. They headed back to Ankwar with Sibaccian in the middle. In dignity, she wrapped me in the burial cloth of winter's kiss, warming the waters to flow through the gully, preserving me where I lay. As my body surrendered to the pass, a lament came with the wind like the sound of a lone wolf, sealing my spirit in the glacier's grip. Together, the swirls of white snow and the flush of water cloaked me gently in a shroud of ice. Cheala had preserved me, the man in the ice. Her work conserved and protected my stories, turning them into secrets for five thousand springs.

I am the Iceman.

# ACKNOWLEDGMENTS

A writer in isolation tends towards insanity and a lack of motivation. I am incredibly thankful, therefore, for my writers' group, The Lavender Ink Society. Katrina Grzankowski and Jeny Sisk, you have challenged my writing to go beyond what I thought possible. And to our other founding member, Lisa Larkin, your desire to share your own story instigated the roots of our group. It is with sadness and affection that I include my gratefulness to you, Lisa, and our conversation on my deck the two years before your untimely passing. Thank you, ladies!

My other writers' group, Write by the Rails, did much to challenge my perspective and expose me to opportunities I hadn't previously considered. Several details are interspersed throughout this story as a result of writing exercises begun at our meetings. Thank you specifically to Maryel Stone, Becks Sosa, Andrea Yarbough, and Katherine Gotthardt. Your friendship and love of writing has been a wonderful balm.

My students, who continually challenged me to stay fresh and consider new possibilities, have also impacted a number of lines and ideas in this story. The phrase "We write what we know" doesn't necessarily mean what we experience but rather what we understand, and my students have helped me understand many depths through our discussions and work with literature. Thank you for taking risks and sharing your hearts and ideas with me.

My project manager, Ashley Barnhill, has been a calm and guiding source of encouragement and wisdom. I greatly appreciate all of the time and effort she put in to keeping me and the production on track. She's been a wonderful help by keeping her eye on the final product and where we needed to go.

A shout out across the pond must go to David Matthew, known as Graenwulf on Instagram. Be sure to check his page out. He has been an amazing help sharing with me his experiences of going into a Neolithic copper mine and all of his experiences as a reenactor of Ötzi. The excitement he had helping me achieve amazing cinematography for my book trailers as well as affirmation that I was on the right path was huge in bolstering my efforts of reimagining life 5,000 years ago. Thank you for your passion of archeology.

Even though I mentioned him in the author's note, this page would be remiss without taking the time to say thank you to Dr. Walter Leitner. To call you my friend has been a tremendous reward. Thank you for all of your council and patience with me as I try to understand a people and time not my own. Thank you so much for your thoughtfulness in guiding my experience to actually see the Iceman. Finding you was the best surprise on our trip!

My trip up the mountain would not have been successful without my husband. Thank you for all of those practice hikes in the Shenandoah and for letting me talk you into our mountain top trip. I trusted you to get me up that slope, and you didn't let me down. I am so thankful for the way you take care of me and let me know that you love me and believe in me. Miluji tě.

Finally, to my children, who this book is dedicated to. You challenge me to take risks and believe more because I try to model for you to reach beyond what you believe possible. I couldn't be prouder of each of you. May you always know the strength and power of God's hand on your life. I can wish you nothing greater. Thank you for helping me understand what it means to love.

# ABOUT THE AUTHOR

**Sharon Krasny** has worked as an educator for twenty-two years in Virginia and taught abroad in both Hungary and Czechia. Through teaching English as a second language, she discovered a love for oral history. Sharon listened as her students explained central European history and culture to her, and she saw how inextricably bound their past is with part of their identity. This began her fascination with people's need to be known and heard.

Retired from teaching English and research in Virgina, she currently writes, grows lavender, and finds adventures for her and her husband to experience.